The Obsidian Stone

Elisabeth Ashe

PublishAmerica
Baltimore

First printing

ISBN: 1-4137-7226-9
PUBLISHED BY PUBLISHAMERICA, LLLP
www.publishamerica.com
Baltimore

Printed in the United States of America

This book is dedicated to my son and my granddaughter, Tayler , neither of whom are far from my thoughts.

A special thank you to my many friends for their friendship, kindness and hospitality along my journey.

Thank you to my father for showing me that change is possible at any age. Much gratitude to my brothers and sisters, Wolfgang, Rose, Margrit, Peter and Denise. A special appreciation for the Weiss family, who have played a large part in my life from an early age.

A special dedication to the memories of Elizabeth, Florence, Martina and Kate. Mothers to me all, you are my guardian angels, and I am forever grateful.

With special thanks to Ramon for his love, care and unshakeable belief in me.

This book happened in part because of my neighbor Elaine, who lived down the hall from me in Mexico and who was the first to tell me that I "just had to write the sequel." Unfortunately, Elaine passed away this year before the book's release, but I would like to believe that she would have approved. To the rest of you who wanted to know what happens next, I hope you will not be disappointed. Your opinion matters, and if you would care to drop me a line, please email me at: www.glassactimports@yahoo.com

Thank you all for your support and encouragement.

-Elisabeth Ashe

The Obsidian Stone

Prologue

The sun dipped its golden rays into the ocean as it made its slow ascent of the day. From the hilltop where she sat overlooking the Bay of Zihuatanejo, Lydia watched its progress with the same awe she had always felt since arriving in Mexico. There for what was to have been a mere one-month holiday but had stretched to twenty-five years, her ritual of watching the sun rise from this spot was well known.

She sipped her coffee and bit into one of the fresh croissants their housekeeper made that morning and sighed in pleasure. She thought for perhaps the umpteenth time that this was her favorite time of day.

Today, after nearly five years, their daughter Jade was coming home from school in Canada. The renewed realization brought a smile to her lips. Jade had been gone for too long in her mind. Only once in all that time had Jade returned for a brief visit. At least until after her schooling was finished, Jade had rationalized to them, adding it was far too expensive to come home on a regular basis. Better, their daughter suggested, she take the money and put it toward school supplies and her future career.

Both Lydia and Jade's father, Rodolfo, had protested they didn't mind the cost, but Jade had been adamant. Finally, they reluctantly conceded, even though they didn't understand fully Jade's reasons. Instead, they compensated by making the trek north twice a year and combining it with business interests. For some reason, this arrangement was perfectly acceptable to Jade. Still, it wasn't the same as having their only child with them on a full-time basis. Lydia could hardly wait to hold her baby in her arms again.

Grown woman now, she reminded herself with a smile. It was hard to think of her daughter in those terms. The realization had hit both she and Rodolfo the last time they visited Jade over six months ago.

Poised and sophisticated, Jade had taken them out for dinner—her treat, she insisted—to one of the best restaurants the city had to offer, and Calgary had many from which to choose. Her parents had watched in amazement as their former tomboy had ordered the correct wines to accompany each dish, in French no less, tipping appropriately the attentive waiters at the end of the meal. Too attentive, Rodolfo had grumbled disconcerted, and they had all laughed.

It wasn't all that surprising really, Lydia mused. Jade was raised in and around the food and hospitality business all of her life. It was normal that she would know these things. Still, it was a shock to their system. In that moment, they realized just how grown their daughter had become. And beautiful.

Lydia couldn't help but be proud of the elegant woman she called her daughter. Luckily, Jade had inherited her father's height rather than her mother's mere five foot two. Combined with her willowy form, Jade favored, as well, the deep blue-black hair of her Spanish ancestors.

From Lydia she received her piercing green eyes, startling in a face with her peaches and cream complexion—a throwback to her German heritage on her mother's side and Irish on her grandfather's. Despite that, Jade managed to tan quickly and easily, a nice golden brown that made her eyes stand out even more. The reaction of people meeting Jade for the first time and peering into those hypnotic eyes never failed to amuse them.

Amie, Jade's best friend and roommate, was coming with her too—her first visit ever to Mexico. Lydia was pleased. The daughter of her lifelong friends Lina and Len, Amie was almost like a second child to them. In return, their friends treated Jade like one of their own, a fact that did much in allaying Rodolfo's somewhat overprotective fears about sending Jade so far away.

Amie was petite and beautiful in a way uniquely her own. Her blonde locks, big, baby blue eyes, dimples and winning smiles disarmed people and drew them to her like bees to honey. Having these features combined with a bubbly, outgoing personality, she was a perfect foil for Jade's more reserved nature. Lydia could not have wished for a better best friend than Amie for her daughter. Even then, she had not had an easy time convincing Rodolfo that going away would be good for their only child.

"Why can't Jade go to school in Mexico City?" Rodolfo had complained in his quiet way when Lydia had first broached the subject with him.

"It's not just school, Rodolfo," she had explained as gently as she could. "It's time that Jade realizes she has two heritages—one Mexican and the other Canadian. You want her to be well rounded, don't you?"

The discussion had gone on for a long time between them until, surprisingly, out of the blue, Jade told them she wanted to go to Canada—the sooner the better.

With that, Rodolfo had capitulated, as Lydia had known he would. The best person she ever knew, Rodolfo was also one of the greatest of fathers. If his daughter Jade wanted something, she was sure to get it. Surprisingly, she was neither spoiled nor tainted in anyway by their indulgence.

Jade had also asked and received permission to bring another guest home this visit—a friend named Eric Foster. Sketchy on the details, Jade assured them they would like him very much, hanging up the phone hastily before they could question her further. Both she and Rodolfo wondered about the mystery guest and what his significance was in their daughter's life. Was he a boyfriend? Of Amie's? Or just a casual friend? Philosophically, they decided to adopt a wait-and-see attitude. After all, Jade had proven time and again how trustworthy she could be. This they felt would be no exception.

Aside from the desire of wanting to see her daughter again, Lydia had another reason for wanting Jade home.

Lately, when her husband thought no one was looking, Lydia could feel his weariness emanate from him in waves. He was working too hard, she felt, biting her lower lip in concern. With all the preparations of opening the new restaurant in Ixtapa, the extra hours were taking their toll. Even though she wanted to tell him to quit and retire, she bit her tongue and kept her own counsel. Lydia knew from long experience how important it was for her husband to feel as if he were worthy of her. It was funny to think that a man judged his success in terms of monetary reward while a woman was more apt to define it in perhaps more spiritual ways. At least that was her perception.

For whatever reason, Rodolfo became determined, almost obsessed with proving himself to her. He promised her when he won her heart away from John Mathews, the rich man from Canada who wanted to marry her, that he would do everything to make sure she never regretted her choice. She never had. Not once. Not ever.

A slight breeze was picking up now, a relief as the sun rose higher in the air, warming the lush green world at her feet. It reminded her of her first full day in Mexico so many years ago. She had gone to the beach. Lying in the sun, as most tourists do for far too long, she had turned a lobster red. Lydia smiled now as she remembered that vacation as if it were yesterday. It was to become a life-changing experience simply by the fact that now she was married to the man that was and always would be the love of her life.

She stood now and stretched her still-lean, slender body, wrapping the wind around her like a shroud. *Some days it just feels good to be alive*, she thought. This was definitely one of them. Her hair whipped around her face, still blonde but streaked heavily with silver. She wanted to color and cut it long ago, but at this Rodolfo had balked. He loved her hair long, running his fingers through its silky length. Most days she put it in a braid, satisfying his wishes while at the same time hers of keeping cool. Each night, Rodolfo would watch with loving eyes as she unbraided it and brushed it the required one hundred strokes before bedtime—he on the bed and she in front of the dressing table his brother Roberto made for them as a wedding present. In this relaxed way, they would talk over their day, eyes meeting in the mirror and smiling. Always smiling.

The sun completed its show, a signal that it was time for her to begin her day. Bending lithely, she picked up her wrappers and cup from the ground, and straightening gracefully, she began the slow descent home.

1

can hardly wait to get there." Amie leaned across the narrow space and giggled excitedly from her seat next to the window. Her turned-up nose pressed tightly against the pane, she watched eagerly as the plane lifted off the ground. In minutes, Calgary was a mere speck in the distance. Other than what Jade had told her, she knew very little about Mexico, but they had dreamed of making this trip together. She could hardly believe that the dream was finally about to become a reality. With a happy sigh, she turned to her companion next to her.

"We are going to have so much fun." She laughed again. "*Oh my god!*"

Amie was always laughing or smiling or acting enthused about something. It was part of her charm, and today especially was no exception.

Jade grinned and turned to look at Eric, who was sitting on the other side of her next to the aisle. He rolled his eyes, and Jade's smile faded a little before turning away. She could never understand the rivalry between Eric and Amie. It wasn't as if she didn't have enough time for both of them. She wished that the two people she cared about more than anything could at least tolerate each other. But they never did.

From the first moment they had set eyes on each other, Eric and Amie became, if not enemies, then certainly not friends. It was a strain for her sometimes to maintain both friendships, but she refused to give up on either one of them. She kept thinking that if only they would spend more time in each other's company, they would see how much they had in common. For one thing, they both liked to ice skate—something Jade never did if she could possibly get out of it. For a Mexican woman, it was simply more than her bones could take, she would laughingly tell them, encouraging them to go without her. But they only made excuses that never rang quite true. She hoped that this trip together would, by some miracle, make them friends, although seeing them now, she had her doubts.

From several conversations, Jade knew that Eric thought of Amie as a pest. Her laugh drove him crazy, and he could never see why people described it as infectious. Then there was that husky, low-pitched voice—incongruous with a face that looked like it was twelve years old—albeit a pretty one, he admitted reluctantly. Most of all, he didn't understand the friendship the two young women shared. Jade was cool and more reserved, while in his opinion, Amie was as silly as a school girl. While Jade favored more classic designers, Amie's attire was more colorful and, in his opinion, outlandish. The list of differences went on and on, but it was even more than that, and he knew it. Truthfully, he had admitted that as silly as it seemed, he was a little jealous of the bond the two shared.

As for Amie, she told Jade she thought Eric was overbearing, insensitive and a boor—and that was on a good day! Most of all, she thought he was stuffy. Sure, he was handsome in his own way, although blondes with blue-green eyes never had appealed to her much. She had never particularly cared for muscle-bound men either, preferring slimmer, compact bodies that suited her own small curvaceous one better. In her opinion, Jade could do much better. Jade needed someone more exciting, dashing and daring. Someone who would pull her out of her shell and make her laugh like in the old days! The first two years Jade lived in Canada, she been like that, Amie had reminded her. But then she went back for holidays and returned a new person—quieter, sadder and more unsure of herself. Amie suspected it was a man, but Jade never wanted to talk about it, even to her best friend.

Jade sighed and turned her attention back to Amie, who had already ignored Eric's slight and moved beyond.

"You are going to love Mexico, Amie, and I can't wait to show it to you." She reached over and took Eric's hand in one of her own to include him in the remark.

"Both of you," she said firmly, as if wishing that the two would reconcile their differences was all that was needed to make it so.

Eric opened his eyes at the touch of her hand and leaned closer.

"I can't think of anyone I would rather see Mexico with either." His warm smile lit his handsome face.

"Me?" Amie loved to goad him, delighted by the flash of annoyance in his eyes.

"Hardly." His voice was dry.

"Stop, you two," Jade told them firmly. "Just this once, I want you to promise me you will get along. Remember that my parents have to think that you are a couple. At least until I can tell them the truth."

Inwardly, she groaned. The way these two disliked each other, they were never going to pull this off. Maybe she should just forget the whole thing and come clean from the beginning.

"Don't worry, Jade." Amie' spoke with uncharacteristic seriousness now. "Eric and I will behave and act like a couple in love. Won't we, Eric?" She flashed her amazing eyes in his direction, daring him to disagree.

The one thing they did have in common was their love of the woman sitting between them like a referee. Neither could imagine a life without her in it. Thinking along the same lines, surprisingly, Eric acceded and managed a polite if not overtly friendly, nod.

"Good." Jade smiled at both of them and changed the subject.

Later, with Eric and Amie fast asleep on either side of her, Jade took the down time to think. While a part of her was easily as excited about going to Mexico as Amie and Eric were, another part of her was filled with apprehension. It was, after all, her childhood home. She had left a naive girl and was returning a woman. What would it be like to see her old friends? Would they welcome her with open arms, or would they shun her? She had heard that some of them had started families and were living lives totally different from hers. A part of her was envious, and she often wondered what would have happened if she had stayed home.

Remembrance of a past conversation burned hotly in her ears. It had been during her last brief visit home. After that, she had sworn she would never return until her schooling was complete. Up until now, she had kept her word.

She knew her absence had been difficult for her parents. They had compensated by combining buying trips to Canada for the gift store they owned adjacent to the restaurant. Although not an ideal arrangement, it had managed to work out, but she missed her girlhood home during that time, and she wondered now with mature eyes whether her decision to stay away had been the right one. Then she scolded herself. Of course it was. She had the business degree she wanted that would help her either start up a business of her own or take the management job offered back in Canada. Or she could even take over the restaurant in Mexico from her parents someday. The possibilities of a bright future were endless and ones she wouldn't have had if she had stagnated in Mexico, married with babies.

Her parents were throwing her a party next week to celebrate her twenty-fifth birthday. She knew they hoped she would return to Mexico for good, but was that what she wanted? She glanced at the man whose head rested on her shoulders, looking adorably angelic in his sleep.

Eric wanted to marry her. He had asked her the first time months ago while they were dining at one of the city's finest restaurants, La Chaumiere. It was where she had taken her parents once when they came to visit, and they had loved it. The setting couldn't have been more perfect for a marriage proposal, and unsuspecting as she was, Jade had been overwhelmed with emotion. Caught up in the moment, she had been highly tempted at the time to say yes. For some reason, instead she had asked for some time to think it over.

Eric was disappointed but accepted it in good grace as she explained her reasons. She felt she owed her parents more than she could ever repay them, and she knew that they had plans for her when she returned. She needed to work them out first before she could make plans of her own. Reluctantly, he had agreed, eliciting her promise to give him an answer once they were in Mexico. She promised he would have her answer on the day of her birthday. Watching him sleep now, she sometimes wondered what it was that held her back. *You know.* The voice she often ignored broke through her thoughts unbidden. Firmly, she turned them back to the man beside her.

Just out of law school a year, where he graduated in the top five in his class, Eric was already the rising star in his firm, Hutch, Benzyl and Simmons. At twenty-seven, he was considered to be the Canadian version of Jack Monroe, the famous American litigation lawyer of Jones vs. Trotsky fame. There was no question that marriage to Eric would be a smart move for many reasons and on many levels.

Aside from his physical attributes, the two of them were a good match. Both somewhat reserved, they made an elegant-looking couple. Everyone wanted to know them. In addition, they shared many of the same interests in theatre and art; they attended wine tastings and gallery openings and sometimes just hung out with their many friends. Avid readers, they spent hours discussing books, sharing many of the same opinions on a wide span of topics. Financially, they would be more than comfortable, Jade knew, although money had never been a big concern of hers. Born and raised in a Third-World country had taught her that.

That first year in Canada, she had been shocked by what she considered unbelievable waste. What some people spent on one night out would feed a family of ten for a week in Mexico. At first, it was hard for her to reconcile the economic differences, but after nearly five years in Canada, she had grown used to the abundance of her rich adopted country. Now it was rare if she gave it a second thought. She squirmed in her seat at the realization. Maybe she had changed more than was good for her. Jade rubbed her eyes wearily, wishing she could fall asleep as her friends had. Then maybe she would be able to forget. Even her dreams were filled, as much as she tried to close off unwelcome thoughts.

The person who haunted both her sleeping and waking moments was Jose Raul Angel Flores, or Raul to his friends. He had been an integral part of her nearly all of her life, it seemed, and her first love. At one time, she thought there would never be another. How wrong she had been. All had changed the last visit home.

With two years toward her business degree, she had been in need of rest and relaxation. When her parents surprised her with a flight home, she had been ecstatic. She decided not to tell Raul she was coming, wanting to surprise him. She even enlisted her parents' aid in keeping her secret.

That first night she had gone down to the pier, the same one where her mother had told her father how much she loved him over twenty-five years ago. Staring out over the water, she looked for and found his sailboat, the *Jade,* in the harbor.

In low season, Raul's primary job was fishing. His secondary one was in high season, taking tourists on tours to the many beaches that surrounded Zihuatanejo. It was this job that made him the most money. He told her he wanted to save enough so that one day they could marry and build a house. With her help and encouragement, he learned to speak English, and the two spent hours practicing together. Bright as he was, his command of the language soon became as good as hers.

The first night home, Jade borrowed a dinghy and rowed out to where Raul was anchored a hundred meters offshore. As she approached, she imagined his surprise and their reunion and smiled in anticipation. It was then she heard a woman's laughter followed by a male's low chuckle. Puzzled, she stopped rowing to listen.

A match flared, and in the light, she saw two people huddled closely in the prow of Raul's boat. In the tiny glow, she could just make out the distinctly proud features of her boyfriend…and next to him sat a woman. For a minute, she was too startled to do anything but stay where she was. She saw him light a cigarette and throw the match overboard, plunging them in darkness again. It was clear he never saw Jade sitting immobile in the dark.

She watched in fascinated horror and disbelief as gracefully tapered arms encircled his neck and she saw his head bend forward. Jade never stayed to find out what happened next. Tears streaming down her face, she had simply rowed away.

The following day, Raul arrived at her father's house to sell him some of the fish he had caught the previous day for the Mi Corazon. His obvious joy and surprise at seeing her was so genuine, it nearly melted her pounding heart. Then, remembering what she had witnessed the night before, Jade turned on him. Too proud to listen to each other, they had fought with the ferocity of wounded animals.

"You think you're too good for us now, Chiquita? Then why don't you go back to Canada and forget us poor Mexicans here, huh?"

"Maybe I am too good for you," she had retorted angrily, tearing herself out of his rough grasp.

She had rubbed her arms where he had gripped her, knowing she would have bruises. She saw the flash of hurt in his eyes her words caused him, and for a brief second, she had felt shamed. But as usual, her pride overruled, and she stayed her tongue from making an apology. With deep, unfathomable eyes, he smiled then, a smile unlike any she had ever seen on his face before. She shivered.

"By the time you come back, I will already be married with babies of my own. Then you can sleep with your fancy degree in business."

The words were cruel. If his intention was to anger her, he succeeded admirably, and she had fought back with the only man that could make her lose her composure, then or since.

"With that *puta* you were with last night?" She spat out the words contemptuously. "Why not? It's what you do best, isn't it? Working on the beach and flirting with the *touristas*. Sleeping with every woman who throws herself at you?"

Her words were equally cruel and vicious, and she watched him struggle to control his temper as realization sunk.

So that was why she was so angry? he'd thought. Somehow, she had known about the visit at his boat the previous night. Raul had grinned a little then, confident he could explain.

"I am not sleeping with Maria or anyone," he began calmly. "She was…"

So that was her name? Jade hadn't known. Hearing it then, Jade had turned her back. She was beyond listening to him and his lies. She knew what she saw.

"I don't care who you sleep with," she lied bitterly. "I want something more than to be with a beach bum who only cares how deep his tan is. There is no future for me with you." The gauntlet thrown, she dared him to pick it up.

They had stared at each other for a long moment, breath fast and furious. His lip curled disdainfully. If she wasn't about to listen then…?

Jade's heart had plummeted to her feet as she watched him walk away from her. Without waiting to see what he would do next, she slammed the door to her father's house and flew to her bedroom. It was time for her to return to school. And a new life.

To her parents' disappointment, Jade had cut her vacation short by several days, citing an unfinished thesis she simply had to have done by the end of the term. It was then she told them she thought it was a waste of time and money for her to come back to Mexico, at least until after she graduated. They thought it was because of the money and had tried to dissuade her. The truth was that she'd needed to put as much distance between her and Raul as she could, but she wasn't about to tell them that. Reluctantly, they had let her go.

Today, she was going back to the source of so much happiness in her life and, at the same time, so much pain. *You're grown up now,* she reminded herself. A big part of her realized that what she had years ago with Raul was a part of her past. If she wanted it, Eric could be her future. It was time once and for all to put the past behind her, and the only way she knew how to do that was to face it. Only then would she be able to move forward.

Eric stirred in his sleep, and Jade smiled fondly and stroked his cheek. She loved him, she knew that much. But did she love him enough to marry him? That was the big question facing her now. With a sigh, Jade closed her eyes and slid lower in her seat. *Maybe a little rest will help,* she thought. She certainly needed all of her wits about her for what lay ahead. Surprisingly enough, she too fell fast asleep.

The tedious work of bookkeeping was never something that Rodolfo liked to do. Today was no exception, especially since he had something else on his mind—the arrival of Jade. He glanced now at his watch, which seemed to be going backwards instead of ahead. Taking off his reading glasses, he rubbed his eyes wearily. He was tired. Lately, it seemed he was feeling that way a lot. Where had the young, strong man he had been gone?

Usually he left the details of the ordering and reconciliation of figures to his manager, but today Raul was off running errands for him. There was so much to do before the second restaurant was ready to open. Thank God he had someone he could trust to help him out.

Thinking about his assistant made him smile. It was no secret that he favored Raul over all of his employees, so much so that last month Rodolfo had made him a business partner with shares. It was like having the son he had always wanted.

He remembered the time the young man had first approached him for a job. It was a few days after Jade had gone back to school. Nervously, the boy told him he was tired of eking out a living fishing and catering to tourists on a budget. He wanted a career—something that would pave his way to a better future. Not only that, Raul assured him, he was willing to start at the bottom. With earnest charm, he alluded that he was doing it as much for someone else as he was himself, and Rodolfo was pleased by the initiative.

Start at the bottom he did. Rodolfo's smile grew as he recalled the first day Raul had reported for work. Dressed in his best white shirt and immaculately creased black pants, Raul's idea of starting at the bottom and his were not quite the same thing. Without a word about his appearance, Rodolfo handed him the toilet brush and instructed him to clean the bathrooms. Although his eager smile slipped a little, to his credit, Raul took the brush and went to work without a word of protest.

That was two years ago. Since then, Raul had worked his way quickly up the ranks from janitor to waiter, then to maitre d', and finally to manager and right-hand man. Rodolfo trusted him explicitly. Rodolfo leaned back in his chair and closed his eyes again. Why was he so tired? It was in this position that Lydia found him a few minutes later.

2

Lydia stopped just inside the doorway to gaze with loving eyes at the man she had married. He was her whole life, as she knew she was his. Unnoticed, she leaned against the door jam, drinking in the sight of him.

His hair, still long and pulled back in his characteristic ponytail, was threaded with silver now, giving his devastatingly good looks a rakish air. In repose, the worry lines that had started to form his face in the last year faded, and he looked like the man she had fallen in love with—a young waiter at Coconuts Restaurant.

She remembered the first time she saw him and her reaction. It was the night before New Year's Eve, and she had arrived only a few days before. Her new friend Ana, a longtime resident of Zihuatanejo in the winter months, had introduced them. The attraction was immediate, and for the next several weeks, they had been inseparable, so much so that when it had been time for her to return to Canada, she found that she couldn't.

The decision made, she and Rodolfo opened a successful restaurant of their own as well as a gift shop that sold Mexican pottery, jewelry and other crafts from around the world. Just when Lydia thought that they had reached the success they worked for, last year Rodolfo announced his intention to expand. His plan was to add a second Mi Corazon, which meant "my heart," at the resort Ixtapa a few miles away. They would call it the Mi Corazon Dos. The idea was that they would give the restaurant to Jade and whoever she married someday. In the meantime, Raul would retain his shares, and the pair would be partners unless Jade decided she wanted no part of the business. Then Raul could exercise his right to buy the family out. That it would work out best if Jade married Raul went without saying. *And if I can ever convince Rodolfo we should retire*, Lydia thought ruefully. As she watched, he rubbed his hands across his face in weariness. Immediately, she glided to his side and, leaning over, kissed his cheek.

Startled, Rodolfo looked up into his wife's face, concern and love easily apparent in her eyes. He relaxed and smiled, pulling her down to sit on his lap.

"Aye, Chiquita." He whispered his pet name in her ear, tickling her with his warm breath.

Lydia laughed and curled up in his strong arms. She leaned her head against his shoulder and regarded him thoughtfully. After all this time, he still had the power to thrill her, although with age, their relationship had mellowed over the years. It had deepened and matured just as his father, the last Shaman of the Tarahumara, had predicted it would just before he died.

She had never met Joseph Perez, but she wished that she could have. Rodolfo told her his father foretold a blonde woman would come for him and that she would make him very happy. Telling the story, he had laughed because he remembered the night that he recalled the prediction. She had kissed him in the moonlight on the first day of the year while walking the neighborhood he lived in. Then, in the next breath, she informed him that she had a boyfriend back in Canada and that he would be arriving soon. At the time, it had been a funny coincidence. Now, with her sitting contentedly on his lap, it was obvious that his father had been right. According to Rodolfo, his father was the most incredible man on earth. Lydia liked to think he would have approved of them had he lived.

As it was, she enjoyed a close relationship with the remaining living members of Rodolfo's family, especially Roberto and Yola, his brother and sister-in-law. At first reluctant to meet the *gringa* that Rodolfo had fallen for, they soon overcame their prejudices when they had seen how suited they were for each other. Even her mother-in-law, Nina, had treated her like another daughter, welcoming her into their hearts and family with an ease and grace that had astonished and gratified Lydia. By the time Jade was born, Lydia was firmly entrenched in the family dynamics.

Her friends Len and Lina, among others, hardly recognized the former driven executive she had been as the softer gentler woman she was today. She had the man on whose lap she was sitting to thank for the change. She kissed his lips lightly and asked how he was feeling.

"Lydia, I am fine." He grimaced, touched by her concern but a little annoyed too. He knew she worried about his health far too much, and it bothered him. As if to reassure her, he bent her back over his arm and kissed her long and hard.

"Are you happy now?" he asked with mock sternness until she had to laugh. She changed the subject.

"Our baby is coming home today," she reminded him, as if there was any need to. "What time should we leave for the airport?"

He looked at his watch.

"I think if we leave around two, we should get there in time. Mexican time." He laughed the deep, self-deprecating chuckle she always enjoyed.

"Everyone wants to come with us, remember?"

Rodolfo nodded. Jade had been greatly missed. Thank goodness he had a big truck and they could all pile in the back. Maybe Roberto would bring his car too. He made a mental note to ask him later. Right now, he had work to do if he was going to be finished in time. For once, he didn't want to be late.

Gently, he squeezed his wife and nudged her firmly off his lap.

"I have work to do, Lydia, and you are distracting me."

She laughed again and complied with his not-too-subtle hint by standing up.

"That's okay, *mi amor*. I have things to do in the store too before I go to the airport. Remember that you are not to work this evening. We are having a family dinner tonight."

"I will see you in an hour then," her husband promised just as the phone rang, and he reached to answer it.

As he kissed the tips of her fingers, she moved away, stopping once in the doorway to look over her shoulder. In the minute it had taken her to cross the room, he was already deeply engrossed in conversation with a supplier. She sighed. Even now she could see the stress forming on his face as he concentrated. It was a far cry from the Rodolfo she once knew, and she wasn't all that sure she liked the change. *He is working too hard*, she told herself for the second time that day, vowing to have a talk with Jade and Raul at her first opportunity. With renewed determination, she lengthened her stride and walked briskly to the gift store next door.

Raul loaded the groceries in the front of the pickup and glanced at his watch. It had been a present from Jade the year he turned eighteen. It never failed to remind him of her every time he looked at it. Today was no exception, but then today was no ordinary day either.

If he hurried, he could take the vehicle to the car wash for a quick rinse and polish. Lydia had told him that Jade's friends, some of the family and, of course, Ana, Lydia's dearest friend, all wanted to be at the airport to greet her. Knowing this, he wanted to make sure the truck was spotless.

Driving through the winding narrow streets at the market, Raul expertly dodged the numerous strays that darted in his path, impatiently stopping for pedestrians that crowded the noisy neighborhood. Finally, he was on Benito Juarez and driving into the lot of the car wash. While the attendants soaped and scrubbed, he sat on the white plastic chairs to wait.

He knew that he should be among the friends at the airport to meet Jade— no one had a better right. But that was before. Not even Rodolfo and Lydia, surrogate parents to him that they were, knew the extent of his estrangement from Jade. They assumed they were going through a cooling off period while she was away at school. He knew differently. Her face the last time they saw each other had been colder than he had ever seen it. It would be hard for her to forgive him for what he had done. *What she thought he had done,* he reminded himself.

Regardless, Raul knew that her parents both felt it was a mutual but temporary situation and that when Jade came back, the relationship would resume as before. Puzzled that he wouldn't be with them later, Lydia questioned him.

"Rodolfo tells me you are not coming to the airport, Raul." There was surprise and concern in her voice.

"I have too much to do, Senora," he lied unsuccessfully and flushed. Jade's mother could always see right through him. "But I promise I will be there at the dinner."

Lydia frowned but seemed satisfied for the time being. It was clear from her manner, however, that she would want answers soon, and he didn't know what those answers were. Not until he talked to Jade.

What he said about dinner was true. He would be there that night, but in a different capacity. He had arranged with Arturo, Rodolfo's closest friend and compadre, to switch shifts with him. Instead of being a guest, he would be the one serving Jade's celebratory dinner. No doubt Jade would think that she had been right about him all along—that he was without ambition and would never amount to anything. Raul grinned, imagining her surprise when she found out that he and her father were partners.

When it first happened, he had asked Rodolfo and Lydia not to tell Jade, explaining that he wanted to be the one to surprise her. Without question, they had agreed, only mentioning to their daughter that Raul was now working for them. Jade had seemed indifferent and had not pursued the issue. To be sure, it had surprised them, but they let it pass.

The words she had thrown at him that day long ago still burned in his ears. Raul vowed that one day he would make her eat them. Then she would relent and beg him to take her back, he thought, confident in the power of their attraction for each other. In his mind, he imagined her throwing her arms around him in admiration and asking him to forgive her for the things she had said. He would kiss her, and she would kiss him back. Maybe they would make love...so real was the fantasy that he didn't see the wet rag flying through the air soon enough to duck. It caught him full in the face.

Surprised, he looked up into the mischievous eyes of his best friend Carlos Garcia. Swiftly, he pulled the rag off his lap where it had fallen and whipped it back, catching his friend in the head. Then they both burst into laughter.

Raul stood and shook his friend's hand. It had been awhile since they had seen each other. Carlos had obtained a job at one of the local resorts in Ixtapa as an accountant and worked long hours during the day. Their schedules never seemed to coincide, and it was rare that they would meet like this.

"Que haces, amigo?" [What are you doing, friend?] Raul asked a wide grin on his face as he attempted to clean himself off. Thankfully, he was wearing his oldest clothes and wouldn't change into his uniform for a few hours yet. Carlos, on the other hand, was wearing his office attire, but as usual, he looked rumpled and untidy, his wide, good-humored face nearly split in two by his cheerful grin.

"I came into Zihua to pick up some office supplies." Carlos puffed his chest a little and told him importantly, "My boss is in Mexico City and has put me in charge while he is away. I saw the truck and stopped. Where have you been?"

"Working, working, working." Raul made a comical face as if he hated the idea, although secretly, he liked his job very much.

Carlos nodded. He knew what that was like. "I hear Jade is coming back today," he said casually, looking at his friend for his reaction. As Raul's closest friend, he knew about their estrangement, but like most people, he never believed that it was permanent. Everyone knew that Jade and Raul were perfect for each other and had been since the first grade. In his opinion, this was just a passing phase.

He felt guilty too. His role in the split was never verbalized, but it was there. Once when he tried to apologize to his friend, Raul had waved him off.

"She'll get over it," Raul had tried to assure him at the time.

But Carlos knew she never had. In all the time she had been away, to Carlos' knowledge, Jade had never spoken to Raul again. He wished there was something he could do.

Raul nodded at Carlos remark about Jade's homecoming but didn't say anything. Seeing his reluctance to elaborate, Carlos changed the subject and asked him about the new restaurant instead.

Raul's face lit up as he talked about the changes they were making, the features and equipment it would have. Carlos was impressed and told him so. Raul smiled modestly and tried not to let his pride show at the praise.

"It's mostly Rodolfo and Lydia," he confided. "I am very lucky they gave me a job. I am learning so much about this business. One day, one way or the other, it will be mine."

Carlos smiled. He was the only one of Raul's friends that knew about the partnership and how much it meant to him to have a business of his own some day—a business Raul would hopefully one day share with Jade.

The pair talked a few minutes more. With real interest, Raul asked Carlos about his family. He was godfather to their little girl, Lulu, a role he took seriously. A mischievous little minx, she had her *padrino* wrapped around her baby finger. He smiled as Carlos told him about some of her latest escapades.

As they laughed, the car wash attendant came over and told Raul his truck was ready. Promising each other they would connect at Jade's birthday party in one week, they parted ways.

Raul hopped in the shining truck and carefully backed out of the lot. He had to hurry now in order to get the truck delivered to Rodolfo in time to meet Jade's plane. He almost wished he was going now, but he resisted the urge. *My time with Jade will come soon enough*, he promised inwardly as he headed the vehicle to the Mi Corazon.

While they waited for their luggage to appear on the conveyor belt, Jade gazed anxiously through the glass doors of the arrivals lounge. At first she didn't see anyone she knew, and her heart sank a little. Did they forget she was coming today? As if reading her thoughts, Amie laughed and grabbed her arm.

"Don't worry, Jade. They're here. Look." She pointed to the left. "There's Aunt Lydia and Uncle Rodolfo."

Straining to see over the crowd, Jade followed the pointing finger. Suddenly, she saw her parents, and immediately her eyes lit up with joy. She watched as their faces scanned the crowd anxiously. In the next instant, they saw her too, and Jade laughed aloud as her mother pulled her father closer to the glass partition for a better look. They waved excitedly, wishing they were on the other side already.

"Oh and look, there's Aunt Ana and Uncle Roberto, and Aunt Yola!" Jade exclaimed. "And some of my friends from school! Is that Delila?" She smiled at the sight of her girlfriends jumping up and down in the airport like teenagers. She knew that in her absence they had gotten married, and she saw that two at least carried small children on their hips. She felt a pang but pushed it away.

"Looks like half of Zihuatanejo are here to meet you." Without thought, Eric kissed her cheek, forgetting for the moment that he was supposed to be Amie's boyfriend and not hers.

Amie reminded him. "Better kiss me too, Eric, or they will be suspicious."

Eric's mouth slid sideways but did what she asked. If that was what Jade wanted, far be it for him to go against her wishes, but he, for one, would be thankful when their charade was over.

Eric's lips were surprisingly gentle, and Amie drew back in surprise and surreptitiously wiped her cheek with a slightly grubby hand. It gratified her when his eyes narrowed in anger.

"Are you sure we have to go through with this?" he complained under his breath, and Jade almost smiled.

"Just for a little while," she pleaded. "I need time to…"

Just then, one of their suitcases appeared on the belt, and as one, they moved closer to claim it. For the next while, they were kept busy pulling the heavy bags off the belt and onto the carts of the waiting porters. What she had been about to say was soon forgotten as they followed their luggage to the outer room and into the waiting arms of her family and friends.

Jade crossed the doors first, and immediately they swarmed and gathered her in their midst. Tears of joy streamed down her face, and she felt whole again for the first time in a long time. She tried to stem the flow, laughing and crying at the same time.

Feeling slightly out of place, Eric and Amie hung back and watched the open and touching displays of emotion. Rapid Spanish filled the air, punctuated with shrieks of laughter and more hugs and kisses.

"Welcome home, *princessa*." Rodolfo's eyes were bright with tears of his own as he held his daughter away from him to look at her. "You grow more beautiful every day."

Pleased, Jade laughed. "You just saw me a few months ago, Poppa," she teased. "And you always say the same thing."

"That's because it is true," her uncle Roberto told her, and his wife nodded in agreement and pride as Jade kissed them both, then their daughter Andrea.

Next in line were her childhood girlfriends. In addition to Delila, who she had spotted earlier, there were Celia and Elizabeth—Eli to her friends. She hugged them warmly and complimented the young mothers on their beautiful wide-eyed children. Jade made them all promise to come to the house soon for a visit and to catch up with all the news. Readily, they agreed and stepped back so that Lydia could spend a few minutes with her.

"We have missed you so much." Lydia tilted her head appraisingly to look at her beautiful daughter.

"Me too." Jade leaned over to give her mother another kiss.

The two had always shared a special mother-daughter relationship. Now, holding her close, Jade realized just how close that connection was. If she decided to live in Canada, she knew that it would be hard to leave her family behind. She felt a sharp pang in her breast at the thought.

Finally, Lydia lifted her head and noticed Jade's friends standing off to one side. Wearing pasted-on smiles and looking uneasy amidst so many strangers, they returned her look with frank admiration. Lydia hurried over to them and apologized for her neglect.

"We are just so happy to have Jade home. Welcome, Amie." She hugged the young woman she loved like a daughter to her breast.

"Thank you for inviting me…us, Aunt Lydia." Amie returned the embrace and then turned to greet Rodolfo.

She was fond of them both, telling Jade often that she envied her parents. Not that she would trade hers for anything, she hastily thought loyally. It was just that the story of Lydia and Rodolfo's romance was like something out of a fairy tale to her. Resolutely, she grabbed Eric by the arm and yanked him none-too-gently forward. Jade wanted them to pretend they were together, and she was determined to do exactly that.

"Aunt Lydia, Uncle Rodolfo, I would like you to meet my…um…friend. Eric Foster. Eric, these are Jade's parents, Mr. and Mrs. Perez."

"Please call us Lydia and Rodolfo." Lydia was insistent as she reached for his hand and brought his head down for a kiss on the cheek in true Mexican fashion. Rodolfo took his hand with a manly grip but settled for a brief hug instead.

At first, Eric drew back in surprise. Jade's parents and indeed all of the people present were so much more open and uninhibited than he was used to, so different from his own rigorous and slightly sterile upbringing. He decided he liked it, and his warm smile lit up his face, instantly winning over the people in the group.

Jade watched from the edge of the circle anxiously. Then she saw Eric's smile, and she relaxed. She should have known better than to worry about Eric in any kind of social situation. His well-to-do background and good manners were sure to help him now. Besides that, he was well traveled, even though this was his first time to Mexico. She wondered how he was going to react to some of the things he would encounter, but then she dismissed it as unworthy. *He will either accept my people or he won't*, she thought determinedly.

As for Amie, she knew she need not be concerned. Already, she was knee deep in the middle of her friends, laughing and joking in the rudimentary Spanish Jade had taught her, her deep throaty voice floating happily above the crowd. Jade sighed contentedly and looked around, catching sight of her Aunt Ana watching quietly from the sidelines. A small secretive smile rested lightly on her face.

Aunt Ana was not really her aunt but a friend of her mother's. As long as Jade could remember, Ana had been a constant part of her life. Her mother had once told her it was Ana who had introduced Lydia to Jade's father.

"And it was Ana who had the courage to knock some sense into my head when it looked like I was going to go back to Canada and marry someone else," Lydia had recalled. Jade hurried toward her now and, leaning over, gave her an affectionate kiss on the cheek.

"So you've finally come home, Jade." Ana stated the obvious in her slight, crisp New York accent. "It's about time."

Jade nodded and smiled, remembering the countless times she had confided in this woman over the years.

"Si, *tia*, I am back. It is so good to see you. How are you?"

"I am well," Ana replied crisply, "but you are not here to talk about my health. You want to know why Raul is not here, don't you?" As always, she was blunt and to the point.

Jade flushed a deep red. Ana could always read her better than anyone, voicing exactly what Jade had been thinking with uncanny accuracy.

Ana watched her carefully. It was just as she had thought. She smiled smugly.

"I haven't seen Raul for two years, Ana." Jade blushed even as she tried to defend herself. "By now, I am sure he is married with babies."

"You don't believe that anymore than I do, Jade." Ana mocked her a little and then changed the subject. "And who is that handsome young man with you over there?" She pointed to the group with her cane.

"That is Eric Foster. He is…um…Amie's boyfriend." She flushed as she saw Ana's eyebrows lift. It was clear she didn't believe her.

"Okay, Aunt Ana, he is my boyfriend." In a guilty rush, she confessed hastily, seeing her mother head in their direction. Lowering her voice, she whispered, "Please don't tell. I promise to tell you all about it later."

Ana nodded regally just as Lydia joined them. No one knew exactly how old Ana was. She was one of those rare women who looked ageless. She never confirmed or denied it, but some would say she must have been in her seventies. One thing everyone knew with certainty was that she was used to keeping the secrets of young women, especially Jade's, just as she had with Jade's mother twenty-five years ago.

Lydia smiled fondly down at her close friend seated on the airport chair. "Our little girl has grown up, hasn't she, Ana?"

"And very well, too." Ana complimented the gratified young woman and held out her hand for assistance to stand.

Jade grasped it and was shocked by the frailness of the woman she had not seen for over two years. She quickly hid her dismay, but not before Ana caught the look and smiled.

The folly of youth, Ana thought, *is that they all think life will go on forever. Everyone knows that this is just the beginning.* She kept her thoughts to herself, however, and walked with her two favorite women to where the rest of the group waited. She was charming to Eric and Amie, complimenting them on their healthy good looks with a frankness that pleased them both. Jade told them that Ana was a part of her family and that they would be seeing a great deal of her while they were there. Amie was enthralled to finally meet the woman of whom Jade talked of constantly, winning Ana over instantly.

The introductions and greetings finally concluded, it was decided that the young would crawl in the back of the truck while Lydia and Aunt Ana rode in the front with Rodolfo. On the way to the parking lot, Rodolfo placed one arm around his daughter and the other around his wife. A man of few words, his love for "his girls" warmed them. Silently he thanked the Creator for his daughter's safe return.

The rest of the group straggled behind the small family. Roberto and Yola walked together with their daughter Andrea, grown now and with a husband, Hugo, and two children of her own. Her husband was working today, and their children, Tania and Rosie, were both in school, but they sent their love, Andrea told her cousin shyly. Jade told her she was looking forward to seeing them soon. Turning at the parking lot entrance to get into their own car parked at the corner, the family said goodbye and invited Jade to visit when she was settled, telling her to bring her Canadian friends with her. Kissing them fondly, Jade promised them she would at the first opportunity.

Eric and Amie followed the others a short distance behind. As usual, they were arguing but trying to keep their voices low so they wouldn't be overhead.

"You don't have to hold my hand," Amie hissed the words under her breath, her smile remaining firmly plastered on her face.

From a distance, they looked like any young couple in love and drew admiring glances from passers-by. Physically, with their blonde hair and good looks, they radiated like the golden couple they were supposed to portray.

"I like holding your hand, Amie." Eric drawled his vowels lazily, delighted he had finally found the perfect way to antagonize Jade's best friend.

"I hate you." She gritted her words through clenched teeth and dropped his hand as if he had leprosy.

After that, she hurried forward under the guise of wanting to talk to Aunt Lydia. From behind, Amie heard his amused chuckle, and her face burned.

"You look hot, Amie. Are you feeling alright?" Lydia asked concernedly.

Amie heard Eric laugh again but ignored it and turned brightly in her aunt's direction.

"No, Aunt Lydia, I am fine. Just need to get used to the weather, that's all."

For the next few minutes, they discussed the climate difference between Canada and Mexico, agreeing adamantly that it was better here.

"I can't wait to get a tan," she told Lydia now, holding up a satiny white arm ruefully.

"Be careful at first," Lydia cautioned her with a few words about her own first experiences in Mexico, and Amie promised she would. As fair as she was, she would eventually tan just as Jade did, but she realized she did have to exercise common sense in the beginning of the process.

By now, they had reached the truck, and the porters began to unload the luggage into the back.

"You can sit on the bags," Rodolfo instructed everyone in Spanish and then kindly translated in English for Amie and Eric's sake.

Eric looked dubiously at the means of transportation before shrugging good-humoredly. Amie was already in the back, staking her claim on one of the brightly colored suitcases closest to the rear window. In a flash, he climbed up and sat next to her. Amie glared haughtily but said nothing. At that moment, Ana looked up and saw the exchange.

Interesting, Ana noted, smiling as Rodolfo opened the passenger door for her and helped her up to sit next to Lydia. The situation was promising to be more interesting than she previously thought. She could hardly wait to have that conversation with Jade later.

Once everyone was settled, Rodolfo put the truck in gear, drove to the gate and paid the parking lot attendant. Then cautiously, he pulled out onto the highway toward Zihuatanejo.

From where she sat squished between Delila and Elizabeth, one small child on her lap, Jade was able to point out some of the more interesting sights. Eric and Amie looked around with fascinated interest. In the manner of a tour guide, she showed them the coconut plantations that lined either side of the road, as well as the pineapple and mango trees in the distance.

Amie—who had never seen a coconut, banana or plantation tree in her life and thought they all grew in a Safeway store—was thrilled. Even Eric found it interesting, although he pretended that Amie was making a big deal over nothing. Embarrassed, Amie looked to Jade for support, but she had her hands full for the moment with the charming child sitting on her knee and didn't notice.

"You are so hateful," Amie hissed, exasperated, and Eric grinned.

This is working out better than I could imagine, he thought, wondering why he hadn't come up with the idea sooner. In reply, he took her hand and held it.

Amie was about to pull it from his grasp when she looked up and saw Jade's friends watching her, curiosity written on their faces. *It's clear they think Eric is some kind of Greek god,* she thought, irritated. With a small, false smile, she returned their envious looks and kept her hand where it was. Then, as the truck veered around the corner, she feigned losing her balance and pulled away to steady herself. She made sure not to let him grab it back.

Jade continued her brief tour now that the child was settled firmly in place.

"Over there is a little neighborhood known as Agua de Correa, which means 'Running Water.'" They followed her eyes.

"It looks very poor." Eric was unable to keep the shock from his voice. Jade nodded. "Do people actually live in those shacks?"

"Yes it is, and yes they do, but there are pretty spots in it too, the old church for one thing. My parents were married there, and I was baptized there. My friends baptized their daughter there, and many of my other friends have been married in it, too. It is where I have always wanted to be married." She said the last part shyly, looking up at him from beneath lowered lashes.

Eric smiled, and for a moment their eyes held.

Watching them, Amie felt a twinge of something indefinable, and she looked away to the right.

"What is that?" She pointed to a modern-looking building as they entered the small city.

Jade tore her gaze from Eric and answered her friend. "That is something we are all very proud of. It is the new municipal building. Now you can go to one place and do most of your city business instead of to a dozen different locations. It's sort of like the city hall in Calgary." Her laughter was infectious, and Amie joined in.

The truck slowed, and Jade turned her head to look forward. They were entering the circle now at Plaza Kyoto. Soon they would backtrack and head up the steep hill toward Playa La Ropa and her home. *Home!* She could hardly wait. As the excitement of being back churned within, she stayed silent and kept her eyes eagerly fixated to the front.

Street after street whizzed by them, and she noticed that while there were new stores and businesses along the way, many things had not changed at all. She was relieved. Finally, they made their way up the last leg of their journey, and Jade pointed out the Bay of Zihuatanejo far below them as they climbed. Eric and Amie pressed forward, shoulders touching as they tried to get a glimpse of the sparkling ocean below. For once, Amie didn't pull away from his touch and even smiled at him briefly, so caught up was she by the sheer beauty of the scene.

At last, the old red Ford screeched to a halt, and everyone laughed as the motion whip-lashed them where they sat. Then, one by one they piled out, Eric jumping to the ground first to gallantly offer his assistance. Jade watched him as he joked with her friends. She could tell they thought he was absolutely wonderful, and her heart warmed at the knowledge. From her standing position in the back of the truck, she almost moved forward as if to kiss him, but she remembered and caught herself. Instead, she grabbed his hand and expertly swung herself to the ground, hurrying forward to help her mother with Ana.

"This is the damndest vehicle to get out of." Ana was complaining loudly even as she eased her small frame out of the cab.

Jade smiled. "You should have gotten in the back with us," she teased, and Ana tapped her with her fan, eyes twinkling.

Belatedly remembering her manners, Jade turned back to her friends. They would have to get home now in time to fix their family lunch. She hurried forward to thank them again for coming and promised once more to visit.

"And bring the guapo." They giggled flirtatiously, their eyes sliding over to Eric before descending the pathway to their respective homes.

"Were they talking about me?" Eric demanded to know.

"You think everyone talks about you." Amie was scornfully dismissive before Jade could answer.

"In this case, yes, they were," Jade admitted with a laugh. "But I think that maybe you will get too swell-headed if I tell you what they said."

Amie snorted as Eric preened, and Jade laughed again at the pair of them. Sometimes watching these two together was better than going to the movies— a favorite pastime of hers in Canada.

They stood outside in the courtyard for a while, chatting and looking around while her parents and Ana went inside. Eric and Amie were amazed at the numerous plants that surrounded the property and the many different kinds of flowers growing in the pots lining the verandah. Jade explained that the garden was her father's pride and joy, although with the restaurant, he was too busy to do it by himself. Now he relied more and more on the expert assistance of Juan Sanchez, a man employed by them ever since Jade had been a small child. His wife Juanita was their housekeeper, and the pair, together with their one son, lived in a small house down the hill.

Eric and Amie were impressed. A maid and a gardener? Jade laughed. She could understand their surprise, knowing that in Canada it would be excessive unless you were very rich. Here in Mexico, she explained, many people had domestic help because it was very cheap to obtain. She didn't add that her parents were considered well-off by Mexican standards, though, and really even by Canadian ones too.

Just then, Rodolfo and Lydia called them into the house for lunch, and they hurried to obey the summons. Suddenly, they were starved. Before they entered the house, Jade stopped and cautioned them once more.

"Remember, you two. You are a couple. At least until I can let my parents know in my own way. I know they have plans for me, and I don't want to disappoint them." She gave them her usual pat explanation, and for the moment, it seemed to satisfy.

Eric nodded his head, threw an arm around Amie's shoulder and squeezed. He was determined that if Jade wanted it that way, he would do everything he could to make sure her wishes were granted. *No matter what*, he thought grimly.

Startled, Amie said nothing. She wasn't sure she could keep this up, not with the way Eric had been acting since their arrival. His open hostility she could handle, but the false intimacy was more than she could bear. She, for one, would be very happy when they could call an end to this game, if that was what it was, and she could be herself again. Hating Eric openly. She smiled at the thought.

Watching them and seeing Amie's smile, Jade misinterpreted and relaxed. It might work after all...at least she hoped so. Turning, she led the way into the cool kitchen, Amie and Eric hot on her heels.

After the fairly substantial lunch of chicken enchiladas, rice and beans, Amie and Eric announced that they wanted to go to the beach. With characteristic generosity, Rodolfo offered to drive them. Jade opted to stay behind and spend time with her mother while Ana exercised her option to take a siesta in one of the cool guest rooms off the verandah. Later, they would drive her back to the hotel The Citlali, where she would change for dinner at the restaurant that evening.

On hearing that Jade was going to stay behind, Amie immediately offered to stay with her. There was no way she wanted to go to the beach alone with Eric.

Lydia interceded. "Go spend some time with Eric, Amie. Jade and I have a lot of catching up to do. I hope you don't mind?"

She gave her daughter's friend her most winning smile, and Amie nodded. When her Aunt Lydia smiled, there was no denying her anything. Eric chose that moment to pull Amie close to him.

"We don't mind at all, do we, Amie? Besides, Mrs. Perez is right—it will give us a chance to be alone." He winked lasciviously, and Amie reddened.

Jade merely stared at her boyfriend, wondering what on earth had gotten into him, while Ana only laughed and retired to the guest room.

"Okay, then. *Vamanous*," Rodolfo said, and Eric and Amie hurried to their bags to find their swimsuits.

They returned a few minutes later and soon were roaring down the road that would take them to the beach they had glimpsed from the back of the pickup.

As soon as they were out of sight, Lydia turned to her daughter and smiled. "Okay, Jade. I think you better tell me what's going on."

Raul put the finishing touches on the main table in the dining room and stepped back to view his handiwork. This was the table where Jade's family and guests would be dining tonight. It was the best table in the house, and he wanted everything to be perfect. As he worked, he frowned. Only that morning Lydia had told him about the two extra guests from Canada. Casually, he asked who they were, but she had been unusually vague.

"One is Amie, Jade's best friend. I am sure she told you about her in the past?"

Raul nodded. "And the other?"

"Now that is something I can't tell you for sure. It's a man. That much I do know. Maybe Amie's boyfriend? Anyway, we will find out soon enough,"

With that, Lydia had hurried out the door before he could question her further. She had a niggling idea in the back of her mind that this unexpected guest was more important to Jade than she let on, and she wanted to avoid talking about it with Raul until she knew more. *No sense in hurting him unnecessarily,* she had thought as she opened the door to her shop.

Raul shrugged now. Worrying about it would get him nowhere. As Lydia said, he would know soon enough. He reached out and straightened a fork, a foreboding feeling niggling in the pit of his stomach. Finally satisfied, he hurried to the kitchen to discuss the last-minute menu changes and make sure that everything was ready on time.

As usual, the kitchen was in full force when he got there. At one time, it had been his job to wash the mountain of pots that looked about to topple on the floor. He glanced in sympathy to where his head dishwasher was now working. At Raul's approach, Jorge looked up and grinned good-naturedly. Raul knew that as disorganized as it looked now, Jorge would be finished in plenty of time before they opened. Then he would have to start all over again in order to be finished in time for closing.

He was proud of their team—completely self contained and dependable, he knew that they were the envy of many of the lesser restaurants in Zihuatanejo. The competition had been fierce, too, but little by little, they had taken over a respectable share of the market. In another week, they would exceed that with the opening of another restaurant. And after that, who knew? One thing for certain, he would never forget that Rodolfo and Lydia had given him the chance to be here. If it wasn't for them, he would still be chasing tourist dollars on the beach or smelling of fish. Now at least he had a future and a dream that was on the way to becoming a reality. Raul walked to the bar to give some last-minute instructions as to the wines he would need that night.

Then, taking a much needed break from his duties, he sat back to wait for the onslaught of business in the night ahead.

3

Rodolfo drove away, leaving his charges alone on a deserted part of the beach "where they could be alone." Even before he was out of sight, Amie turned and lashed out at the blonde man beside her.

"You can cut out the crap, Eric." Her furious face was reddened and molted with anger. "There's no one around you have to impress anymore."

She was referring to the fact that Eric had grabbed her hand and held tightly to it during the ride to the beach, going so far as attempting to cuddle her. It had been all she could do not to push him out of the truck.

"Crap?" Eric tried for an innocent look. "Why, Amie, you do have the cutest expressions."

Amie stared at him for a second, seething with anger. Then, disgusted, she turned on her heel and stalked off without another word. As far as she was concerned, he was carrying this charade a little farther than necessary. A boorish Eric she understood. A charming one, she had no idea what to do with. Emotions high, she decided the best way to handle Eric was to ignore him. She began by snatching her beach bag off the sand and retrieving a giant towel from its considerable depth.

Bending slightly, she gave it a shake and spread it out on the sand. Back to him, she shimmied out of the sundress she had changed into before leaving the house, revealing a near perfect curvaceous body. Still miffed, she lay down on the warm earth to tan. In spite of her anger, it felt good, and almost against her will, she felt herself relax and her tensions ease. Content, she burrowed deeper into the soft sand.

Eric stared at the woman as she went through her motions. He had never seen Amie in a bikini before, and it stunned him into silence. He could barely take his eyes off of her. Perfectly proportioned, her white skin gleamed in the sun like a marble. *Stop it*, he admonished inwardly. *This is Amie you're looking at.* She was lovely.

Unaware of the effect she was having on him and mindful of Aunt Lydia's advice, Amie reached into the bag once more and pulled out a tube of suntan lotion.

"Here, boyfriend." Sarcastic words dripped from her pink mouth. "Why don't you make yourself useful?"

She stretched her arm, holding the super-strength sunscreen in her hand and waiting.

Eric gulped and scowled mightily. After a moment's hesitation, he stepped closer and took the lotion from her hand. Kneeling, he unscrewed the top of the tube and squeezed a small amount into his palm. Mouth suddenly dry, he rubbed his hands together before placing them on the small of Amie's back.

"Hmmmmm," Amie murmured as she lay, face buried in the towel.

Encouraged, Eric's hands roamed her creamy body, luxuriating in the feel of the satin skin beneath him. His hands slid under her bra strap and then to the top of her back, across her shoulders and down her slender muscled arms, causing him to lose himself in the sensations.

Amie started to feel a tingling in her body. When his strong fingers reached to the top of her thighs, Amie's eyes flew open in alarm. Sitting up quickly, she grabbed the tube out of his hand.

"I can do that," she snapped rudely, and he reddened.

Amie watched him stride away, his back erect and stiff. She knew she should apologize. After all, she did ask him to help her. And it had felt good too, she had to admit. She tried to push the remembrance of it away.

Angry with himself for getting so carried away, Eric stood at the water's edge, his errant thoughts tumultuous. The feel of her skin on his fingers lingered, and impatiently he shook his head and tried to concentrate on something else. As the waves lapped at his feet, he struggled get a hold of himself.

At this time of day, most of the beachgoers were beginning to head home, and now it was almost deserted, as Rodolfo had assured them it would be. He wondered why he wasn't there with Jade instead of that bossy little.... He left the thought unfinished and fought to control his anger. He felt a tap on his shoulder and, thinking it was Amie, he snarled over his shoulder without turning around.

"Get lost."

"Pardon?" A shy and very young male voice spoke, and he whirled.

Before him stood a slight Mexican boy of about twelve, he guessed, looking at him with a wide smile and a question in his eyes.

He was instantly apologetic. "I'm sorry. I thought you were someone else." Looking over the boy's shoulder, he could see that the "someone else" was face down once more in the sand. With an effort, he turned his attention back to the youth in front of him.

"You want to go for a sail, senor?" The boy spoke with carefully accented English. "A romantic sail with you pretty lady?" He jerked his thumb over his shoulder.

"No thanks. She's not my..." Eric started to explain, then shrugged and stopped.

The idea of a sail on the ocean, with or without the "pretty lady" was suddenly appealing to him. It was a beautiful time of day—the waves were calm, the lighting was perfect, and it would at least help him get rid of the restless energy he suddenly seemed to have. If he couldn't be with Jade, then at least maybe he could enjoy it on his own. He smiled at the young lad.

"How much?" he asked.

He was favored with a wide disarming grin. "For you, *barata*, very cheap. Only twenty dollars."

"Fifteen dollars, and you got yourself a deal." Eric stuck out his hand to seal the bargain, and after a brief hesitation, the boy took it.

"Deal," he said, and Eric smiled again.

He wondered if he shouldn't have just paid the asking price and vowed that he would leave a five-dollar tip at the end of the hour instead. His conscience eased, and he looked around for a boat. There wasn't any.

"What's your name? You speak very good English." He decided to compliment him instead.

At that, the young lad's chest puffed with pride at the blonde man's words. "I am Jose Juan Roberto Sanchez. You can call me Juanito though. Everyone does. I study English in school."

"I am pleased to meet you, Juanito. I am Eric Foster, and that pretty lady over there is Amie Le Blanc. Why don't you tell her we are going sailing?"

With a perpetual smile, Juanito strutted across the sand to where Amie lay baking in the late afternoon sun. As Eric watched, he saw Amie sit up and almost immediately stretch out her hand to be shaken by the small stranger. *At least she's not a snob*, he noted with approval as their laughter rang out across the sand. He saw her turn her head and regard him. With the sound of the surf on shore, he was unable to make out what they were saying, but a few minutes later, Juanito returned, a huge besotted smile on his face. With a new swagger, he informed Eric that Amie was agreeable to a short sail.

Eric looked around again. "Where is your boat?

Juanito smiled. Then, placing two fingers between his lips, he blew hard and shrilly, nearly deafening Eric in the process. Ears ringing, Eric watched in awe as, from around the crest of the bay, a multi-colored catamaran glided into sight, carrying two boys of about the same age as his new friend. Within a few minutes, the crewmen were out of the water and pulling the craft from the surf onto the sand.

Eric reached into his back pocket, quickly peeled off three five dollar bills and handed them to Jaunito with a smile. Then he waded in the water. A splash alerted him, and he turned to see Amie grinning excitedly beside him, her earlier displeasure completely gone. He couldn't help it—he grinned back.

Amie scrambled onto the deck and settled herself so that she faced forward. With the help of the three boys, Eric pushed the catamaran out into the surf, with a promise that they would be back in an hour's time. Amie and Eric waved at the young entrepreneurs and were soon headed out to sea.

"I repeat, Jade," Lydia spoke slightly more forcefully. "What is going on?"

"I don't know what you mmmean..." Jade felt like a child as she stammered and flushed under her mother's stare.

"I think you do, Jade," Lydia replied quietly. "You can start by telling me just who Eric Foster is and what he means to you."

Jade mind raced as she struggled for a minute, unsure as to what she was going to say.

"Eric is a friend of mine and Amie's..." she began hesitantly.

"I think more a friend to you than to Amie." Her mother's eyes were bright as she noted shrewdly, "Yet you have passed him off as Amie's boyfriend. At least, that is the impression both your father and I got. Why is that? Are you ashamed of us or him?"

Jade stared at her mother in astonishment. "I could never be ashamed of you or Poppa. You must know that."

Lydia nodded that she did. "Then it must be Eric?"

Jade shook her head vigorously in denial, "Never that either. Eric is wonderful." Then she looked closer at her mother, who was trying to hide a grin.

"How do you know that Eric is my boyfriend not Amie's?"

At the look on her daughter's face, Lydia burst out laughing. There were some things that couldn't be elucidated, but could she tell that to a soon-to-be twenty-five-year-old? One day when she had children of her own, Jade would understand what a mother's intuition meant.

"I guessed," she would only say with a wide smile, waiting patiently as Jade struggled to find the words. Ana chose that moment to enter the spacious kitchen and, seeing them, stopped in the middle of the room.

"It's too quiet to sleep," she complained humorously, and they laughed.

She was used to the noise of the downtown hotel, although she would be the last person to admit it. Now she looked at the faces of mother and daughter and smiled knowingly.

"Ahhh, Lydia. You've figured it out." Admiration was evident in the tone of her voice.

Pleased with herself, Lydia merely nodded and smiled.

Jade sighed resignedly. All her life, these two women had been able to see right through her. She was never able to put anything over them, and she wondered now why she bothered to try. She waved her hand in an invitation to Ana to join them at the table. Eyes twinkling and full of mischief, the older woman complied.

On cue, Juanita entered the kitchen with a pot of tea and filled three cups. With a hug, she greeted Jade, a young woman she had practically raised whenever business kept Jade's parents occupied. She placed a plate of sweet rolls and pastries on the table, leaving the three women alone to talk. She knew that Lydia would tell her everything later anyway.

Jade took a deep breath and began. "It started when I was here two years ago. Do you remember, mother?"

Lydia nodded and leaned forward in her chair. Arms on the table, Ana followed suit.

With a calm that belied her stress, Jade told Ana and Lydia that Raul and she had broken up but not the reason. Implying only that it was because she was tired of his apparent lack of ambition, she said she decided to end it all before she returned to Canada.

Lydia frowned in surprise, sure there was more to the story than Jade was telling, but for the time being, she was willing to keep her thoughts to herself. She had wondered more than once about the day that Jade decided to leave so suddenly. Jade's behavior at the airport should have clued her in. Jade had turned around countless times—right up until the time she was ready to board the plane. Lydia had noticed her distractedness but had not known the reason. She realized now her daughter had been expecting Raul to show up. She wondered why he hadn't.

"Don't look so sad, Momma." Jade reached out across the table and patted her hand. "Things did work out for the best."

Intent on reassuring her, Jade related what happened next. Back in Canada, Jade threw herself into her schooling, excelling at all of her classes and making the dean's list on a regular basis. Other than Amie and a few friends she went to movies with, most of her free time was spent studying.

She met Eric by literally running into him at Stanley Park one day. As was her habit, she ran several miles each morning. It was her way of burning off excess energy that she could not get rid of sitting behind a desk at school. In some ways, other than the occasional movie, it was her only recreation. She liked running down the path by the Bow River. Sometimes she would pretend she was back in Mexico and running down the beach at Playa La Ropa. One day, she decided to vary her normal routine and cut through the wooded trail instead. It was while she was turning her last corner for home that she ran smack into Eric Foster. When she looked up, it was into gorgeous blue eyes.

Lydia and Ana covertly exchanged smiles as Jade confessed, "Eric and I started dating after that. We've been seeing each other for almost a year and a half now. I guess you should know he has asked me to marry him."

"I see." Lydia's eyes automatically flickered to her daughter's hand, looking for an engagement ring. There was none.

Jade followed her glance and, reaching into her pocket, pulled out a beautifully cut diamond solitaire. She slipped it on and shyly held out her hand for Lydia and Ana to admire. Eagerly, they moved closer.

"It's beautiful," they breathed in unison, and Jade laughed.

"Does this mean you're engaged?" Ana asked, bluntly curious.

"No," Jade admitted. "I told Eric I would give him an answer on my birthday. He asked me to wear this in the meantime, and I told him I wouldn't until I had made a decision. We meant to tell you together, but since you already guessed..." Her voice trailed away helplessly.

She took the ring off again and put it back into her pocket. Once again, Ana and Lydia exchanged meaningful looks.

"How do you feel about being married to Eric?" Her mother spoke gently, concerned by the look of restlessness in her daughter's eyes.

"I think I love him. I know I do." Jade amended the statement and tried to sound convincing. "I know that he would make me very happy."

"Loving someone and being in love is not the same thing," Ana put in sagely. "You only have to ask your mother to find that out." The pair shared another secret smile.

When Lydia had first come to Mexico, there had been someone else in her life, but once she met Rodolfo and fell in love, there was never any question that he was the only man for her.

"Why haven't you told us before, Jade?" Lydia was puzzled.

Jade hesitated, reluctant to speak her mind. "Because you and Poppa have plans for me, and I know that Eric is not a part of them. How could he be? You've never met him before. I wanted you to get to know him first. I should have known you would see through my stupid idea."

Lydia laughed, even though she knew what her daughter said was true. She and Rodolfo did have plans for Jade, and part of those plans certainly included marriage. She had to admit that in the back of their minds, Raul was always the one they hoped Jade would marry, especially now that he was such a big part of the restaurant and their lives. She realized now that the assumption was a mistake on their part. Most of all, they wanted her to be happy. They would never force Jade to marry someone just to satisfy their wishes.

Lydia explained this to Jade then, adding, "You should have told us, Jade. The last time we visited you, your father and I thought that you and Raul were still a couple, even though you haven't talked about him much. At least, that is what he has had us believe."

She frowned, thinking back on conversations with Raul. Never in all that time had he indicated there were severe problems, although, to give blame where it was due, they hadn't thought to ask either.

"He told you we were together?" Jade asked incredulously.

"Not exactly," Lydia admitted. "I guess we just assumed."

The normally calm Jade exploded. "How dare he let you think we were together? Of all the low-down—"

"Settle down, Jade," Ana spoke sternly and immediately. Jade quieted and obeyed. When Ana gave an order, it was to be listened to. One of the blessings of getting older, she would say.

Lydia continued. "I am sure that Raul did not mean to lead anyone astray. I mean, it is not the first time that you have had a spat before. Maybe he thought that it would blow over. You know how men can be."

"I know how Raul can be," Jade said this with a frown. *And he is a snake.*

Lydia admonished her daughter as if she had spoken aloud. "He is a trusted member of our staff, Jade."

For a minute, Jade looked startled, and Lydia paused. She was about to tell her that they had made Raul a partner, but just in time, she remembered her promise and kept silent. She wondered now if that was wise. The spilt between her daughter and Raul seemed to be more severe than they had suspected.

Jade stared at her incredulously. "But he's just a waiter?"

Lydia nodded calmly. "Yes, Jade, he is a waiter," the censure in her voice was strong. *And much more*, she thought but again stayed quiet. "Remember that your father was 'just a waiter' when I met him too, and now look at him."

At the reproach in her mother's voice, Jade flushed. She knew that it was wrong to judge someone by the job they did. Her parents had taken great pains to teach her that, and she was ashamed of herself. Maybe she had changed more than she thought. She loved her father more than anything—if he was a ditch digger, she would love him. She apologized for her thoughtless remark, and her mother smiled to show her she was already forgiven.

At the same time, Lydia's mind was churning. While it was true they had promised Raul the opportunity to buy them out if Jade didn't want the business, they had never really believed in their hearts that things would come to that. Rodolfo could not continue to work forever, and if Jade turned her back on the business, all that they had worked for would leave the family. She could not imagine Eric wanting to stay behind in Mexico to run a restaurant with Jade. And with Raul as a partner? If Jade married Eric, there would be no question that they would return to Canada. The thought saddened her.

"You should have told us, Jade," she said again without elaborating.

Jade hung her head. Her mother was right. Why had she thought that telling her parents the truth would be a terrible thing? She should have known better. Her parents had always stood behind her no matter what happened. She smiled apologetically and patted her mother's arm.

"Don't worry, Mother," she said with more resolve and determination than she felt. "I haven't decided anything yet, and we have lots of time. Eric and Amie will go to Canada the day after my birthday…" Her face brightened, and Ana and Lydia looked at her curiously.

"The one good thing is that I can tell Eric and Amie they don't have to pretend to like each other anymore," she laughed at the thought.

"Don't be too sure," Ana smiled but declined to offer any explanation when Jade eyed her curiously.

"We only want what you want, Jade," Lydia was saying now. "I had hoped that with you home, Rodolfo would start taking some time off. Lately, I have been…"

She was about to say worried about him, but she stopped. This was not the time to discuss her concerns about her husband's health, even to Jade. The last thing she wanted was for Jade to turn down Eric's proposal out of some family need or guilt. She meant it when she told her they wanted her to be happy. If that meant that their only child returned to Canada, then so be it.

"…I have been hoping to get him to go on vacation," she improvised now. "With Raul here, I think I will anyway."

"You'd trust the Mi Corazon to Raul?" Jade was incredulous, forgetting her earlier apology.

Lydia shot a warning glance at Ana, her eyes sending a silent message. Privy to all the secrets this family had or ever would, Ana understood and kept quiet.

"Yes, Jade, we would." Lydia's countenance was stern. "Over the last two years, Raul has proven himself to be someone we can depend on. We would have no hesitation in letting him take over if we were to go on a vacation." She smiled to take the sting out of her words.

Jade was silent. Her mother hadn't come right out and said it, but her own experience with the restaurant was sadly lacking, at least since she went away to school, that is. Stung, she offered her assistance in the restaurant while she was there. With a genuine smile, Lydia thanked her but refused just the same.

"That won't be necessary, Jade, but I appreciate the gesture. I think what you need is some fun and relaxation, and don't forget you have two guests with you. They certainly wouldn't have nearly as good a time if you were slaving away in the restaurant while they were basking on the beach. There's time enough to make any long-term plans, but for the time being, we are all under control."

Jade nodded. A part of her was very relieved her offer had been turned down. She was tired. Studying for her degree was much harder than people thought, especially this last year.

At that point, Ana discreetly yawned and stood up. All the drama was making her sleepy. Maybe she would try again to take that siesta. Tonight promised to be even more entertaining than previously thought, and she wanted to stay awake for it. With a kiss and wave, she stood and made her way back to the spare room.

Alone, Jade and Lydia switched the topic to safer ones like what was going on with some of her friends from school and who was building what new house where. In this way, they were able to keep the serious considerations at bay for a little while and concentrate on more pleasant topics.

Amie decided she was enjoying herself immensely, even if her companion was that over-muscled blonde at the helm! The feeling of the wind in her hair and the soft spray of the ocean on her skin was sensuous and warm. She never wanted this day to end. Alongside them, a school of porpoises jumped and performed for them, and she laughed out loud with sheer pleasure. She wished Jade were there to share it. Glancing back over her shoulder, she saw that Eric had noticed their playful guests. Like her, he was grinning from ear to ear. Catching her look, he winked, and unaccountably, she blushed and turned her attention back to the antics of their guests. After a few minutes, they dove deep into the ocean and then disappeared from view as quickly as they had come.

"We have to go back now!" Eric shouted over the wind that had picked up unexpectedly, hoping he could be heard.

Childishly, Amie stuck her tongue out at him. "Not yet," she replied stubbornly. Hoping the porpoises would return, she faced forward again.

Eric sighed. Amie was a real pain in the ass. In just a few minutes, he could see the waves were higher and choppier than they had been when they first set out. The last thing he wanted was to be out here if a storm came up. Besides, it was close to an hour already, and he had promised they would be back. He had no intention of breaking that promise just to keep "Miss Amie," as he had taken to calling her, happy.

Angered, he swung the tiller sharply to the right and tried to turn into the waves. It wasn't easy, and he knew he had to be careful. He saw Amie topple to the side, and he gave a grunt of satisfaction. Then, without warning, he watched as she rolled across the decking, vainly trying to grab something to hold onto as she slid. He laughed aloud. *It serves her right*, he thought.

As the catamaran turned around, it tilted higher, and an errant wave washed over the slippery surface. With a sharp cry, Amie lost her tenuous hold and slid further toward the edge. In a blink of an eye, she was in the water.

At five fifteen even, Rodolfo was starting to get worried. After dropping Ana off at the hotel, he had gone down to the beach at Jade's request to pick up her friends. He became alarmed when there was no sight of them. It was getting late, and soon the sun would be completely set. Thinking they may have returned on their own, he headed back to the house to where his wife and daughter sat in the kitchen.

Jade and Lydia were worried too. Lydia because she thought something might have happened to them, and Jade because she feared they had killed each other during one of their many arguments. As the three worried and wondered, the back door slammed. Anxiously, they turned to see a young boy enter the kitchen where they kept their vigil.

"Juanito, is that you?" Jade exclaimed and hurried over to the son of their trusted housekeeper and gardener.

She had known him since they first brought him home from the hospital, and to her, he was the little brother she wished she had. She could hardly get over how much he had grown and told him so.

Jaunito beamed. He was nearly eye-level with Jade now. Soon, he would be taller than her. He was already taller than the blonde woman he had met that afternoon at the beach. Thinking of her, he frowned.

"What's the matter?" Always susceptible to his moods, Jade regarded him with concern.

"Senor Rodolfo, Senora Lydia." Juan nodded to the employers of his parents, belatedly remembering his manners. "This afternoon I rent the catamaran to two gringos, and they no come back. I am very worried."

Jade's heart sank. It could only be Eric and Amie. A moment later, Juanito confirmed it by saying the names aloud.

With that, Rodolfo jumped up and headed over to the door. Jade and Lydia were about to follow, but he asked them to remain, saying it would be better for someone to be here should Eric and Amie find their way home on their own. Although it made sense, Jade chafed at the thought of waiting behind.

Calling for Juan, the three men left for the marina. There they would get the dinghy and search for the missing pair. Looking for something to do, Lydia went to the kitchen and made a pot of coffee while Jade made sandwiches. It seemed a silly thing to do given the fact that they were going out later for dinner, but it kept them occupied. After those minor chores were completed, Lydia and Jade poured themselves a cup of the strong brew and sat back anxiously to wait.

4

Hold on!" Desperately, Eric yelled over the side to where Amie was floundering in the rough surf. He didn't feel like laughing anymore and was a little ashamed that he had—especially now that he could see the panic in her eyes. Anxiously, he cast about for something to throw to her. A red life jacket lay wedged under a box, and with a quick tug, he pulled it free. He tied the rope lying at his feet to it, securing the other end around his waist. With a heave, he tossed it into the sea.

Amazingly, she caught it on the first pass. Relieved, Eric watched as she clung to it, the waves crashing over her head. Although he knew she could swim, no one would ever accuse her of being good at it.

Eric pulled Amie closer to the catamaran, hand over hand until she was at the edge. Then he bent at the waist, grabbed beneath her arms and pulled her up onto the slippery deck. The elapsed time couldn't have been more than five minutes, yet he felt as if it had been an eternity.

For a minute, Amie laid motionless, coughing and trying to regain her breath. She felt that she had swallowed a whole ocean, a fact she readily shared with him.

"Need some mouth to month?" Eric quipped without warning, and she giggled despite herself.

Amie looked up in surprise. It was the first time they had ever laughed together, she realized, seeing the answering grin on his face.

He sobered. "I'm sorry, Amie." His whole manner was filled with sincere apology. "I should have given you some warning that I was going to head back." His eyes looked haunted. *If anything had happened to her...* He didn't allow the thought to finish.

Amie blinked at his apology. Another first! "You did tell me, Eric. It was my entire fault. I acted like a child. I'm sorry, too."

She pulled herself up off the floor of the catamaran and watched him warily. He was busying himself with sailing and did not notice her scrutiny. For the first time, she saw him as something other than her best friend's boyfriend and her enemy. She had never been attracted to his blonde good looks, as everyone knew, but she could see now why Jade was. *As well as half our friends on campus and nearly everyone else we know,* she thought ruefully.

The short time in the sun was already turning his skin a golden brown, unlike hers, which would be pink first before deepening. She thought enviously of this as the setting sun glistened off the hairs on his muscular arms and legs. He had thrown off his shirt when they had first boarded, and she wondered now why she had never noticed how wide his shoulders were before or how flat his stomach. His chest hair, only slightly darker than that on his head, trailed down his front into the band of his trunks. Her tongue darted out between her lips, and she swallowed hard.

Just then, Eric looked up and caught her staring at him. "See anything you like?" he drawled and then grinned as he saw her blush a deep red.

"You are a jackass," she shot back without thinking, any good feelings she may have entertained about him gone in a flash. With a flounce, her back was firmly to him, their momentary truce already forgotten. The quick motion almost caused her to lose her balance, and she threw out a hand to steady herself.

Eric caught her with a vise grip before she could tumble back into the water. He pulled her to him.

"Careful," he told her, a sardonic grin on his face. "I saved you once, but after a remark like that, I may not want to do it again."

She tossed her head, the rocking boat pressing her near naked body against the full length of him. Pinned, she was unable to free herself.

Eric looked down at her upturned face at the lips that quivered with anger or fear, he wasn't sure, the blue eyes so like his filled with tears. Something about that vulnerable face touched him, and he softened. Then realization hit that save for the tiny bikini she wore, there was little between them. Abruptly, he lessened his grip and roughly pushed so that she could hold on to the mast.

Grateful to be out of his arms, she grabbed it firmly.

"Stay there." Like a drill sergeant, he ordered harshly.

Giving a disdainful look, she nevertheless obeyed him without question. If her heart was beating a little too fast, she put it down to the shock she had of nearly drowning. What else could it be? Out of the corner of her eye, she saw Eric concentrating on maneuvering through the waves, avoiding her look entirely. *Fine.* She sniffed and eased forward to a more comfortable position. Two can play that game.

A short time later, they spotted land. The sun was almost completely below the horizon, and Eric didn't like to think what could have happened if they had had to spend the night out there. Besides that, Jade and her parents were sure to be worried about them. Thinking about Jade, he flushed guiltily, making him angrier than ever with the woman before him.

As he drew closer to land, he saw what looked like searchlights. Relieved, Eric made for them until soon they were on the crest of waves and gliding into shore. A shout went up, and he saw figures running down the beach in their direction.

As they landed, Juanito splashed into the surf to help pull them in, followed closely by Jade's father and another man he assumed, correctly, was Juan. That he was also little Juan's father struck him as a big coincidence, having heard all about the family that cared for Jade and her family many times over.

Wisely, Rodolfo kept his curiosity to himself, hugging Amie in sheer relief and shaking Eric's hand. Amie and Eric stumbled over themselves trying to explain, but he only smiled and told them no explanations were necessary. All that mattered, he assured them, was that they were safe. As they sped up the road to the house, he questioned them as to how they were feeling and was relieved to know they were completely unhurt. Eric tried to apologize for causing so much worry, but Rodolfo waved it away again.

"Jade and Lydia will be very happy to see you, I know, and tonight we have a welcome home dinner. Now we have a celebration dinner too."

Amie smiled fondly at the man she had called uncle since she was a little girl. Rodolfo always knew how to make people feel better, she remembered, and this was no exception. Sitting next to him in the cab of the truck, she squeezed his hand in gratitude just as he pulled the truck into the driveway of his home.

The front door flew open, and Jade darted out of the house and straight into Eric's arms, nearly knocking him to the ground. In return, Eric wrapped his strong arms around Jade and held her tight. Looking over the top of her head, he caught sight of Amie, and their eyes met and held.

Instantly, a curtain fell over Amie's eyes, and there was only a blank stare.

She turned to Lydia, who closed her arms around her while Rodolfo watched Jade and Eric in astonishment. He looked to Lydia for explanation.

"Later," she mouthed, and he nodded his head in confusion.

Jade broke free from Eric's arms, hurried toward Amie and gave her a big hug. "I am so glad you are alright. What happened? Did you get lost?"

She fired questions at her friend while leading her into the house. The rest followed behind.

"It was my fault, Jade," Amie confessed. "Eric rented Juanito's boat, we went for a sail, and I fell overboard. He saved me."

Jade's mouth hung open for a minute as she tried to take it in. Then, turning around, she beamed in Eric's direction.

"That makes you a hero." Raising herself on tiptoes, she pulled his head down for a kiss.

A stab of envy struck Amie, and she looked away into the shining eyes of Juanito, whose face was full of admiration for her. Mollified slightly, she basked in the glow of his unabashed worship. Even if he was only twelve years old, something had to assuage her bruised ego.

Again, Rodolfo looked to Lydia for an explanation, but she shook her head. It was obvious she would tell him later, but now wasn't the time. While he was still mulling it over, Lydia took charge.

"I think that we should all have a little rest, and then it will be time to get ready for dinner tonight. Eric, your room is down the hall to the left; Amie, you are to the right; and, of course, Jade, your room is where it always is."

They all laughed and moved away to do as she suggested. The sound of the three young people's laughter drifted back, and Lydia and Rodolfo smiled at each other. It was good to have the house full again, they silently communicated across the few feet that separated them.

Juanito and his parents, seeing that their assistance was no longer required, said goodbye for the day and made their way out and down the path toward their own cozy home.

Finally alone, Rodolfo turned to regard his wife. She held out her hand, and he crossed to her, pulling her close and kissing her long and hard. She was as beautiful today as she had been that first night he had met her. At the time, she had looked like an angel to him in her summer dress and silver sandals. Now he knew that it was her essence as much as her looks that made her that way for him.

"Maybe we should take a nap too?" His hint was anything but subtle, and she smiled even as her pulse heart sped up.

"Don't you want to know what's going on?" she teased, inclining her head in the direction of the young people.

Rodolfo swiftly bent over and picked her off the floor. "Later," he whispered. Lydia laughed and half-heartedly insisted he put her down. He ignored her demands.

"What about the children?" she giggled helplessly against his shoulder.

"They can have their nap in their own way." He growled into her neck, and she laughed again as he carried her to their room.

Later, as they lay naked and curled in each other's arms, Lydia told Rodolfo about the new development in Jade's life. Unsure as to what his reaction would be, she spoke carefully, explaining as best she could what Jade had confided to her just hours earlier.

For a long while, Rodolfo said nothing, staring into the darkened room, his mind racing in a dozen directions. The news stunned him, and he needed time to digest it all. Everything he had planned for and assumed was no longer, and he knew it would take him a little time to get used to that. But used to it he would get. He loved Jade more than life itself, and he would do anything to make sure she was happy, even if it meant that the restaurant he had started left the family and went to Raul, as promised. There was no doubt in his mind that if Jade decided on marriage to Eric that that was exactly what would happen. He sighed. On the other hand, anything could happen.

He remembered how hopeless he had felt when Lydia's boyfriend had come to Mexico to meet her. Up until that time, he and Lydia had been dating, and without warning, both had fallen in love with the other. Despite that, they had decided that they should end it and walk away.

Rodolfo smiled into the darkness as he recalled how Lydia had come to the restaurant at closing time to tell him she had changed her mind and that it was he she wanted all along. It took a lot of courage, he knew. At the time of their breakup, he had been standoffish and proud, belying a hurt that he tried to hide. He certainly hadn't been all that friendly and approachable, but she saw through it and took a chance. Years later, they still laughed over all the wine glasses he had broken upon seeing her standing at the door of the restaurant where he worked—too afraid to come further but too determined to give up and leave.

Later, they had taken a walk down to the pier. Standing in the moonlight, Lydia had poured out all her feelings for him, melting his proud heart. Gladly, he had capitulated. They had never been apart a single day since.

"What are you thinking about, mi vida?" Lydia asked him softly.

He kissed the top of her head and tightened his grip on his wife. "I was thinking about how you and I got together. It was a miracle to me that you would choose me over your rich boyfriend," he teased her, and Lydia playfully swatted him.

She stayed quiet, however, interested in what he would say next.

"I think that we should just wait and see what is going to happen. Jade has not seen Raul yet. He hasn't said anything to me, but I have a feeling he is looking forward to it. I have to admit that I was hoping Jade was coming back to marry him. Come to think of it, she never asked about him very much when we went to visit her. I guess I just assumed she was in contact with him and already knew what was going on in his life. Shows how much we know, huh? Not that I think that Eric is a bad guy," he hastened to add.

"If Jade is thinking about marrying Eric, then he must have good qualities," Lydia agreed diplomatically. "So far, I like him. I still don't understand why we didn't see the problems."

"Maybe because neither of them said anything. This makes me think that all might work out."

Lydia rose up on her elbow to gaze down at him. "You think so? What makes you say that, Rodolfo?"

She had long ago learned to trust her husband's instincts. His father had passed on to his son an almost magical intuitiveness. He had shown her over and over in many ways just how useful that gift was.

Rodolfo grinned and pulled her over and down to lie on top of him. "Well, look at it this way—if they were both sure that it was over, wouldn't they have been up front about it? What stopped them from telling anyone they were through? Neither said a word."

Lydia smiled slowly. "You're absolutely right."

"Don't worry, Chiquita," he told her playfully. "Trust me on this. What will be will be."

He kissed her hard to forgo any protest she might have until he felt her press against him. As for Lydia, anything she was about to say was soon forgotten as she threw her considerable enthusiasm and energy into kissing him back.

5

Raul stood impatiently by the entranceway to the restaurant. He looked at his watch once more and wondered what was keeping them. At the same time, he almost wished they wouldn't show up and he could choose the time and place to see Jade—somewhere other than the Mi Corazon. He was so busy thinking what it would be like that he jumped when Marcos suddenly approached him and asked him about tonight's specials.

Marcos looked at him strangely but only repeated the question. Everyone knew that the usually calm, inscrutable Raul was uptight tonight, and they all knew the reason for it. They had been placing bets all week as to what would happen. Marcos was positive that Jade would ignore Raul. He was convinced that she would return a snob. Arturo, oldest and with the most seniority, assured them that she wasn't, and he should know, he'd said—he had known them longer than anyone, hadn't he? From the time since they were babies, practically. It was only too bad he wasn't going to be there to watch the drama. That night, he was spending the extra time with his family courtesy of Raul, he told him proudly.

Marcos agreed it was a shame that he would miss it, but he promised to report back anything that happened.

Raul recovered his equilibrium quickly and moved from the doorway to answer Marcos' question. As luck would have it, his back was turned just as the party he was waiting for appeared.

Jade's first look at Raul was from behind, and she drew a deep breath in relief. It would give her some time to compose herself, and she wanted to be at her most confident, cool self when she talked to him. She tried to control the erratic beating of her heart, sure that at least everyone in the room was able to hear it. While the rest of the group moved forward, she paused and covertly watched.

She saw Raul lift his head at their approach and beam a warm smile of welcome. Then, with a quick nod, he dismissed Marcos and stood waiting at his station for their approach. Only someone who knew him as well as she did would know that he was not quite as confident as he appeared. She saw it in the way he drummed his fingers against the podium—a sure sign he was nervous. She used to tease him about it in the past. Yet, despite his nervousness, even Jade was amazed by how polished and self-assured he looked.

Eric stopped when Jade did, a quizzical smile as he noted her suddenly pale, taut face. His eyes followed hers to the man who was now shaking Rodolfo's hand and bending over to kiss Amie's, and he wondered who he was. He heard Amie's pleased laughter ring out over the stone corridor, and he grimaced. Wasn't it just like her to fall for any handsome man that paid attention to her?

Leaning over, Eric whispered in Jade's ear. "Now maybe she'll stay occupied so we can be alone," he teased.

Jade's faltered slightly, but the remark had at least the power to propel her forward. Smiling, she took Eric's hand, and together they crossed the threshold to rejoin the others.

At their approach, the first thing Eric noticed was that the man's eyes never left the woman beside him. *It is almost as if he thinks she is the only person in this room.*

If Raul had known what Eric was thinking, he would have applauded his insight. As far as he was concerned, there *was* only one person in the room, and she was walking straight toward him, looking more beautiful than he had ever seen her. Time stood still, and everything appeared to move in slow motion. For long moments, they stared as if unable to tear away.

Jade wondered a bit hysterically if they ever would. Like a thunderbolt, a thousand emotions coursed through her body. She heard voices and laughter in the distance and knew that people were making introductions, but for the life of her, she couldn't open her mouth to speak.

Finally, Lydia came to her rescue. Placing a hand lightly on her daughter's shoulder, she spoke close in her ear as if talking to small child. "Look, Jade, here's Raul, after all this time."

Somehow, Jade came to and reached her hand out for Raul to shake. He held on to it, his thumb caressing her palm, and lifting it, he brought it to his mouth and kissed it.

Smooth, thought Eric admiringly even as a jealous streak raced over him. Then he smiled as Jade snatched her hand back. With a grin, he offered his hand and gave Raul's a manly shake. Raul turned away from Jade and regarded him with a reserved smile.

This must be the Canadian man Lydia told me about, he realized as he looked his potential rival up and down. Lydia confirmed his thoughts.

"Raul, this is Eric, Jade's...er...friend from Canada. What are you doing working the door tonight, Raul? Where's Arturo?"

The spell broken by the mundane question, Raul faced Lydia and answered politely, "Arturo couldn't make it." His face was impassive as he white-lied, knowing that the switch was deliberate. "I told him I would take his place tonight."

Lydia was not fooled. "That's too bad. We were hoping you would join us for dinner tonight," was her only comment.

"In a way, I will." He laughed. "Emilio isn't here either, and so it looks as if I will be your waiter tonight." He didn't bother to explain that he had arranged that too. She would already know that.

Raul bowed to Jade, and for the first time, addressed her personally. "I hope you don't mind, Jade?"

Her name slid off his tongue, sounding intimate somehow, and she flushed.

Coolly, she replied. "Not at all, Raul. You do work here, after all. I think that you waiting on us is exactly the way things should be."

"Jade." Rodolfo's voice came from the left of her, low and stern and filled with rare disapproval.

Jade flushed, knowing she was being rude. Even Eric and Amie were staring at her in surprise. It was not like Jade to be so condescending.

But Raul merely tipped his head back and laughed, his white teeth flashing in his brilliant smile. So Lydia and Rodolfo had not told her. *Good.*

"That's quite alright, Senor Perez. I can think of nothing better than to wait on Jade and her friends."

He turned now to Eric and Amie, who were both fascinated with the young man before them, but each for different reasons. "I am hoping I will see a lot of both of you and that you will like our part of Mexico."

That was the last thing Jade wanted, and she turned to him, the smile still plastered to her lips. "I am sure you are too busy these days, Raul, what with working here and your family, I would think that there weren't enough hours to go around. And how are your wife and children?" Her voice was hard but equally polite. "Maria, isn't it?"

Gratified, she saw her words had hit their mark as his eyes narrowed slightly. She knew perfectly well Raul wasn't married.

Amie looked confused by the tension between the two. "Oh, you're married?" She looked a little disappointed. *Why were all the good ones taken?*

Raul only laughed and shook his head, not bothering to reply. *Touché, Jade.*

Amie looked from one to the other, puzzled, then decided she was pleased. So he wasn't married? She wondered why Jade had thought he was. She decided it must be some kind of joke between the two of them. *Just how well do these two know each other?* she wondered quietly, looking from one to the other and back again.

Eric was wondering the same thing. He had never seen the tenderhearted Jade be rude before, and it interested him. Astute in most ways, he decided that it would behoove him to watch and see what was going to happen next. Still, maybe if Raul fell for Amie's somewhat childish charms, he would get to spend more time with Jade. He flashed a grin in Raul's direction, seeing immediately that it would be in his best interest to forge a friendship.

The preliminaries over, Raul decided it was time to seat the party. With a flourish, he waved his hand and asked them all to follow him. Eric and Amie eagerly stepped behind. Jade followed woodenly, a mutinous look on her face while Rodolfo and Lydia brought up the rear. Amused by the drama, they caught each other's eyes knowingly and smiled. This was proving to be interesting.

Ana was already seated at the table and observed the procession as it approached. Raul placed one hand lightly on Jade's arm, and Jade was looking as if she wanted to fling it off. Ana had always been able to recognize that stubborn look her godchild wore for what it was, and she hid a smile behind her fan.

Approving, she noted the deep jade green dress she had bought for Jade the last time she had been home, and she smiled at the compliment. Ana told her it was chosen to match her name, suiting perfectly her dark wavy hair and coloring beautifully. Around her neck was the jade pendant that Rodolfo had given Lydia years ago, long before they were a permanent fixture in each other's lives. She peered closer and saw that it was the female version of the pair, and she wondered if Rodolfo was wearing the male one. She decided to ask him at dinner later, feeling it would make a good story for Eric and Amie to hear.

Just behind Raul was Amie, looking beautiful and lightly tanned in a pretty pale pink dress. Her silver sandals had a little heel, which made her stand taller and showed off her shapely legs. Like Jade, she wore her hair up in a clasp, giving the illusion of even more height. A single strand of pearls hung from her neck, sophisticated and elegant.

Behind them trailed Eric, looking dapper, as they said in her day, and already brown from his afternoon in the sun. His blue Hawaiian-style shirt highlighted the color of his eyes. He wore a pair of casual pants, pressed and creased. Looking relaxed and confident, Ana quite approved of him, although not necessarily as the man for Jade. That would remain to be seen.

Lydia, she saw, wore a midnight blue dress slightly above her knee. The material shimmered in the soft candlelight, the hem slightly flared to allow freedom of movement. It was a look that suited her best, given her small frame. Like Amie, her heels were a little higher tonight than usual. Standing next to Rodolfo, her head fit neatly into the cradle of the arm he had placed around her shoulders. As always, he was perfectly groomed in a deep blue shirt to match Lydia's dress, paired with a khaki pant. She had always thought they made an excellent-looking couple, and tonight was no exception.

As they neared the table, the group caught sight of Ana. Immediately, Jade removed her elbow from Raul's firm grip and hurried forward, claiming the seat on her right. She patted the chair next to her.

"Eric, why don't you sit here," she purred, watching Raul out of the corner of her eye. She was amused to see his mouth tighten slightly, but other than that, he gave no further sign he was annoyed.

"Where should I sit?" Amie asked brightly, and Ana patted the vacant chair on the other side of hers. Happily, Amie complied and was soon regaling Ana with the tale of their adventure that afternoon.

"It was my fault entirely," Eric injected humbly. "I should have given Amie warning that I was turning."

"No, Ana, it was my fault," Amie confessed.

Jade turned to stare at both of them, and simultaneously they flushed. "You two remind me of that cartoon *Tom and Jerry*. Do you know the one?"

They all laughed heartily, and the next little while was spent discussing cartoons and the merits of which ones were better.

Raul listened while he poured water into the goblets. They were talking about things that were beyond his realm of experience. Briefly, it made him feel like an outsider in his own country, and his smile faltered slightly in the chatter that floated around him.

Lydia reached out a hand and touched his lightly. "Don't worry, Raul," she told him. "Things have a way of working out."

Uneasy, Raul stared in surprise. He knew that both Rodolfo and Lydia thought the world of him, as he did them, but she had never said anything about his relationship with their daughter before. After his argument with Jade, he had gone to them for a job. Thinking he was still Jade's boyfriend, they hired him without a second thought. The one time he had tried to come clean about the true nature of his relationship with Jade, Lydia had told him the same thing as she was telling him now. That things would work out. Not wanting to hurt his chances with them, he had not really tried to make them understand. Instead, he had allowed them to think it was just a little spat and would soon blow over. Watching her with the blonde, handsome giant, he knew with a sinking heart that he had been living with false hope for a long time, and he felt a stab of jealousy.

Turning away, Raul caught another encouraging look on Lydia's face, and visibly he relaxed. With renewed resolve, he decided that there was plenty of time to worry about the future. Adeptly, Raul finished pouring the water into the crystal goblets and moved to Rodolfo's side to discuss the wine.

Unnoticed, Jade lifted her head and watched Raul with her father. In some ways, they looked very much alike. Both sported deep dimples on either side of their cheeks and had gentle, chocolate-colored eyes. While her father still wore the ponytail of his youth, Raul's longish hair was of a more modern style and minus the silver grey. Although not quite as tall as her father or Eric, Raul was still taller than she. It was his proud air and posture that gave him the appearance of being a much larger man than he really was.

He was not as heavy as Eric either, but she knew that well-defined muscles rippled down his arms and across his chest beneath the starchy pressed shirt. His thighs, one of his best features, were strong and hard. Her eyes clouded over as she remembered lying next to him on the sand, one strong leg thrown over her possessively, pinning her to the ground. Shivering, she snapped her eyes open only to find Ana watching her as if she had read her thoughts. Forcing a smile, Jade pretended to understand the conversation that had been going on around her while she had been daydreaming. Inwardly, she sighed. She didn't think this interminable evening would ever end.

Later, when everyone else had retired, Jade and her father sat on the front porch of the sprawling ranch style home and discussed the evening. The night had been a success in his mind. Jade's friends were amusing and appreciative of everything, complimenting profusely the excellent food and the ambience of the Mi Corazon. Rodolfo had watched with interest as Amie flirted with Raul, who, although polite and friendly, had eyes only for Jade. Jade, on the other hand, had kept most of her attention firmly fastened on Eric, treating Raul as if he were a servant more than a part owner, which, of course, she had no way of knowing that he was. It was a side of his daughter he hadn't particularly wanted to see. If that was what her fancy education had gotten her, he wished that he would have fought harder to keep her in Mexico. At least here maybe they could have watched her more closely. Despite these thoughts, now he hadn't the heart to say anything. He was too happy to have his daughter safe at home.

Thankfully, Ana had kept the table amused, regaling them all with funny stories about her adventures during the months she wasn't in residence in Mexico. Amie was particularly taken with her, fascinated by the dramatically flamboyant yet classic-looking woman. She hoped she was as active and as beautiful at her age.

It was Eric who inadvertently brought up the subject of the necklace Jade was wearing, complimenting her on it. With real interest, he asked her where she had got it, never having seen it on her before.

Jade explained with a smile, "That's because it belongs to my mother. I borrowed it tonight. It has a great deal of power."

While gentle, her voice was serious in its truth. "The jade is the symbol of love. My father has the matching pendant, don't you, Poppa?"

As Ana had predicted, Rodolfo was wearing the male version of the pendant, and to illustrate Jade's point, he pulled it from beneath his shirt now to show her Canadian friends.

Eric and Amie leaned across the table for a better view. Even Raul stopped what he was doing to look closer. Knowing the family as well as he did, he already knew the story behind the pendant, but he listened as Rodolfo recounted it again for the benefit of Jade's friends.

"I made the wire casing and bamboo shoots and beads." He held it closer to indicate the decoration. "But it was my grandmother that carved the jade stones. See, this one is a male face, and the one that Jade is wearing is female. My grandmother told me the two should never be separated, and they never have. When I gave it to Lydia, it was when we were dating. It was my insurance that she would never leave me." He laughed and patted Lydia's hand fondly.

"And this pendant is why my name is Jade," his daughter finished proudly.

"Remember the time that I thought I lost it, Ana?" Lydia directed her question to her friend. Ana nodded as Lydia turned to the rest of the group and explained, "It had fallen behind the bureau of my hotel room, and I was frantic that I would never see it again. Thankfully, one of the maids noticed it when cleaning, and it was lying on my bed when I returned from an outing. I can't tell you how relieved I was. It was funny, though, once I did get it back again, I took it as a sign that Rodolfo was the one I wanted." She leaned over to kiss her husband's cheek.

Jade was silent for a minute, thinking about what it was she wanted. If only she could find the love that her parents had. She turned to Eric, and her face softened. He was a good man, a trustworthy person. Would he be the one?

She felt a tingle, and sensing she was being watched, she looked up to find Raul staring at her from across the room. A sardonic smile twisted his lips. He looked at Eric and then back again, one arched eyebrow raised in question. Or was it contempt? Flustered, Jade looked away quickly and made a point of not looking in his direction for the rest of the evening.

Now sitting on the porch with her father, they talked about what was going on in her world. Rodolfo asked Jade about her schooling and life in Canada, something he had only glimpsed at on visits there. Proudly, she recounted her grades, and he complimented his daughter warmly on her successful marks. For the third year in a row, she had made the dean's list, and he was proud of her. He asked a great deal of questions, curious about her time away from home.

Jade answered truthfully, although her replies were somewhat tempered. She felt he would be shocked by some of the things she had witnessed there. Things were more regimented and stricter in Mexico, although in some ways, that was changing too. Parties she had occasionally attended were much different in Canada than here. For one thing, people in Mexico were more inclined to socialize as a family. She noticed in Canada that parties were often with her own age group and could get carried away sometimes. She decided to gloss over some of those details, saying only that she had made a few good friends.

Rodolfo smiled to himself in the darkness. He knew without her telling him that her life was much less sheltered there than it would have been in Mexico. He remembered his wild times in the United States very well. He had gone there one year to live with his friend and compadre Daniel Forbes after his first marriage had disintegrated. To say it was an eye-opener would be an understatement, but he trusted Jade implicitly. To her relief, he changed the subject. Curious to what her answer would be, he instead posed the question that had been on his mind for a long time.

"And are you sorry we sent you to Canada, Jade?"

"I am very glad I went to Canada," Jade answered truthfully, and he smiled. "It was very hard at first. My English was not so good because all of my friends here are Mexican, but with Amie's help, I learned. And thanks to you and Momma insisting that I speak both languages, too. I couldn't have done it without all of you."

He replied quietly, "Yes, you could."

He had no doubt whatsoever that this young woman before him could accomplish anything she set her mind on to do. It was no secret that he had initially resisted the idea of his only daughter going away to school, only agreeing after Jade herself said she wanted to go.

"And Eric? Did he help you too?" He teased her now in a light a voice.

Jade flushed a little in the moonlight. As close as she was to her father, she was unused to having this kind of conversation with him. Usually they talked about school, what she had done on the weekend, or if she needed any money. For the intimate details of her life, she confided more in her mother or Ana. She almost wished her mother could be here.

"Yes, Poppa. Eric, too." Then she surprised them both by confessing, "He has asked me to marry him." She blurted it out.

Rodolfo nodded. Calmly, Lydia had told him the news earlier, wanting to prepare him.

"I told him that I needed time," Jade assured him solemnly.

Rodolfo nodded again but wisely kept his counsel. What was there to say? He regarded her thoughtfully, and finally he asked "Do you love him, Jade?"

Jade hesitated as she remembered what Ana had said earlier about loving and actually being in love. Finally, she nodded.

"I think so, Poppa, but..."

"But what, Jade?"

"If I marry Eric, we will go to live in Canada. I don't know if I can leave Mexico for good," she told him now in a rush, all of a sudden seeing that, for her, it was the biggest stumbling block. She continued. "And if I go to Canada, then what will you do with the restaurant? Would you sell it eventually?"

Her tone was almost angry, and Rodolfo fought to hide a grin. His daughter was so cool on the outside, yet on the inside, there burned passion as yet untapped. It was interesting to see what part of her would win out—the calm Caucasian or the volatile Latina.

"And would selling be so bad, *princessa*?" He asked curious as to what her answer would be.

Unthinking, she flashed her reply, "I don't want to see the Mi Corazon in another's hands. With a stranger." A thought hit her. "You wouldn't sell it to Raul, would you?"

This time, Rodolfo did laugh out loud. "I don't think that we can consider Raul an outsider, do you?" he hedged.

He was both amused and perplexed by his daughter's response, but he didn't answer her question. Like Lydia, he had promised Raul he would allow him to be the one to tell Jade about their business arrangement. He too was unsure if this was the right thing to do given the circumstances.

"There was a time when we all thought that the two of you would marry."

"That was before," Jade shot back hotly.

"Before what, *princessa?*" Rodolfo thought she might shed more light on the subject than what she had told Lydia and Ana earlier. He wondered briefly if Raul had cheated on his daughter and if that was the reason for the estrangement. In all the years he had been with Lydia, he hadn't looked at another woman—not even once. The thought that Raul could have betrayed his daughter with someone else was not a good one. Deep down, he couldn't reconcile that thought with the man he knew, but whether he did or not, it was clear that something had happened to cause such an apparently deep rift.

Jade was as evasive as she had been with her mother earlier, saying only that she didn't want to talk about anything serious her first night home. Rodolfo sighed and stretched out his arms to his daughter in comfort. Immediately, Jade flew into them.

Curling around her father's feet, Jade put her head in his lap as she had done since she was a child. *It's so good to be home*, she thought. They stayed like this for a long time, Rodolfo stroking the side of her face in comfort, murmuring words with little meaning but in a soft hypnotic voice that soothed her. Finally, Jade stood and announced she was tired and wanted to go to bed. As she turned to go, she looked tenderly back at her father, his face turned skyward, illuminated by the moon. *He does look tired*, she realized in shock, overcome with guilt that she was only adding to his problems. Stooping, she leaned over and kissed the top of his head.

Rodolfo looked up and smiled gently. Then, with a touch of her hand on his shoulder, she bid him goodnight.

Rodolfo stayed where he was. He loved watching the moon glide across the sky and wished that Lydia was here beside him so he could share it with her. As if by magic, he felt a light touch on his shoulder, and he looked up into Lydia's face. Immediately, she curled up on his lap. Tonight, she wore a full length white peignoir, its iridescent material translucent in the moonlight. He rubbed his hands along the length of her in the manner she liked, as if stroking a cat. He could almost feel her begin to purr, and he laughed.

Lydia was content to lie here for hours, but she knew that Rodolfo needed to sleep. Tomorrow things would be more or less back to normal now that the initial excitement of Jade's return was over. She wanted to make sure he got all the rest he could before another grueling day of dealing with contractors and workers for the new restaurant. Besides that, she needed to get some rest too. Jade's birthday was in one week, and she still had a great deal to do before then. *Thank God for Ana*, she thought with a smile. This party promised to be larger than the *quince años* they had thrown for Jade on the day she turned fifteen.

Neither she nor Ana had been in favor of it, feeling, as foreigners, that it was a way of putting a young girl on the marriage block far too early. Personally, Ana thought it was almost a barbaric custom. Regardless of their feelings, however, in this, Rodolfo had won out. "This is a part of Jade's heritage," he had told them firmly. He would not like them to interfere with that, especially since Jade was the only daughter he was ever likely to have. Reluctantly, Lydia had capitulated. It wasn't often that Rodolfo insisted on anything, so when he did ,she made sure to listen. Besides, a brief five years later, she got her way about Jade going away to school. In her opinion, the trade off for one day was worth the years of education her daughter had received.

They were going to have some surprise guests too, which was sure to cause a great deal of happiness but add to the stress. Amie's parents Len and Lina had called earlier in the week and asked if they could come to Mexico for Jade's party. Lydia had been ecstatic that two of her best friends were going to be there for such an auspicious occasion and had excitedly extended them the offer to stay at their house. Surprisingly, Lina had graciously declined, saying that she and Len would prefer to get a hotel room in one of Ixtapa's nearby hotels.

"Len and I need to have a honeymoon." Lina had laughed, a little embarrassed but sounding giddily happy. "Besides, with Eric and Amie both there and Jade home, you have your hands full. Also, do me a favor and keep this a secret, will you, Lyd? I want to surprise everyone."

Lydia had eagerly agreed ,although she wondered how she would be able to keep it to herself. Just as they were about to hang up, Lina reaffirmed that they wouldn't see her until the night of the party since that was the day they were coming in.

"And, no you're not to worry about getting us from the airport to the hotel either. I've been there enough over the years, Lydia. We can find our own way. Just keep a seat at the table for us." With a low chuckle, Lina had said goodbye and hung up.

Lydia smiled in the dark. It was much too long since they had been here. She had known them for over thirty-five years, Len first and Lina later. They had been through a lot together. Tragedy had struck them over the years too, like the time that Lina developed cancer. It had been touch and go as to whether she would survive, but somehow she had.

When Lydia first heard about Lina's illness, she had immediately flown to be with her with Jade in tow. It had been Jade's first introduction to the other half of her heritage, and she had loved it. It had also been the first time Amie and Jade had met and forged the bond that had spanned all these years.

When she was sure that Lina was safely out of danger, she returned with her young daughter to Mexico and to her husband, but the seeds for Jade in her adopted country were already deeply sown, and Lydia had much to be grateful to her friends for. It looked like there was not going to be a shortage of things to celebrate for the next while. The thought made her smile again, and she wiggled to a more comfortable spot on Rodolfo's lap.

At her stirrings, Rodolfo kissed her nose and suggested they go to bed. Unresisting, Lydia slid to the floor in her bare feet. Then, arm-in-arm, the two quietly made their way into the house. *Tomorrow will take care of itself,* she thought as she closed the bedroom door.

6

Jade awoke to the sounds of voices low and muted in the far recesses of the house. She stretched, luxuriating in the feel of the cool cotton sheets her mother bought in Canada and wondering who could possibly be up so early. She punched the pillow and placed it over her ears in an attempt to close out the sound, but it was no use. By habit, Jade was usually an early riser, so the sound of people did not disturb her. In Canada, she would be pulling on her sweats and heading for her morning run. In frigid cold winter weather, she would haul her running gear to the indoor track at the university, getting as many laps in as she could in an hour before showering and changing into her usual uniform of jeans and a t-shirt before class. But now, while Amie and Eric were here at least, she was on official vacation, and she wondered what they should do today. Excited to get started, she rose from her bed just as someone rapped at her bedroom door. It was her mother.

"Jade? Are you awake?"

Jade smiled at the tentative voice. "Come in, Momma."

Lydia poked her head around the door.

"Good." There was obvious approval in her glance. "You're up already." She stepped all the way into the room. "Raul's here." She searched her daughter's face for a reaction.

Jade shrugged and turned her back to hide the annoyance she felt. She grabbed her hairbrush from the bureau and began to brush vigorously.

Oblivious, Lydia continued. "He's talking to Eric and Amie now. They've accepted his invitation to go to Manzanillo Beach for snorkeling and a picnic."

Jade whirled around angrily. "Really? And just what gives him the right to—"

Lydia interrupted her. "Raul is here because he wants to be nice to your friends and to invite you all for a nice outing. I think you should go."

Jade stared at her mother. Didn't she hear what Jade had told her yesterday? Then Jade remembered that she hadn't elaborated, and she stopped abruptly. As far as Lydia was concerned, it would be perfectly natural for Raul to come over, even if they were no longer *novios*. She peered into Lydia's serene face and scowled. Apparently, nothing she could say would change the fact that he was here so she might as well deal with it.

"Fine," she groused. "But believe me, Raul and I are going to have a little talk very soon."

Without waiting for an answer, she grabbed a towel off the back of the chair and stomped grumpily off into the adjoining bathroom for a shower. The least she could do was make sure she didn't look terrible, she thought, not bothering to analyze why looking good in Raul's presence should concern her so much.

Alone in her daughter's room, Lydia smiled. *That's exactly what you should do, Jade*, she thought to herself before leaving to rejoin the others, closing the door softly behind her.

When Jade emerged a half an hour later, she was freshly scrubbed and attired in a matching shorts and tank top set. She found Raul and her friends bent over a guide book at the kitchen table. As she crossed the floor, they looked up with welcoming smiles on their faces. The first to react, Eric stood to greet her, planting a light kiss on her cheek and inviting her to join them. Raul pretended not to notice the gesture and instead moved closer to Amie on the pretense of seeing better. Jade frowned and looked away.

"Here's the beach we're going to today, Amie," Raul was telling her now. "The snorkeling is excellent. Someday, I will take you to the others off the bay—beaches like Contramar and Las Gatas."

"I think I can manage to do that myself." Jade spoke dryly, and Eric and Amie turned to stare at her in surprise.

She had remained standing and was looking at Raul, her face disapproving and unapproachable. This was the second time they heard the normally polite Jade behave rudely. Jade flushed.

"Of course, there is no better guide then Raul." She smiled to take the bite out of her words. "I just meant that I know Raul must be too busy to go gallivanting off with us like this."

"It is my pleasure." Raul's quiet answer made Jade feel even more like an ungracious fool.

Coolly, she smiled but kept silent.

Raul's eyes stayed on Jade's face, knowing she was angry he was here. Pretending not to notice her reaction, he purposefully goaded her now. She had changed so much from her time in Canada that he hardly recognized her. The Jade he knew before she went away had been a passionate young girl on the brink of womanhood. Always laughing and teasing, she had been considered the leader of any group she was with. She was as quick to smile as she was quick to anger, but she had never carried a grudge and would forgive anyone who displeased her quickly and easily, never referring to it again.

The person who had returned was unsmiling, sharp-tempered and inflexible. And cold. At least with him, he amended, realizing that part of that was his fault. Of all the things he could say when describing Jade, frigid was never one of them. Remembering their hot embraces, he wondered idly if Eric and Jade shared those moments, too. Unable to resist, he had pulled Lydia aside as they were leaving the night before and asked her what Eric meant to her daughter.

Lydia had been brutally honest, sorry that she was the one he had chosen to impart the news. "He is her boyfriend, Raul."

It was hard for her to see the hurt in his eyes, and wanting to comfort him, she had patted his arm and told him to make sure to drop by in the morning. To her pleased surprise, he had.

Now, watching Jade charming and happy with her friends but cold towards himself, Raul knew that he wanted her love directed at him again…the way it used to be when he was the center of her world. He was determined he would make that happen, even if it meant risking her anger. It was better than her apparent indifference now.

Feeling his interest, Jade looked at Raul and scowled. She moved to the counter and helped herself to a cup of coffee. It was apparent that the three were quite happy to be together, with or without her, and she felt another flash of anger and something that felt like envy. With a twinge, she saw Eric clap Raul on his back, nodding eagerly at something he was saying while Amie threw back her head and laughed that infectious chuckle of hers. She felt like an outsider.

Just then, Amie noticed Jade standing by herself. Excusing herself, she hurried over to her friend on the other side of the vast kitchen. Neither Eric nor Raul paid attention, intent as they were on the maps in front of them.

"Jade, are you okay?"

Amie's gentle face looked concerned, and immediately Jade softened. She didn't know anyone who could stay mad when Amie was around. Berating herself silently for what she knew was childish behavior, she smiled and put her free arm around her shoulder.

"No, Amie, I think I got up on the wrong side of the bed. Why don't you and I get the snorkeling equipment ready while Eric and Raul plan the outing? I'll ask Juanita to make us some sandwiches."

Across the room, Raul lifted his head.

"Already did," he stated.

Jade's face darkened, and instinctively he grimaced

How dare he? Then, remembering her resolve, she forced a smile to her face.

"Well, aren't you the proficient one."

As a compliment, it failed miserably. *At least she's warming up to me,* he thought with an inner chuckle. Then, deliberately to annoy her further, he turned to Eric, who sat thoughtfully silent throughout the brief exchange.

Ever the peacekeeper, Amie pretended not to notice and grabbed Jade's arm. "*Vamanous,* Jade."

Her attempt to command in her deep, throaty voice caused Jade to burst into giggles despite her rotten mood. Somehow Amie always made her feel better. Even when she suffered her worse bouts of homesickness, Amie knew just how to cheer her up. Gratefully, Jade threw an arm around her friend and led her toward the outside door to where their nautical gear was already waiting in readiness as Raul said it would be. The screen door slammed behind them, and the sound of their laughter drifted back to the kitchen and then was gone.

Eric regarded Raul thoughtfully. "You have been friends with Jade a long time."

It was more a statement than a question. Raul nodded his head but kept his eyes glued to the guide book in front of him. Even so, he was still unprepared by the Canadian's next words.

"I think you should know that I've asked Jade to marry me."

Raul looked up in surprise, feeling the sharp blow in his solar plexus. By some miracle, he kept his face impassive; only a tic by his right eye betrayed his thoughts. He willed it to stop even as he wondered why no one had thought to tell him. Then he shrugged. Maybe they didn't know. Or maybe Jade didn't want them to. He tired to ignore the pain seeping through his entire body, numbing him. He waited until his heart slowed before speaking.

"Congratulations. When's the wedding?" he asked nonchalantly.

Eric's mouth twisted. "I don't know. She hasn't accepted yet. She says she'll let me know the night of her birthday party next week."

Suddenly, he sounded a little unsure, and Raul almost felt sorry for him. The band around his heart eased a little. *There is still a chance.*

Eric squared his broad shoulders and looked him in the eye. He chose his next words carefully, dashing Raul's hopes swiftly and cruelly.

"I can offer her a great deal in Canada. I think she will say yes. She will have everything she could ever want with me. A nice house. A job and career if she wants it." He sounded more confident now, and Raul's heart sank

"She can have all that here, too." Stung, Raul felt the need to respond.

Eric nodded slowly. "Yes, she can," he allowed. "But with me she will never have to worry that I would cheat on her."

He watched as Raul flushed guiltily. It had taken him a little while, but Eric congratulated himself on having figured it out. This was the guy who had broken Jade's heart. She hadn't gone into great detail, but being a man, Eric figured it must have been something to do with another woman. Women were funny about things like that, he knew.

He also knew that this man was in some ways the barrier to his future. He could see the tension between them the night before at the restaurant, and he had wondered about it then. It was made more obvious today that they shared some history. Before they went further, he needed to find out if that part of her life was over. If it wasn't, he had a right to know.

He thought back to the day he met Jade. It was plain that at first she was not overly impressed with him, but it didn't take him long to see it wasn't just him. She was standoffish and cold to nearly every man that came within a mile of her. He had always thought there was a reason for that and had taken it as a challenge to win her over. It didn't help that her best friend Amie thought he was a toad, as she had overtly called him one day. Over time, however, Jade had come to trust him and open up.

"It's not what you think," Raul began, wondering why he was defending himself to this man.

Eric agreed on that point and held up his hands. "I'm not the one you have to convince."

"But I do," Raul told him sadly, seeing Eric as the man who stood between he and the woman he loved. Unknowingly, he was echoing Eric's own thoughts.

Intrigued, Eric sat back in his chair and regarded him carefully. It was true he didn't know Raul, but if Jade had once been in love with him, it would be in his best interest to find out more. He tipped his chair back and drawled, "Fine, pal. Shoot."

Raul snorted at the expression, but just as he opened his mouth to explain, Jade and Amie reappeared, laughing and giggling like the best friends they were. They crossed the room to stand beside the men, Amie grabbing Raul's arm and flirtatiously hauling him to his feet.

"Come on, Raul. Are you two going to stay here all day and yak? I swear, you are worse than a pair of little old men."

Raul looked down at the petite blonde next to him, then back at Eric, as if to say, *Who could resist such a woman?* But Eric had his arms around Jade and was not paying attention to either one of them. Raul felt another twinge, but he turned back to the smiling Amie at his side and grinned.

"You're right, Amie. We are ready when you are."

With that, he grabbed his knapsack off the chair with one hand and Amie's arm with the other. Eric and Jade had no choice but to follow.

At the door, Eric pulled Jade back, and once again his arms circled her small waist. Surprised, she looked at the man who had become such an important part of her life and smiled, startled as he bent to kiss her. He was usually more reserved and not prone to outward displays of affection, and she wondered at his actions.

Eric took his time, loving the taste of her soft lips beneath his. He felt her body mold against his, and his kiss deepened. With a small groan, he pulled back, an amused grin on his face. Then, without a word Eric took her hand and ushered her outside to the courtyard where their companions waited in the sunlight.

Lydia walked purposefully from the gift store to Rodolfo's office. Hard at work as she knew he would be, his head was bent low over his desk. She moved closer and kissed his cheek.

Rodolfo looked up and smiled warmly. He was concentrating so hard on the project before him, he hadn't heard her come in. Happily, he held it up for her to admire.

"Do you think she will like it?" He looked expectant and then gratified when she smiled.

"She will love it," Lydia told him honestly and kissed him again.

"How are the plans for the party coming along?"

"Thank heavens for Ana is all I can say." Lydia smiled wryly. "You know how difficult it is to get things done here. Remember how impatient I used to be when I first came?"

Rodolfo chuckled. What Lydia said was true. The first months after she had decided to stay in Mexico with him permanently were very difficult for her. It took her a long time to realize that in Mexico you were never able to accomplish everything you wanted to in a single day. Sometimes it would take many days for what in Canada would be a simple task.

She smiled at him, remembering how patient he had been when she had railed that, "this is not how we do it in Canada." Over time and with his help, she learned to become much more relaxed and accepting about things. That didn't mean she didn't still find it frustrating sometimes.

"I am hoping that everything will go smoothly," she said now with a shrug.

"It will." Rodolfo was quick to give her a reassuring hug around her waist. He had no doubt that Lydia would be able to pull the party off. It was one of her strengths as an organizer. He looked around him. The restaurants had been her idea, and now look at where they were. The gift store was a huge success too, and he knew he owed much of that to her business savvy.

At first when she had approached him about the idea of going out on his own, he had been reluctant. After so many years working for someone else, he had to admit he was complacent, secure in his job. Gently, Lydia convinced him he was wasting his talents as a waiter when he could own something and build on it for himself.

It had been a struggle for both of them. After Lydia's business, an advertising company that collapsed in Canada, they had made their way back there to take care of the disaster and find new jobs for themselves. Inga and Richard, owners of the Log House Restaurant in the northern community of Prince George had given Rodolfo a summer job while Lydia picked up a consulting job for a publishing company. Between the two of them, they saved every dime they made, enough at least to put a down payment on the building in which they now sat. In all, it had taken two years of working in Canada before they had enough money to buy all the equipment, furniture and dishes they would need to open, but they had done it. And they never looked back.

Lydia looked down at what Rodolfo was working on and smiled again. Then, straightening, she gave him a swift parting hug and headed for the door.

"Speaking of plans, I'm supposed to meet Ana for breakfast and go over some details. See you later at five?"

Rodolfo was already at work and distractedly threw his wife a quick smile. In minutes, he was totally engrossed with what he had been doing before she interrupted him.

Raul dug into the sand, his mind remembering the events that had changed his life. Was it only two years ago? It seemed like forever. If only his pride had not gotten in the way. He should have forced Jade to listen to him. She would have understood. In hindsight, he was sure of that, but he was young then. What did he know? Looking across the small beach to where Jade was sitting laughing and talking with another man, her knees pulled to her chest, he wished now that he had.

"Raul...Raul." A woman's voice sounded over the water, immediately waking him from his sleep. As usual, he had been dreaming about Jade. He flew to the side of the boat before he remembered. Jade was far off in Canada at school. With an ache, he missed her all over again. He focused his sleep-filled eyes and, squinting, peered out over the water.

Disappointed, he saw that it was only Maria, someone he had known all his life. Then he was curious as to why she would be coming to see him. As her boat drew closer, he smiled a friendly but cautious greeting.

"Hola, Maria," he called, and she waved her hand in reply but did not return his smile. She looked distraught to him, and straight away he was on guard.

"May I come aboard?" she asked quietly, and for a minute he hesitated.

No other woman but Jade had ever been on his boat alone. Then, seeing her forlorn face, Raul relented.

Maria threw the rope of her dinghy to Raul, and he caught it expertly and tied it to his stern. Then, reaching over, he pulled her onto his boat. He sat as far away from her as he could and waited patiently for what she had to say.

Maria took a deep breath and looked up with huge, liquid eyes. "I'm pregnant," she blurted as Raul stared at her in shock. Then promptly, she burst into tears.

The day turned out to be not nearly as bad as Jade had thought it would. In fact, if she were being totally honest, it was one of the best days she had spent in a long time, she grudgingly admitted.

Raul had been the perfect host, treating Eric and Amie like royalty in a gracious and easy manner. Earlier in the day, she had thought that there was some tension between her former love and her present one, but seeing them examining shells companionably on the sandy beach, she wondered now if she had imagined it.

There was no question what Amie thought of Raul, Jade realized with a pang. On the boat ride over, Amie had asked her if it would be alright if she went out with Raul. As Eric had, she guessed that Raul was the boyfriend in the past she never wanted to talk about. The last thing she wanted to do was hurt Jade in any way.

At first, Amie's probing had taken Jade aback. It never occurred to her that other women would find Raul attractive too, but then she realized how ridiculous the assumption was. Unsure as to how to respond for a long while, she had not said anything.

Finally, her innate sense of fairness and common sense prevailed, and Jade told Amie what she wanted to hear. She had Eric now, a man who loved and wanted to marry her. With a false cheerfulness, she told her friend that as far as she was concerned, Raul was open game. As she said the words, she tried not to think about the dull ache in her chest while Amie smiled happily, glad to have that out of the way. The last thing Amie wanted to do was hurt her in any way.

"If only Raul would look at me as if I were more than the family pet maybe I would get somewhere," she complained with a laugh, making Jade laugh with her.

She tried to look interested as Amie chatted away about how attractive she found the Mexican man—much more her type that those big hulking men from Canada, she said, her eyes casting over at Eric.

Now, sitting beneath the palm tree on the near-deserted beach, Jade wondered how she would really feel if she were to see Raul with someone else, especially her closest friend. *Probably the same way he must feel about seeing me here with Eric,* she thought then with a flash of intuition. She frowned. If he did, he sure wasn't giving any indication that it bothered him.

For the most part, Raul ignored her, speaking occasionally to get his little digs in. He seemed to delight in getting her angry. Sometimes she wanted to slap the self-satisfied smile off his face.

Pleased by the fantasy, she grinned as she imagined what the reaction of everyone would be. With renewed energy, she started digging in the sand with some of the sand toys Amie had found in the shed and laughingly included along with the picnic basket.

"Digging to China?" A voice spoke low into her ear, and immediately her heart sped up.

"No. I'm digging to Canada," came the quick retort, and she looked up into smoky eyes close to hers. *Too close for comfort*, she thought as dimples deepened in his face. Her heart jumped again, and she looked around for Eric and Amie, sitting up higher to try and spot them. Surprised, she saw the pair walking slowly down the beach. Heads down, she deduced they were searching for seashells. In a minute, they disappeared around the bend and were gone from sight.

Raul followed her eyes. "They make a good couple. Just like us."

His voice sounded satisfied, and she bristled and curled her lip disdainfully.

"That shows how much you know. They hate each other." Then she smiled sarcastically. "On second thought, maybe you're right. They are exactly like us."

"Ahhh, but Jade," Raul leaned closer, "I don't hate you at all." His whisper was low and seductive, his breath caressing her cheek as he leaned forward. "You should tell him you are going to marry me, Jade."

His words caused her jaw to drop, and she felt naked as he ripped away her secrets. "Who told you?" She sounded confused.

Raul's grin was smug. "Eric." *So it was true?* He tried to ignore the pain.

Jade's hand fluttered in the air. That Eric would tell Raul was the absolute last thing she expected to hear, and her eyes narrowed in disbelief.

It's good to see her off balance, Raul decided self-righteously. He decided it was time to push her a little more. Without warning, he reached out and cupped one hand around the back of her head, his face mere inches from her. Then he kissed her, gently at first then more insistently.

Jade tried to push away, but somehow his arms had wrapped around her, imprisoning her in his embrace. She felt the air leave her body and exhale into his, his mouth warm and wet. With a moan, she returned his kiss.

From somewhere far off, she heard a triumphant chuckle. The sound froze her, and with a Herculean effort, she pulled away. Then, without thinking, she raised her hand and slapped his face.

The surprise in his eyes quickly turned to anger, and she saw his eyes narrow and grow dark. Suddenly afraid, she drew back her breath, coming in ragged gasps for air. Then, before he could make a move, Jade jumped up and fled down the beach in the direction of her friends.

Raul sat back on his heels and rubbed his cheek. He was more furious than he had ever been in his life, and his first thought was to go after her and... *Do what?* He knew he would never lay a hand on her no matter what she did— never mind that she had the strength of a burro and was almost as stubborn as one too. He grinned ruefully. Well, at least he knew that the Jade he had always loved was just inside that cool façade she portrayed to the world. That was something at least.

A small smile of satisfaction wove its way across his features. She still thought she hated him, of that he had no doubt. But everyone knew that hate was just a short step from love. Feeling better than he had for a long time, Raul stood and brushed the sand from his legs. Then, turning to the knapsacks, he set about arranging the picnic Juanita had so thoughtfully packed for them on the makeshift table of rocks nearby.

There were sandwiches of baked honey ham and turkey with lettuce and cheese. In deference to the guests, Juanita had made some of them with sweet rolls while others she had wrapped in flour tortillas. There were also individual containers of flan and fruit for desert, a few cokes he kept in the cooler of ice and some chocolate bars. He grinned again, knowing Jade's appetite for food from the past. It wouldn't do to let her starve, it might make her mean. He laughed and sat back down in the sand to wait for everyone to return.

7

The next days flew by for Jade and her friends. Raul often found time to join them on the various day trips they took. Sometimes they would go to the beach, spending long hours lying in the sun, acquiring healthy bronze tans. Other times, Jade would take Eric to visit out-of-the-way cantinas in the poorest sections of town. He was always amazed that these were the places that could produce the best food he had ever tasted in his life. Taco Bell has nothing on this, he would joke with her afterwards, making her laugh.

On those excursions and when seeing they wanted to be alone, Amie would take long walks into the hills outside of town, a strong walking stick against stray dogs her only protection. Sometimes Raul would go with her, and she would come back from the day trips chattering excitedly about Raul this Raul that, so much that Jade felt irritated, but for what reason even she was unsure. She told herself it was because she didn't want to see Amie hurt.

Mindful of the last time they were together alone, Jade made a point of always being with either Eric or Amie whenever Raul was around. If Raul noticed, he never made mention, only regarding her with that knowing grin he had and infuriating her all the more.

They went dancing a couple of times at the local discos, but Jade only danced with Eric or occasionally some of her school friends. Amie, by default, was Raul's constant partner. After a couple of attempts, he stopped asking Jade to dance at all, concentrating only on teaching Amie the Meringue or how to Salsa. If he was unfailingly polite to Jade, he was even more attentive to Amie, who basked in the warm glow of attention. Jade pretended not to care, but inside she seethed. Cautiously, she tried to warn Amie that Mexican men had a different philosophy about relationships than what she was used to, but Amie had only laughed.

"Jade, that is the most prejudiced thing I have ever heard you say. Since when have you believed in generalizations?" she teased unmercifully as Jade tried to explain, failing badly.

"Don't worry, Jade," Amie assured her. "He is a friend of yours. I'm sure he wouldn't do anything bad to me. Besides, I'm just having fun."

Jade had smiled then and agreed with her, but she vowed to keep a close eye on her "friend" just the same.

Jade noticed too the cautious relationship that appeared to spring up between Eric and Raul, and she wondered about it. It looked to her as if they were becoming friends, and for some reason, it annoyed her even more. She felt that Raul was up to something, but she didn't know what that could be. Casually, she tried to bring up the subject with Eric, but he only looked at her blankly and shrugged away her concerns.

"He's a good guy, Jade, even if he did screw up things with you. I guess I can afford to be generous. I have you now, and he doesn't," he said, sounding a little too sure of himself, and for some reason it irritated her. *It seemed that everything does these days*, she recognized and hated herself for it.

Later, when she was alone, she thought how foolish she sounded. Still each time she saw the two men together laughing and joking, her doubts came to the forefront again, and she was instantly on guard. She shrugged. There were more important things to worry about—like what she was she going to tell Eric in only a few days.

Her birthday was fast approaching, and planning it was taking up a great deal of her free time. Occasionally she stayed behind with Ana and her mother while Eric and Amie and sometimes Raul went off on outings. The three women would spend countless hours going over the myriad of party details— everything from what she would wear to the mariachis they hired and the color of the decorations.

Knowing she was a former window dresser at Bloomingdale's department store in New York, both Jade and Lydia bowed to Ana's suggestions and expertise with a grateful humbleness that amused the family friend. It had been a long time since she had had the opportunity to be a part of something of this magnitude, and it breathed new life into her.

After much deliberation, they had decided on silver and jade green streamers and balloons, along with spectacular centerpieces for the tables in matching colors. Each one would have small, silver-dipped candles with a white baby rose and baby's breath wrapped artfully around the base.

In addition to being her birthday, it would be the debut of the restaurant too, a double celebration, her parents told her proudly. Anyone who was anyone was invited—in all, over two hundred and fifty guests. A live band would play during dinner and for the dancing that would follow the elaborate five-course meal. Jade had asked that they play mostly Mexican music. She missed dancing to a Latin beat when she was in Canada and wanted to get as much of it as she could while she was here. Amie agreed. She was becoming adept thanks to Raul's tutelage and wanted nothing more than a chance to show off her new-found talent as a salsa virtuoso.

In a rare moment of sweet remembrance, Jade told Amie that she and Raul had gone dancing often when they were younger, even winning dance competitions. She knew that it was pride that kept her from accepting his invitations to dance now. Yet watching Amie dancing with him sometimes made her nostalgic for those days.

To counter those feelings ,Jade wondered if Eric would be interested in learning some dances and decided that she would teach him a few steps between now and the party. When she suggested it to him, he had only laughed.

"I think you and I will do the slow ones and leave the wild dancing to you and your friends. Safer for everyone that way," he told her, remembering the moves he had seen the other night at the nightclub.

Jade had danced then with some of her childhood friends who had all been delighted to see her again. To see her so dancing freely and expertly had shown him a side of Jade he had never known before. Part of him had been excited by the passion he glimpsed as she moved to the intricate steps, but another part realized it was if she were a stranger. Both sentiments gave him a great deal to think about.

Jade, seeing that she was not about to convert Eric to learning something new, made sure there was also music that he would know and recognize and that would allow them to do the "slow ones."

Entertainment plans set to everyone's satisfaction, the next step was to make preparations for dinner. Rodolfo told her that Raul requested that he take complete charge of the meal, to which Jade sarcastically remarked she hoped he wouldn't poison their guests. Her father didn't answer but had looked disapproving. It was just one more thing to make her resent Raul.

One day, as she was hurrying down the alleyway between her mother's gift store and the Mi Corazon, she accidentally bumped into him. With a mumbled apology, she tried to brush past, but his hand shot out and grabbed her arm. Pulling her into the shadows, Raul pressed her into one of the alcoves of a bordering building. Not wanting to give him the satisfaction of seeing how much his presence affected her, she merely stared coldly into his eyes until, with grudging admiration, he stepped back, but not so much that she could move around him. Defiant, she waited.

Raul grinned, wanting no more than to have her in his arms so he could kiss away the hurt he saw in her eyes. He knew she was hurt, even if she was too proud to admit it. Resisting the overwhelming urge, he kept his voice light and teasing instead.

"Where are you going in such a hurry Jade? Remember, this is Mexico. In Mexico, we don't rush around so much. Here we work to live, not live to work."

She pretended to smile, but her eyes remained cold.

"You would know all about that, Raul, wouldn't you?" He looked confused, and ruthlessly she continued. "Somehow, you managed to wriggle your way into a nice easy job with my family, but don't think it will last long. I'm back now."

Arrogantly, she lifted her chin higher, her voice pure honey as the words dripped disdainfully from her lips. "Things will be different for you very soon, I think."

Raul leaned closer and lifted one hand to touch the tendrils of her hair that had escaped the severe bun on her head. He felt her flinch, but only a little, and once more he was filled with admiration for her courage. Then, suddenly, he was ashamed. Pure sadness swept over him, and straightening abruptly, he took a step back.

"You are right, Jade." His quiet comment surprised them both. "You are back now, and soon things will change. It will be interesting to see what those changes will be and if you will stay to see them made."

With that, he spun on his heels, his footsteps clacking loudly over the cobblestone streets until they could be heard no more.

Jade leaned back against the wall, her legs trembling in relief. At one point, she hadn't known if he was going to strike her or kiss her. No, she amended, he would never hit her. Of that she was certain. Kiss, then? She didn't know what was worse. Either way, she was relieved he was gone. Slowly, she started down the alleyway. She had no idea what he meant, or, for that matter, what she meant either. Even she didn't know yet what she was going to do about her future.

The previous night, she had had a chance to talk to Eric alone on the wide front porch of the hacienda. In the moonlight, he told her his plans for their life together, quietly and firmly painting a picture of security and happiness with him in Canada. For a moment, she had almost said yes, but she held back, only promising an answer on her birthday. She knew Eric had been disappointed, but like the gentleman he was, he agreed to wait a little while longer. The day was almost there, and she wasn't any closer to knowing than when she had first arrived.

It was so easy in Canada to believe that her future was with Eric, but here in Mexico, she realized that it was much more complicated than that. There were her parents to consider, of course, and the rest of her family. She doubted that she would see her friends if she moved away. At least not regularly! The one time she had gone to visit them since her return made her realize just how many light years they were from each other. After the first hour, though, things had lightened up a little, and soon they were laughing and chatting as much as they ever had. It was almost like old times. But what would happen if she went away permanently with only yearly visits to sustain them? Would they accept her then? Or would they pretend she never existed? Either way, she doubted it would be the same.

Then, of course, there was the business itself. What would happen to it if she decided not to stay? Who would run it? Her father certainly couldn't do it forever. If she had been a boy, there would be no doubt that she would take over. And if she stayed? Could she do that on her own now?

It had been many years since she had worked in the restaurant, although as a kid, it had provided some of the happiest times of her life. She had enjoyed setting the tables, prepping food when the chef allowed it, and generally doing any of the tasks they gave her. She remembered fondly times when Arturo had explained the tiny details that went into being an excellent waiter as opposed to only a good one, while Alfredo the bartender had taught her how to make more than a dozen drinks by the time she was twelve.

When she had gone to Canada, her parents insisted that she not work while attending school. In their opinion, it was more important for her to concentrate on her education and get good grades. She wondered now if that had been a good idea. What if she had forgotten everything she had ever learned?

But now is not the time to think about this, Jade thought as, with renewed determination, she straightened her shoulders and continued down the alleyway. At the gift store, she opened it to find her mother, Ana and Amie waiting impatiently for her.

"There you are!" Amie cried out happily. "We were just about to call the police, weren't we, Ana?"

Ana only smiled while her mother regarded her daughter closely. She noted the flushed cheeks with interest but decided not to mention it. Instead, she calmly asked if they were ready to go.

Today was set aside for a shopping excursion that they unanimously looked forward to all week. First on the agenda, however, was a visit to Lavender and Roses in Ixtapa, a new beauty shop owned and operated by long-time friend, Kimberly. Once in the cab, Ana told the fascinated Amie the story of Kimberly and her husband Gonzalo, how they first met and how they fell in love in Zihuatanejo, but only after a tragic accident that caused her to fall many feet over a balcony to the rocks below. It was while Kimberly was recuperating in the hospital that Gonzalo realized he wanted to be with her for the rest of his life. Now, many years later, their two daughters, Tenisha and Lily, worked in her beauty salon as masseuses and hair stylists respectively, while Kimberly did the business side of things. Today, however, she would be doing Ana and Lydia's hair personally, as a special favor to her preferred clients, while her daughters would take care of Jade and Amie.

Amie was thrilled by the story. Wishing aloud that something romantic would happen to her while she was in Mexico, her inner voice turned to Raul. *If only.* She sighed inwardly, imagining Raul and... Her daydreams were abruptly interrupted by Jade, who confided, "I've known Kimberly and her daughters for a long time. I promise you will love the experience."

"I can't wait," Amie groaned. "I need some pampering. I'm beginning to think I'm losing my touch with men."

Jade frowned and looked at her best friend in alarm. "What do you mean? Have you and Eric been fighting?"

"No, Jade." Amie waved away the concern in Jade's voice. "At least no more than usual. Eric and I will never change. It's Raul. He barely looks at me."

Amie exhaled noisily in comical frustration, rolling her eyes until, amused, Jade couldn't help but laugh.

Pleased she had made the pinched look Jade wore too often these days disappear, Amie looked out the window of the cab at the lush, green scenery and thought about the comment she had made about Eric. While it was true they were not friends, things had definitely changed since that time on the boat. Now, on top of their dislike, there seemed to be an underlying tension between them. Other than the day they went snorkeling, they were almost never alone. A strange distance had sprung up recently, whereas before they were able to at least talk, even if it was only to trade insults.

"Why? Why do we have to go for a walk?" she had argued stubbornly, reluctant to leave the handsome Raul's side to go with someone who clearly didn't appreciate her in the slightest. At least Raul made a pretense of being interested in what she had to say. He always laughed at all of her jokes, even when she didn't think he understood them. All Eric did was look as if he wished she would disappear off the face of the earth. It really was enough to make a girl feel unattractive—even if it was only boring old Eric who thought so. Why what he thought should even matter, she had no idea, but somehow it did. *Mostly because of her pride,* she realized now as the cab whizzed by, and she sighed again.

At the sound, Jade caught the eye of her mother, who looked about to make a comment, but just then, the taxi pulled up in front of the Ixtapa Palace, and the moment passed. Relieved, Jade got out and moved to the passenger door to help Ana while Lydia and Amie climbed out on their own. With eager anticipation, the foursome made their way into the cool, marble-floored Ixtapa Palace.

Kimberly was there to greet them when they arrived, her two daughters standing shyly by her side. Every time Lydia saw the two girls, she smiled. The elder, Tenisha, took after the Mexican side of the family in coloring and features, while Lily was much like her blonde American mother. Unlike Jade, who had inherited a little of both Lydia and Rodolfo, there were never two sisters who looked so unalike. Despite the differences, they were both beautiful in their own distinctive way.

Introducing Amie, Ana held up her hands and proclaimed, "I need maintenance," just as she always said every time she came.

Obligingly, a laughing Kimberly led her to a booth in the corner of the room. It was decided that Lily, the younger of the two, would cut and style Amie's hair, while Tenisha would begin Lydia's massage in the other room. Then Jade would trade places with whoever finished first so that, by the time everyone was taken care of, it would be lunch. After that, they would go to a couple of the best boutiques the resort had to offer and try to find new dresses for Amie and Jade to wear to the birthday party.

Jade absentmindedly grabbed a magazine from the stack next to her chair and turned the page. It was one she had read before since Amie had subscriptions to all of them. Uninterestedly, she thumbed through it anyway, but her mind was not on the article. After realizing she had tried to read the same page for the last five minutes, she gave up and put the magazine back on the rack.

Looking around, she caught part of the conversation Kimberly was having with Ana about the upcoming party, to which they had of course been invited. Ana was saying it would be better than the one they had thrown for Jade's fifteenth birthday party, and Jade smiled. It was hard to believe that she would soon be ten years older. Ten years wiser too, she hoped.

From the divide in the next room where her mother was being massaged by the capable Tenisha, she heard the soft, instrumental sounds of Zen-like music being played, designed to relax and soothe. Her eyes moved to where Amie sat happily in the chair with Lily listening intently to her ideas on how she wanted her hair done. Jade smiled and closed her eyes contentedly. Maybe if she could rest her eyes a little, she could relax before it was her turn for her own "maintenance," as Ana so aptly called it. In a minute, she was fast asleep.

The streets of Zihuatanejo were filled with people. Jade strolled among the rows of stores and shops, smiling happily at everyone she met. It was another day in paradise, with fading sunlight and a soft, warm breeze. In the main square of the plaza, she heard music and noticed a large crowd of people gathered. Intrigued, she pushed her way to the front.

A lone girl of about twelve stood at the edge of the stage, dressed in the costume of a folk dancer. Poised and quiet, she shyly smiled at the people who applauded her. It was clear she was about to perform, and delighted, Jade decided to stay and watch..

An announcer stepped to the microphone, and in flowery terms, he explained the meaning and origin of the dance. It was from the region of Chihuahua, he told them, and Jade smiled in recognition. It was the Mexico of her father's family and a part of her heritage. Intrigued, she waited with the crowd.

The music began—a catchy tune that soon had the crowd clapping and taping their feet, Jade included. The young girl dipped and swayed, her toes clacking loudly on the plywood stage, her fingers snapping in time to the music. All eyes were on her.

Just then, two young men emerged from the crowd to stand beside the dancer. They were dressed in snow-white pants and shirts, red bandanas tied nonchalantly around their necks.

Each man carried a rooster, the plumage of the birds bright and colorful against the white clothes. It was clear that they were a part of the performance. Fascinated, Jade watched as the men moved toward each other, the birds held at arm's length before them. Moving cautiously to the time of the music, they thrust the roosters to the middle of the stage briefly. Then they withdrew. The young girl, her smile firmly in place, continued to dance to the seductive drum beat.

Jade watched, fascinated, as the dance unfolded. Her hands flew to her mouth in horror as the birds latched together with hooked beaks, their clawed feet scraping their rivals' sides. Feathers flew and landed on the ground, picked up by giggling little boys in the crowd and borne triumphantly away.

The beat slowed, and along with it, the movements slowed too. Then, bending over at the waist, the young men placed the birds on the crude wooden stage and let them go. Instinctively, the birds flew at one another's throats, seeking to kill or at the very least main. The music sped up and reached a crescendo as the crowd roared its approval. Sickened by the sight of blood, Jade moved to flee the crowd. As she did, she collided with the hard bodies of two men, and she looked up fearfully. Grinning wolfishly down from their great heights were the faces of Raul and Eric.

With a jerk, Jade sat up disoriented and afraid, her heart hammering in her chest. She looked up into the concerned eyes of her mother, who had one hand on her shoulder.

"I had the strangest dream," she tried to explain, but it sounded lame even to her ears. "I dreamt there were two roosters fighting, and there was a dance and…" She stopped, sure that she sounded every bit as idiotic as she looked at the moment. She ran her hands through her unruly hair and tried to smile.

Lydia patted her arm soothingly and told her Lily was waiting to cut her hair. With relief, she emerged from the chair and gingerly crossed the room to where an impassive young woman greeted her warmly and invited her to sit. Gratefully, Jade obliged, happy to put her thoughts elsewhere for the moment. Firmly erasing the strange dream from her mind, she tried instead to concentrate on the task before them—which was to bring her hair under a more manageable condition.

As Lily worked, Jade asked about everything that had been going on with her life and whether she was coming to her birthday party. Lily assured her that she wouldn't miss it for the world.

Later, under the strong hands of Lily's sister, Jade's mind kept going back to the strange dream. What could it mean? As Tenisha worked her magic, Jade felt her eyes grow heavy. As relaxed as she was feeling, though, this time she decided to stay very much awake.

Rodolfo sat at a table in the bar of his own restaurant, his right hand man on one side and Jade's new love interest on the other. They were drinking tequila, the bottle in front of them almost empty. Earlier, Eric had thrown a couple shots back quickly, something that had made both Raul and Rodolfo laugh out loud. It was easy to see by the way he hunched over the bar that they were already beginning to affect him. *Good*, Rodolfo thought with some satisfaction. Maybe it would give Eric the courage he would need to approach him.

Approach him he had no doubt he would, although probably not in front of Raul. It would definitely happen soon, though. The pair of them reminded him of two roosters fighting for control of the barnyard. It would be interesting to see which one would win. He smiled, filled up his glass again and then the glasses of his companions.

This time, Eric took a cautious sip of the fiery liquid. He was a little embarrassed by the way he had thrown the first two shots down his throat. After they had stopped laughing, Raul had explained to him, not unkindly, that this was the finest tequila money could buy, certainly not something you slammed but instead sipped and enjoyed. Like a fine woman, he had said, a gleam in his eyes. Eric could only imagine who he was thinking of. His head swimming, he tried to focus his eyes, but they refused to cooperate.

From the other side of Rodolfo, Raul eyed his rival through narrow eyes. Despite the fact that he was Jade's new boyfriend, Raul could see he was a good person. He was funny, kind and seemed tolerant and interested in everything around him…eager even, if truth be known. *He's a man's man*, Raul thought approvingly, but he could tell that Eric was gentle and kind too, especially with Jade. As much as he wanted to dislike the guy, it was impossible for him to do so.

He picked up his glass and took another swallow. The tequila was going straight to his head. If he didn't know any better, he would think his partner and mentor was trying to get the pair of them drunk. He shook his head in an attempt to clear his mind, nearly losing his balance and falling off the chair. The room spun dangerously around him.

"Careful, son." Rodolfo reached out a hand and steadied him, his face neutral as he tried hard not to smile. *I'm enjoying this*, he thought as he raised the now empty bottle in Alfredo's direction. With a smile, the bartender quickly replaced the empty with a fresh one.

It was a strange sight that greeted four women who had exhausted the day being good to themselves. Not only had they spent several happy hours in Kimberly's shop, but they had been dress shopping too. Now, carrying their bundles and parcels into the restaurant, their mouths opened in shock at the considerably tipsy men before them. Then they burst into peals of laughter.

Rodolfo, the only one who looked marginally sober, lifted his head and grinned happily at the sight of his wife, calling out boisterously *"Mi amor!"*

Lips twitching in amusement, Lydia crossed the terra cotta floor to stand before him, her hands on her hips in mock dismay.

"I can't leave you for a minute," she scolded roundly, then kissed him on the forehead to show him he was already forgiven.

Rodolfo laughed and pulled Lydia on his lap, something he did whenever he had the chance. Lydia grinned widely and kissed him again.

Jade rolled her eyes in Amie's direction as if to say, "See what I have to live with?" Amie wasn't fooled for a minute. She knew Jade secretly loved the fact that her parents were so much in love, no matter how many times she said it was embarrassing.

Eric tried to stand to greet them, but the room tilted dangerously. Wisely, he changed his mind and decided it was better to stay put. As for Raul, he merely grinned lazily and waved his hand, his eyes nearly disappearing into intoxicated slits. Amie went to stand beside them and picked up the shot glass from the table. Holding it to her nose, she took a whiff.

"Ugh," she commented, wrinkling her nose with distaste. "No wonder."

Lydia helped her husband to his feet, and he leaned heavily on her shoulder. From years of living with Rodolfo, she knew he wasn't as tipsy as he let on, and she wondered about that. She knew one thing more: her husband would have a good reason for the pretense, and she could hardly wait to hear what it was. With a smile and farewell that they would see everyone later, they left the room for home.

During this time, Ana had remained quietly amused, scoping out the situation but making no comment. Now she decided it was time for her to leave this party too and go back to her room.

"Take care of your fellow," she ordered Jade with a wave of her fan and a quick flick of her scarf before she disappeared from the room.

It was only after she left that Jade realized she hadn't bothered to tell her which man was "her fellow." She certainly didn't know anymore. The decision was soon made for her.

"You heard the woman." Raul stood and moved catlike to stand next to her.

All trace of drunkenness had mysteriously disappeared, and Jade thought she must have imagined it. He looked dangerous. She had no more time to think about what that would mean when he grabbed her hand and started to drag her from the room.

"Hey," Eric protested but without much enthusiasm. Halfheartedly, he tried to stand and follow, but Amie placed a hand on his chest and easily pushed him back. Good-natured though he was, he nevertheless felt it was his duty to resist—at least a little.

"Hey," he said again stupidly. "Who do you think you are, anyway?"

Amie bestowed a wicked smile on him as Raul led her friend out the back door. Then she sat down at the table across from her enemy and poured herself a hefty shot of tequila. With a grimace, she tipped it up and shot it back.

"Ahhh, Amie," Eric warned as he saw her fair face infuse with color, but then he stopped and shrugged.

With a drunken laugh, he reached for his own glass and filled it again, along with another one for her. *What the hell,* he thought as they toasted companionably and threw back two more.

Outside the restaurant, Jade was unsuccessfully struggling to pull her hand away from Raul's determined grip.

"*Quierda,*" he whispered close to her ear. He wrapped his arms around her and stroked her back until she stood still.

"Where are we going?"

He didn't answer but instead took her arm and began to walk, leaving her no choice but to follow. Woodenly, she allowed him to pull her along the alleyway. She got her answer soon enough, though, and her heart sped in anticipation. It had been a long time since she had set foot on the *Jade*. All of a sudden, she was looking forward to boarding the boat named after her.

The sun was beginning to set, and soon night would be on them like a dark curtain falling swiftly on a stage. She shielded her eyes against the glare on the water and looked out across the bay where Raul's boat bobbed merrily a few

ELISABETH ASHE

hundred feet away—exactly where it always was. Just as it had been the last time she saw it.

The *Jade* looked much as it always had, except now it sported a fresh coat of paint, and something else waving from the mast. She looked questionably at Raul, who was busy untying the dinghy from the cement block where it was chained on the beach.

He followed her glance and grinned.

"The Canadian flag," he said and bent over his task again.

Against her will, Jade's lips twitched, but she stayed silently amused. Soon the boat was freed, and she moved to help Raul push it into the water.

"Why do you have it?" she asked, more for something to say than anything else as she tried to hide her nervousness.

He shrugged nonchalantly. "Your father brought it back for me a couple years ago. I hung it to remind me that was where you were." She was oddly touched

Soon, with a few swift strokes, they were alongside the *Jade*, and Raul helped her aboard. She sat on the padded bench, uncertain what to do or say next. Feeling Raul's gaze on her, Jade closed her eyes, the lull of the waves making her sleepy. Remembering the dream at the salon, she forced them open again to find Raul bringing up the anchor. Alarmed, she sat up quickly.

"What are you doing?" Jade stood up on the rolling deck, her eyes casting around incredulously as he eased the craft out of the bay toward open sea. "Take me back this minute."

He ignored her.

Jade sat down again with a thud and folded her arms across her chest. *Fine*, she thought. She would wait him out. He would have to bring her back sometime. Besides, she reconsidered, this was as good a time as ever to have the talk she had promised her mother earlier that week.

Cruising out of the bay as the sun began to set was normally her favorite time of day. Already the moon was rising in the sky, even before the sun said its final farewell. The breeze was minimal, hence the necessity for the motor, but its quiet hum was unobtrusive. Today, however, she was too intent on her raging emotions and thoughts to pay attention. Purposefully, she turned her back on Raul and stared, unseeing, straight ahead.

Raul watched Jade out of the corner of his eye and hid a smile. It would never do to have her know he was laughing at her. In her present mood, she would probably push him over the side. He was counting on the magic of the rising moon and the *Jade* itself to calm her down as it always had before. Maybe then she would at least listen to what he had to say.

Finally, after an hour of strained silence, he put the sailboat on auto pilot and crossed the deck to where she sat hunched over and shivering. He pulled a sweatshirt from an overhead compartment and handed it to her. She looked at it for a minute, and he thought she was about to refuse the offer, but common sense prevailed, and with a mumbled thanks, Jade slipped it over her head.

He sat down and, with a gentle tug, pulled her back into his chest, wrapping his arms around her. Outraged, she tried to move away, but he held fast until she finally realized the futility of further struggle and gave up.

"Shush," he whispered as if she were a child.

She tensed, and he felt her body grow stiff and rigid against him. Alternately, he stroked her hair and back until finally he felt her relax. For a long time, they said nothing.

"I think you've had enough to drink."

Amie was disgusted and more than a little amused by the man sprawled on the chair in front of her. *Why were there two of him?* She narrowed her eyes until she could only see one again.

Eric grinned crookedly. Funnily enough, he was nearly sober now. At least, he was not as intoxicated as he was before. With real amusement, he regarded the disheveled woman before him with interest. He'd never seen her tipsy, and rather than making her look pathetic, it actually made her look...what? Adorable? *Sheesh*. He grimaced. He must be drunker than he thought after all. Still, it was funny seeing the normally together Amie looking slightly less than her usual perky self.

Seeing the wry twist of his mouth and mistaking the reason, Amie pointed her finger sternly.

"Come on now, Eric," she admonished, her words sounding as if her tongue had somehow swollen. She bit down lightly and winced. "It's time for you and me to go to bed."

Eric grinned again. "Together?" he asked, delighting in the red flush of color that infused her neck and stained her cheeks.

Amie giggled. "No silly...oops!" she exclaimed mid-sentence as Eric scooped her off the chair and flipped her over one broad shoulder.

"Put me down, you big ape." She giggled again as obligingly he obeyed.

Swaying slightly, Eric reached out to steady her. The contact electrified him, and immediately he pulled back, startled by the feelings that raced through his blood.

Oblivious, Amie leaned forward, her face muffled somewhere slightly above his waist.

"You better hold me up," she suggested as the room spun around her.

Eric grinned despite his reluctance to touch her again. Grabbing her shoulders firmly, he marched her to the door.

"Come on, Miss Amie." It was a command. "It's beddy-bye time for you."

Amie grinned sloppily, for once not offended by the nickname. She tried to obey, placing one foot unsteadily in front of the other. With his help, they made their way outside and into a waiting taxi.

"You know what, Eric? For a bad guy, you're not so bad after all." With that profound observation, Amie laid her head on his shoulder and promptly passed out.

Eric looked down at the impish smile on her face, and his heart did a funny flip-flop. Without thinking, he reached out a hand and touched the golden hair on her head. It was as soft and silky as it looked. For a few minutes, he gave himself over to the sensation before realizing what he was doing. Abruptly, he tried to ease away from the warm body next to him.

Even in her sleep, Amie felt his withdrawal and gave a small sound of protest. She moved closer, one small hand finding its way to his chest. With a little wiggle, she snuggled in, a smile of contentment resting on her lips. Eric gave up and stayed where he was. It was going to be a long ride home.

Lydia regarded Rodolfo as he lay sleeping on the hammock on the porch with a fondness that never diminished. It wasn't often that he drank, and she smiled now thinking how funny he could be when he did. *And affectionate.* She grinned, remembering the ride home. It had been hard to drive the old red truck when all he wanted to do was… She laughed to herself. It was a wonder they hadn't gotten into an accident.

She thought about what he told her once they arrived home. From what she could gather, two things had come from the "male bonding" afternoon. One was that both Eric and Raul thought they were in love with Jade, and the second was that it was a toss up as to who she would choose. Both things Lydia already knew, but it had been interesting hearing it from Rodolfo's perspective. She smiled again, remembering her own difficulty when she first met Rodolfo and still had a boyfriend in Canada.

John Mathews had wanted to marry her too, proposing on the balcony of the Citlali Hotel by dropping a huge diamond ring into her martini glass. She looked at the simple gold band she wore now. Rodolfo had promised that one day he would buy her as big a diamond as the one she had refused, but she knew none would mean as much to her as this one did. She wondered when all was said and done who Jade would choose. A thought struck her, and she nearly laughed out loud. It would be just like her headstrong daughter to turn her back on both suitors. Just as quickly, she sobered.

Lydia had seen many changes in Jade since her return, not all of them good. That she had been spoiled by an easier life in Canada was apparent. Lydia had caught her tuning her nose up disdainfully on seeing some of the earthier sides of Mexico, like the market with its fish smells and dirty bare-footed babies, for instance. In the old days, Jade would swing through there without a thought to the squalor and mayhem, stooping to kiss the children and compliment the shy young mothers on their beautiful broods. Surely she hadn't been gone that long?

Another thing Lydia noticed was that Jade seemed more reserved and quiet then the last time they had seen her in Canada. Perhaps part of it was that she was here with Eric? In spite of her earlier misgivings, though, Lydia had to admit she seemed more her old carefree self the last couple of days. Maybe Zihuatanejo was working its special magic on her again. She fervently hoped so.

Just then, a taxi pulled up, and Lydia stood to see who it was. She saw Eric get out, pulling an unresisting Amie up the path behind him. Lydia grinned. Unlike Jade, who seemed upset that Eric and Amie could never get along, she found the situation between the pair laughable. *Methinks thou doth protest too much.* The quote came unbidden to her mind. She looked past the pair, expecting to see Jade behind them and not finding her, and lifted her eyebrow in question.

"She's back in town with Raul," Eric said somewhat grimly as he half-carried a grinning Amie up the stairs.

She looks like a rubber doll, Lydia thought, amused.

With a sigh of impatience, Eric bent again and, with a practiced ease, once more flipped Amie over his shoulder and headed back to the front door into the house. Her long blonde hair swayed down his back like a fan. Lydia bit her lip to keep from laughing.

"Excuse me." Eric's manner was apologetically formal as he eased his way past.

Watching their retreating backs disappear into the house, this time Lydia did laugh out loud, the sound waking her husband. Wordlessly, he held out his arms, and without hesitation, she crawled back in beside him, the hammock swinging wildly before settling down. Rodolfo dropped a kiss on her cheek before tightening her arms about her. In a second, he was dreaming again. *Together we will wait for Jade*, Lydia thought. As it should be. Then, following her husband's lead, she closed her eyes and fell contentedly fast asleep.

8

Jade crept up the stairs at dawn and stopped abruptly at the sight of her parents sleeping peacefully in the hammock. *Good!* She breathed a sigh of relief that they hadn't been waiting up for her. Carefully, she tread lightly toward the screen door.

"Happy birthday, Jade," her mother's voice whispered in the shadows of the early dawn.

Startled, Jade whirled and stared into her mother's smiling face. Immediately, she relaxed.

"Thank you, Momma," she whispered back hoarsely. "Is Poppa…?"

"He's fine," Lydia tried to reassure her. "We were waiting for you. Don't worry, I will get him to bed now, and you better get some more sleep if you can, too." She said it all without a trace of censure in her voice. Her daughter was a grown woman and had a right to make her own decisions.

She continued, "Tonight is the big night. We can talk later if you like?"

She peered through the dawning light at her daughter's face. There was something different about her. She wasn't sure what it was, but she bet her life it had something to do with where she was all night. And with whom. She sighed. "What will be will be," her husband had told her earlier, and she knew that, as usual, he was right.

Jade nodded and blew a kiss before turning and entering the house. She wondered what she would tell her mother when she was so confused she didn't know what to think herself. Quietly, she made her way to her bedroom, pausing in the hallway in front of the door behind which Eric slept. She debated whether or not to go in, then decided that now was not the right time. In a few hours, it would be time for them to get up. She hoped he didn't realize that she hadn't come home all night.

Careful not to make any noise, Jade stripped off her clothes and stepped into the shower. She gasped as a stream of cold water hit her full in the face. Blindly, she reached out and added hot, allowing the steady flow to course down her body. Washing quickly, she shut off the taps and dried with a fluffy white towel. Naked, she crawled between pressed sheets and, closing her eyes, willed herself to sleep. But as she had known, sleep would not come easily. Her mind was too filled with her night with Raul.

In near silence, they had sailed out of the bay toward Contramar. Frequented mostly by Mexicans, it was sure to be deserted. Instinctively, Jade had known that that was where they would go. A special spot for them in the past, it was where they had made love just before she left for school. It had been the first time for both of them.

They anchored a few feet off shore, Raul busying himself with the ropes while Jade watched him. His movements were quick and precise, and in a few minutes, the boat was secured. Grabbing a line, he clung to it, swaying on the deck of the boat as if unsure of to what to do next. Jade said nothing, watching him from the corner of her eye.

Finally, after what seemed an interminable length of time, he made his way toward her and resumed his seat on the bench. This time, he made no attempt to hold her but only looked deeply into her eyes. Then, as if coming to a decision, he began to talk.

"I'm pregnant, Raul," the woman wailed between her tears. "What are we going to do?" She flew into his arms.

At first, Raul had stared at her, confused. How was that possible? Then he mocked himself. Of course he knew, but what could they do about it now? He held the crying woman and tried to calm her down. For a long time, he talked to her in a soothing voice until her sobs quieted, and she was able to understand what he was saying to her. Finally, in gratitude, she smiled, and reaching up, she pulled his head down and kissed his lips.

"The baby isn't mine, Jade. It is Carlos'. Maria was afraid if she told him she was pregnant that he would abandon her. I only told her that Carlos would be sure to stand by her no matter what and that she should go to him. The kiss you saw was gratitude, Jade. Nothing more!"

The baby wasn't his; Jade hugged the knowledge close as she digested what Raul told her. She felt the shell around her heart crack a little. It had been a misunderstanding. All this time lost was based on a misunderstanding. Two years, wasted and never again recovered.

That Raul was telling her the truth, she had no doubt—she only had to look into his anguished eyes now to see that. Why hadn't he told her the next day? Or contacted her in Canada when they both had a chance to calm down? Would she have listened? There were a million things she wanted to ask, but she asked none of them. Instead, she placed her arms around his neck and kissed him, a move that surprised and gratified them both.

With infinite tenderness, Raul had lifted the heavy sweater she wore over her head and tossed it on the deck. Then his fingers went to work on the buttons of her summer dress. Her breath catching in her throat, she made no move to stop him. His eyes were fixed on hers, chocolate and endlessly deep. Without thought, she dove into them even as her dress pooled at her feet.

Hungrily, she kissed him, reveling in the passion that was taking over her body. Nothing else mattered but the feel of him. Impatient then, she pulled at his shirttails until they cleared the waist band of his jeans. He groaned in her mouth as, hands shaking, she began to work the buttons. Her fingers had never seemed so clumsy. Nearly groaning with frustration, she finally accomplished the task and was able to run her hands across the hard expanse of his chest. Jade had pressed closer as his hand ran down the length of her naked back, pulling her against his erection. Spine tingling, she slid her hands lower to undo the silver buckle of his belt and ease his zipper down.

When finally they were both naked, he had taken her hand and led her, unresisting, to the small narrow bunk a few steps below deck. There, as the waves rocked lightly against the boat, he had laid her down and covered her with his body.

Remembrance of the night of lovemaking with Raul made Jade smile in wonder. It had been the true homecoming she wanted even without knowing it. More wonderful than she could have imagined, she knew it changed everything. After they had made love, they had talked about their future. There was no longer any question in her mind that she would stay in Mexico. Jade told him that there would always be a place for him at the restaurant when she took it over. Raul had looked startled then, and she thought he was going to say something, but he had only smiled. She decided he was probably ill at ease because she was the boss's daughter and so had changed the subject.

Raul told her how much he had missed her and of his regret that he had been so obstinate and cruel the last time they were together. There was no excuse other than his pride and stubbornness. Not a day went by when he didn't wish he could have taken back the words he had thrown at her. And then he told her that he loved her.

Jade had sat perfectly still while he poured out his feelings and regrets of what was and what might have been. She admitted she hadn't been exactly rational herself and that she should have trusted him more. Vulnerable at last, she told him she loved him too. They had ended the evening by promising each other that nothing would come between them again.

Finally, it was time for her to go home, and Raul expertly sailed back toward the Zihuatanejo harbor. He wanted to tell her family the good news, but it was too early, and she begged him to allow her to talk to Eric first. She felt she owed him that much at the very least. Reluctantly, he agreed and, kissing her tenderly, told her he would see her at the party that night. Then they could tell her parents together.

Alone in her bed, her joy was marred by thoughts of Eric and how she was going to tell him. It seemed she was her mother's daughter in more ways than one.

There will be enough time to figure things out, she thought smugly and stretched her long limbs. She closed her eyes and fell asleep instantly. This time when she dreamed, it was of a life full of promise—a life that centered on a future with Raul.

The sun streamed in the window and hit Amie squarely in the eyes. Blinking rapidly, she looked blearily around, trying to focus. *This isn't my room*, she realized and sat up in alarm. *Where am I?* She eased the covers from her body, saw that she was fully clothed and breathed a sigh of relief.

A rustling sound caused her to snap her head to the right, reflexively pulling the covers up to her neck. From seemingly, nowhere a strong muscular arm snaked its way across her belly, effectively pinning her to the mattress. Incredulously, she gave a yelp, scrambling wildly in an attempt to ease her body from beneath the arm's weight. Her head lifted off the pillow, and she caught sight of the other person in the bed. In shocked disbelief, Amie found herself staring directly into the blue eyes of Eric Foster. *Oh my god!*

Hours later, the household woke to the sounds of Juanita in the kitchen and the delicious smells of tortillas and eggs. Lydia and Rodolfo were the first ones to emerge from their bedroom. Lydia chided her husband but compassionately poured him a cup of coffee and spooned three teaspoons of sugar into it.

Noting the gesture, he smiled at her gratefully as he sipped the sweet beverage. Normally she would allow him only one, telling him it was for his own good and she didn't want to be married to a fat man the rest of her life. Rodolfo grinned and patted his flat stomach. *No worries there,* he congratulated himself. Working as hard as he did, there was little chance the pounds would pile on the way it did with so many men his age. He watched Lydia as she moved around the kitchen, chatting in a low voice with their housekeeper about the festivities later. She hasn't gained an ounce either, he saw approvingly, admiring her lithe, shapely body with a sudden lust. He grinned again, thinking that tequila was a more powerful drink than people realized. Just as Rodolfo's imagination threatened to become rampant, Eric appeared in the doorway, wearing a sheepish smile. Reluctantly, Rodolfo thrust his errant thoughts away and managed to greet him heartily.

"Have a cup of coffee and some breakfast," Rodolfo invited. *It wouldn't do to let this pup see me hurting,* he thought with an inner smile.

Gingerly, Eric crossed the room and sat down in the chair offered. Juanita appeared magically by his side and handed him a cup of coffee from the pot on the stove. With a smile and a, "Gracias, Juanita," he accepted gratefully. In a minute, she was back with a steaming plate of eggs smothered with *salsa verde*. His stomach heaved at the green concoction, but somehow he managed another smile and picked up his fork. Determined to eat the eggs even if it killed him, he dug in. His first bite detonated in his mouth in an explosion of taste and flavor. It was delicious.

Rodolfo watched the young man plow into his breakfast and thought that the good thing about youth was its ability to recover quickly. He needed another hour of sleep in order to feel up to his usual self, something he knew was not likely, given the schedule of the day. It made him weary thinking about it, and he rubbed his eyes just as Amie sailed into the room.

"Good morning, Uncle Rodolfo," she sang out cheerily and kissed him on the top of his head before taking a seat on the other side of him. She nodded briefly at Eric, her smile dimming only slightly.

Eric looked up in surprise, his eyes narrowing at the sight of her sitting so chirpy across from him. He flushed guiltily. *What is she up to?*

Amie paid him no notice, greeting Lydia, who joined them at the table with a plate of eggs for Rodolfo. Fondly, she favored the young woman she thought of as her second daughter with an answering smile and asked her if she would like some breakfast. On hearing confirmation that Amie "could eat a horse," Lydia nodded at Juanita, who hurried to fill the request.

"And what plans do you have today, Amie?" Reseating herself next to her husband, Lydia looked expectantly at the young woman.

"I thought you may need some help today, Aunt Lydia. You know, for Jade's party tonight?" The last was said as a question.

"All under control," Lydia told her with a smile of thanks. "Why don't you and Eric go someplace exploring instead? You could go swimming or hiking or horseback riding...or..."

"Horseback riding?" Eric looked up now in sudden interest. "My grandparents had horses as a kid, and I spent many summers with them on their farm. That sounds like fun." He looked wistful at remembrance of happier times.

Amie looked dubious. "I don't—"

"Chicken?" He taunted, gratified to see the quick anger in her eyes.

"Not on your life," she hurled swiftly before turning to Lydia. "Horseback riding it is," she complied. "How do we get there?"

Rodolfo smiled, listening as Lydia explained that they could take a taxi to Playa Largo, turn right at the beach and follow the dirt road less than a quarter of a mile to the stables. There they would ask for Jimmy, a good friend of hers with whom she rode every chance she got. "Not often enough these days," she realized aloud, vowing that after Jade's party she would change that. In fact, she said she would make the reservation for them.

"Thank you, Aunt Lydia." Amie tried to hide her trepidation.

She had never ridden a horse in her life. She looked over at Eric, who was watching her carefully. There was no way in hell she was going to admit it to anyone now. Quickly, she hid her nervousness and proclaimed with false bravado, "I can hardly wait!"

"Make sure to wear shoes with hard soles and a pair of long pants," Lydia warned them. "In fact, Amie, you can borrow my cowboy boots. I think we are about the same size. And Eric, do you have a good pair of shoes?"

"Yes, I do," he smiled at the woman who was behaving so maternally towards him. "I wore my cowboy boots down, remember?"

"Yes, drugstore cowboy that he is." Amie muttered a few other choice comments under her breath.

Only Rodolfo heard her, and he shot her a puzzled glance. *What is this drugstore cowboy?* He shrugged, thinking that even having spent all this time with Lydia, there were still English expressions that stumped him.

Just as he was about to ask, Jade strolled nonchalantly into the room.

"Good morning, everyone." Her voice sang out similarly to Amie's, and Rodolfo wondered as he held his aching head if that was something they taught them in school. He tried a wan smile in return. Seeing it, Lydia gave his hand a sympathetic squeeze.

Jade neatly avoided eyes as she helped herself to a cup of coffee. Delaying as long as she could, she paused to say a few words to Juanita, who was busy scrambling eggs for Amie. Finally, when there was no other reason not to, she joined the others at the table.

"Did you sleep well?" With one sweep of her lashes, Jade took in everyone at the table.

Eric regarded her carefully, but his mind was busy elsewhere. He wondered if his guilt was written on his face, and he flushed slightly. Succinctly, he pulled his thoughts back to the woman he cared about. *Love*, he amended quickly.

"Good morning, Jade. I slept like a log, actually." He smiled at her tenderly. "I bet I didn't move an inch all night."

Across the table, Amie gave a snort, and everyone turned to look at her.

"Excuse me," she apologized, delicately blowing her nose into her paper napkin and blushing a deep pink. "I must be getting a cold," she said hopefully. "Maybe going riding today is not such a good idea after all."

"Nonsense," Lydia told her firmly, waving away her concern. "In fact, sunshine and fresh air is the absolute best thing for you. Just make sure you drink plenty of water and some orange juice today. You should be fine." To emphasize the point, she poured some freshly-squeezed orange juice into Amie's glass.

"Yes, Aunt Lydia." Amie hung her head meekly in compliance. She didn't dare look at Eric for fear that she would throw the glass at him. The thought nearly made her smile, and she took a huge gulp under Lydia's approving nod.

Jade looked up from her coffee cup with an expectant smile. "What's this? Are we going horseback riding?"

"Eric and Amie are," Lydia said. "I need you to stay with me today, Jade, if you don't mind. Some of your childhood friends are coming over to decorate the restaurant, and I would like you to be here. I know you haven't been able to spend as much time with them as you would like." Her voice brooked no argument, and Jade nodded, trying her best to look disappointed. Secretly, she was relieved she wouldn't have to have the talk with Eric just yet.

"You're right, Momma," she agreed and neatly avoided everyone's eyes.

"Are you absolutely sure I can't help decorate, Aunt Lydia?" Amie was still hoping to change her aunt's mind.

But Lydia was shaking her head, and she knew there was no longer any point in discussing it. She was going, and that was it. She sighed heavily.

Rodolfo patted her hand. "Don't look so worried, Amie." He lowered his voice to whisper confidently when no one else was paying attention. "All the horses are very well trained and tame. Even I can ride them."

Relieved, Amie shot him a grateful smile. Somehow, this man had guessed her secrets, as always, and understood the reason for her reluctance. One of them anyway. She wondered if he would understand the betrayal of his daughter so easily. She frowned deeply, her mind skimming reluctantly to just a few hours ago.

"What the hell are you doing here?" Amie had gasped and sat straight up in bed.

"This happens to be my room," Eric drawled lazily and pushed the covers from himself, revealing a bare chest. In a minute, Amie shot out of bed to stand shaking beside it, the covers wrapped virginally in front of her.

At her look, he grinned. "Relax." He rolled over to stand on the other side, showing her he still had his pants on. "Damned uncomfortable," he remarked sarcastically, "but you can be assured your virtue was safe with me."

Relieved, Amie sagged against the bed weakly. "How did I get here?" she asked, suddenly suspicious.

Feeling more unwell than she had ever felt in her entire life, she put a cool hand to her hot forehead.

"You insisted we have a talk," he told her simply, glossing over the details and watching her closely for a reaction. "Then you fell asleep. Passed out, more like it." He had shot her a look of disdain. "Some people just can't hold their liquor."

"I did?" She racked her brain for remembrance. "Did we…?"

"Are you kidding me? I already told you we didn't." He sounded harsher than he really felt as he tried to push the thoughts of *that kiss* from his mind.

Stung, she retorted. "I meant did we talk?" She didn't understand his attitude, despite her relief at his answer.

But Eric had turned his back on her, giving all signs of ignoring her. "I'm going back to sleep. I suggest you go back to your room and get a few more hours too before someone sees you here." His intent was clear as he slipped the pants down and over his feet before sliding back into the covers. "Unless you want to stay here?" His face twisted in an evil leer.

At the slightest suggestion that someone would catch her in his room, Amie didn't wait to be told twice. With a yelp of distress, she had fled the room towards her own across the hall.

"Are you ready to go, cowgirl?" Amie looked up to discover everyone staring at her. Her Aunt Lydia was holding her cowboy boots at arms length for Amie to take.

Flustered, Amie reached for them and put them on. They fit perfectly, and Lydia smiled with satisfaction.

"Thank you, Aunt Lydia. I'll just go put on some long pants." Amie rose from her chair and headed for the bedroom.

Lydia called after her retreating back. "Bring a bathing suit, too. There are a couple of nice restaurants out there where you may want to stop for a swim and a cold drink."

At the words "bathing suit," Eric shuddered, remembering the sight of Amie's body in the tiny strips of material that supposedly passed for one. He nearly groaned aloud, cursing his cave-man machismo of the night before.

With as much dignity as he could muster, he had strode past Jade's parents down the hall to where his bedroom was. At any other time, it would have been funny and something he and Jade would be able to laugh about later. The sight of Amie hanging limply down his back would have set her into a fit of giggles. As it was, it had looked to him as if Lydia had been trying very hard not to laugh herself, although that may have been wishful thinking on his part.

He stopped in front of the closed door of her bedroom and tried to turn the knob. It was locked. *Who the hell locks the door to her bedroom?* he had wondered disdainfully as he turned a semicircle in the narrow hallway, debating what to do next. Amie stirred and made a sound that was suspiciously moan-like, and he froze. *What if she gets sick?* he thought, imagining something gross and disgusting running down his back. He had spied his own open doorway and made a quick decision.

Carefully, he stepped into his room, closing the door behind him. A few steps, and he was easing Amie's considerable weight off his shoulder. "She's a hell of a lot heavier than she looks," he had groaned under his breath as he dumped her on the bed, watching as her body bounced inelegantly on the mattress. She never stirred.

His face softened slightly as he looked down at her angelic face. Why this woman brought out the protective side of his nature when she was sleeping, he had no idea, but he had to admit that it was true. Too bad she only managed to infuriate him when she was awake. He sighed and eased himself next to her, careful not to touch her. Then, exhausted, he too had fallen asleep.

Eric had awoken a few hours later to find sweet-tasting lips on his and warm hands roaming his body. Without thinking, he had responded immediately. Rolling over, he pinned the lush body beneath his and ground his weight in downward strokes. Pleasure shot through him in waves, waking him fully to erotic consciousness. Lovingly, he opened his eyes just as the moon spilled through the open window, illuminating the passionate figure below him. In alarm, he gazed down at Amie' face where he had expected to see Jade's, and instantly he tried to move away.

But Amie had other ideas. Her grip tightened and pulled him down, and once more, he was drawn toward her delicious mouth and wet tongue. She moaned deep in her throat, igniting him even more while at the same time bringing him to his senses.

With an effort, he finally pulled back, gazing in shocked wonder at the writhing form beneath him. What had gotten into her? His eyes narrowed in anger, his mouth open to curse her for the slut she was. It was then he realized she was fast asleep.

Eric had chuckled softly and pulled away, easing his body from hers in a way that would allow her to stay sleeping. When Amie reached out reflexively, he thrust his pillow into her arms. With a satisfied smile, she curled up into a fetal position, hugging her cushion to her breast like a child would a teddy bear. So much for thinking he was the reason for her unbridled passion, he had thought mockingly to himself. For a long while, he lay there, eyes open wide in reflection. Now what was he going to do? It was a long while before he was able to go back to sleep.

"Eric?" Jade's uncertain voice sounded close to his ear, and he looked up to see her standing by his chair.

The expression on her heart-shaped face was of deep concern. He looked around at the room, devoid of everyone but the two of them. He had been so deep in thought, he hadn't even seen them leave. Eric smiled automatically up at Jade, loving the way her thick, curly hair wove around her face, framing the luminous eyes she had inherited from her mother. Standing, he gave her a hug and felt her stiffen in his arms. Immediately, he released her, a quizzical look on his face as she stepped away from him.

"I have to help my mother, Eric." She smiled to take away the sting of rejection

Relieved, he fell in with her behavior easily.

"No problem, Jade," he assured. "I know you have a ton of things to do, and we would only be in the way. We'll be back later this afternoon and will see you then."

He stepped forward and chastely kissed her cheek in an almost brotherly fashion, a gesture she allowed.

Jade softened and remorsefully put her arms around his neck, pulling him toward her in a warm embrace.

It was while they were sharing the tender moment that Amie walked unseen into the room. Neither paid any attention to her as she stopped in the doorway and watched them. A niggling thought tickled the back of her mind, but she pushed it away. She coughed loudly, interrupting them, and they both jumped back, looking somewhat guilty. Amie pretended not to notice, even as she wondered about their reaction. She apologized and then addressed Eric, barely meeting the contemptuous look in his eyes.

"Uncle Rodolfo said we can use the scooter to go to Playa Larga if you like. He's outside waiting to give you directions on how to get there."

Eric nodded, his eyes lighting up at the thought of riding a motorcycle rather than with one of the wild taxi drivers he had experienced so far.

At his obvious pleasure, Jade laughed aloud, her own joy when riding her scooter evident anytime she did so. Up until now, she had almost forgotten she owned one. All of a sudden, she was looking forward to the day when she could go for a spin. *After Eric leaves*, she realized with sadness in her heart at the pain she was about to cause him, as well as at the thought of Amie's departure. Before she could tell him to be careful, however, he was already bounding enthusiastically out the door to talk to her father.

Amie and Jade stood alone in the kitchen. For the first time since they met, there was an almost uncomfortable silence between them. Finally, it was Amie who bridged the gap and put her arms around her best friend in a warm hug.

"I forgot to wish you a happy birthday, Jade. You must be so excited about tonight." She observed the bright glint in her friend's eyes and thought she knew the reason why. "When are you going to tell Eric?"

"Tell Eric?" Jade blinked stupidly.

"Eric. Remember? Your boyfriend?" Amie teased lightly, determined to ignore the pang in her breastbone. "About his proposal? You are going to say yes, aren't you?"

Again, that unmistakable sharpness hit somewhere near her heart. Must be something she ate, she rationalized.

"Amie, there's something…" Jade started, just as her mother appeared, briskly eager in the kitchen.

"Ready to go, Jade?" She paused to bestow a bright smile at Amie. "Eric is waiting for you outside. I'm not sure what is exciting him the most—riding the scooter or the horse. I think it's a toss up." She laughed merrily, pretending not to notice the tension in the room.

Whatever Jade was about to say was lost in the moment ,and reaching over, she returned Amie's hug and told her to be careful and have fun.

"Make up your mind," Amie joked as she left to join Eric in the front yard. She heard Jade and Lydia's laughter behind her.

Lydia reached for Jade's hand and enveloped her in a motherly hug. Then she stepped back and brushed the hair from her daughter's brow in a maternal gesture. When Jade looked about to say something, Lydia waved a finger, effectively silencing her. There would be time enough to talk later, the gesture said. Then, without a word, she turned and walked outside, leaving Jade alone with her thoughts.

9

Raul strolled down the cobblestone streets of Ixtapa, a huge smile of contentment resting lightly on his face. People who had known him nearly all their lives stopped to stare as he went whistling past with a wave and a greeting for everyone he saw. *Ahhh, amor*, they thought, smiling at the idea of romance. It wasn't hard to guess that the cause of such unbridled happiness had to do with the return of Jade, and they were happy for him. Many of them were invited to the birthday party that evening, and those that weren't were sure to hear about it later. It would be interesting to hear what other announcements would be made tonight. Perhaps an engagement?

Raul himself only knew that he had not been this happy for a long, long time. The only thing that marred his joy was that he hadn't been entirely honest with Jade last night. He knew he should have told her about his partnership agreement with her father, and what that would mean to them as a couple, but he had been so caught up in the beauty of her, the moment, and of course, making love to her again as he had dreamed of doing every night since she had left. Was it any wonder that something as mundane as business would completely fly out of his mind? Besides that, they had promised each other that nothing would ever come between them again, and surely this would be good news, wouldn't it? He tried to put the niggling feelings of doubt from his mind and think only positive thoughts as he approached their newest restaurant, the Mi Corazon Dos.

Stepping through the back doors, he watched the hum of activity before him with satisfaction. Good-natured shouting between staff hanging off of stepladders and holding onto balloons and streamers filled the air. Below them, a group of pretty women he recognized as childhood friends were laughing and issuing orders as to where they should hang them. Waiters and busboys were busy shuttling between tables, attempting to set up the dining room for the festivities ahead. He grinned as he witnessed Rosie, his hapless kitchen help, collide with Bernardo, his newest busboy, sending a tray of napkins into an empty box near the doorway. Quickly he went over to inspect them, deciding promptly that they would need to be replaced. He wanted everything to be perfect, he told them with a gentle smile.

Sure that Raul had been about to yell at them for their clumsiness, the pair could only stare at him in wonderment. Raul was an easy person to get along with, it was true, but today he was unusually tolerant and forgiving. Considering the pressure they were all under, they expected he would be a bundle of nervous energy. Instead, he was smiling benignly at everyone as if he hadn't a care in the world. With genuine bewilderment they shook their heads and hurried to complete the rest of their tasks.

Raul changed direction and followed them into the kitchen, first stopping briefly to greet the women decorating the main dining room. Flirting outrageously, he complimented them on their expertise and artistry, and flattered, they turned to stare at him. Like the hapless Rosie and Bernardo, none of them could believe how calm he was. "See what love does for you?" they giggled among themselves.

As usual, Heike, their main chef looked as if he had everything under control for all the shouting and chaos that greeted him inside the kitchen. Raul grinned, unconcerned, as the Swiss genius threatened a cowering busboy with his raised butcher knife, and Raul decided it might be a wise idea to step in and protect the boy from harm. With a sweet smile, Raul addressed his temperamental employee in calm, measured tones.

In a few minutes, Heike was his usual jolly self, apologetic and shamefaced that he had lost his temper with someone who was "his culinary inferior" as he arrogantly put it. Luckily, he spoke in his heavily accented English. The poor busboy had no idea what his immediate boss dubbed him. He only knew that it was safe once more to continue doing his job. With smiles all around, Raul left the kitchen to inspect the washrooms.

One of the things that both Lydia and Rodolfo insisted on was that the washrooms were immaculate and up to North American standards. When she had first come to Mexico, Lydia had told her husband it was one of her pet peeves that restaurants there had a limited concept of what a bathroom should look like. Other than a few, like the ones at Coconuts and the El Mediterranean on the *Malecon,* most were in deplorable condition. It had been after those successful restaurants that they had patterned the ones their restaurant sported now.

Poking his head around the small men's room, he noted with satisfaction that everything looked shiny and clean. Paper was in abundance in the towel racks, and extras were stashed neatly on a shelf to the right. The same thing was evident when he inspected the women's room, with the added feature of small lotions and creams. Should anyone want them, they were placed attractively in colored, hand-woven baskets on the large marble countertops. In addition to extra stalls (another pet peeve of Lydia's was that there were never enough in most places), there were a couple of high-backed whicker chairs where women could sit and gossip in quiet privacy. Large mirrors adorned the room, some over-hand painted Mexican sinks and others in front of counters where women could freshen up their makeup while seated on the upholstered stools. Double-checking there was plenty of tissue, Raul closed the door. Turning, he collided with Jade and her mother, who were standing directly behind him.

They looked at him in amused silence as he tried to explain his presence in the ladies' room. Finally, Lydia gave him a teasing smile and waved his stumbling explanation aside. She knew full well he was only following her orders that the bathrooms be pristine. Still, it was funny watching the normally calm Raul redden like that. She suspected, however, that being caught visiting the ladies' room was not the only reason. With a certain amount of satisfaction, she watched her daughter and Raul grin at each other like the lovebirds they once were. *And probably are again*, she amended astutely. Excusing herself, she told her daughter that she needed to take care of something in the dining room and hurried away. She doubted very much that either of them noticed her departure.

"*Hola.*" Jade sounded shy even as her hands reached out automatically for his. Without words, he pulled her close, kissed her gently on the each cheek, then lingered on her mouth before releasing her. For a while, neither said anything, the night before still fresh on their minds.

At that moment, Danny, head waiter and long-time friend of Lydia's strolled around the corner, and hastily, they took a step back. Seeing the couple, he only smiled. Married to Marvelis for over twenty-five years, he knew what it was like to be in love. He easily recognized that look now. With a murmured apology, he slid past them into the storeroom.

Jade laughed, a little embarrassed, and stepped out of reach of Raul's arms. "I think I better go and help everyone decorate, or they will send out a search party for me." She made no move to leave.

Raul smiled, remembering Lydia's knowing look. "I think they would have a good idea where they could find you." He agreed with her but somehow could not find the will to walk away. "When do you want to talk to your parents about us?" He watched her face closely.

"I haven't talked to Eric yet," she hedged. "Not until then, Raul."

He nodded, impatient to have everything out in the open, but at the same time, he didn't want to hurt anyone. Despite his misgivings, he had come to like Eric in the short time he had been there.

He tried to sound casual. "When do you think that will be, Jade?" He looked around as if somehow Eric would magically appear and they could put it to rest.

She intercepted his look. "Amie and Eric have gone horseback riding today."

She frowned as she thought about the two of them in the jungle together. If they killed each other, it would be days before their bodies were found. She laughed aloud, realizing her imagination was running away with her again. "I'm sure they will be back in plenty of time for the party. I should be able to talk to Eric then. I promised him an answer today."

Raul nodded, disappointed but knowing that it was the best he could expect given the circumstance. Once Jade told Eric, he planned to talk to her about the agreement he had with her parents. Then the two of them could approach her parents together. He smiled with satisfaction. Everything seemed to be falling into place exactly the way it should.

Jade smiled as she watched him come to some sort of conclusion. She leaned forward and kissed him softly again before moving away. Over her shoulder, she threw him a saucy look, then disappeared around the corner.

Raul grinned. *Soon you won't be farther from me than the length of my arm, quierda.* That couldn't be soon enough.

This isn't so bad, Amie thought with pleasure as they rode slowly and sedately down the beach. With the ocean to the right and coconut trees on the left, she was able to appreciate the beauty around her. Ahead, she could make out small huts and what looked like restaurants dotting the shoreline. She hoped they would stop at one of them on their way back. Lydia had suggested they visit a place called The Jungle Bar. Julian, the owner, was a friend of theirs for years, she told them, and they had the best seafood on the playa. It was where she and Rodolfo would escape to when they wanted to get away. At the very least, Lydia suggested, they would want an ice cold brew after the hot, dry ride. Amie had grinned and teased her aunt. If she didn't know better, she would think she was trying to get rid of them for the day, at which Lydia had laughingly protested.

"There are just a lot of things to do today, and it would be better…"

"If we were out of your hair for a while," Amie had finished for her with a grin.

Embarrassed at being found out, Lydia laughed and good-naturedly shooed them away.

Happy in her daydreams of what the night would bring and the fun they would have at Jade's party, Amie sat back farther in her saddle. The gentle swaying of her horse and the sound of the waves washing to shore lulled her into peaceful security.

Eric trotted his mount at a brisk pace, marveling at the smoothness of the gait. The horse was well trained, and he knew he had the guides at the stables to credit for that. Upon their arrival, they had introduced themselves to the head groom, liking immediately the affable Jimmy, who welcomed them warmly. Lydia, who had called ahead to make the reservations, had raved that Jimmy and his brother Alejandro were two of the best horse trainers in the country. Eric believed it. It was easy to see that a lot of time and attention had gone into making his mount a good lead horse for trail riding, while Amie's "Taco" was more sedate. *Perfect for a beginner*, Eric thought with a grin. It hadn't taken anyone very long to realize that Amie had never ridden in her life, simply by the way she had tried to mount on the wrong side of the horse.

Suddenly impatient with the leisurely pace, Eric spurred lightly. Immediately, Capitan responded to his touch and leapt forward as Eric tightened his thighs and clung tightly. With a cowboy whoop, he was galloping down the beach, unknowingly startling Amie's horse in the process.

Amie's eyes flew open, and in desperation, she gripped her mount as he lunged forward in hot pursuit. Her bottom bounced inelegantly up and down as it slapped the hard leather and wood saddle, nearly unseating her. Cursing the man in front of her with every fiber of her being, she clung to the saddle horn with a deathlike grip. With each jarring breath, she sent up a prayer to her guardian angel to watch over her.

Suddenly, she felt Taco rear up on his hind legs and shy hard to the right. She felt herself lose her tenuous balance, and without being able to stop, she slid to one side. The ground rose to meet her. *This is going to hurt*, she thought as she flew into the air. Her last thought as she hit the ground was that she was right—it hurt a lot.

When she came to seconds later, it was to see Eric bending over her, deep concern in his eyes. Deciding this was a perfect time to punish him for his reckless behavior, she decided to feign unconsciousness. Pretending to faint, she closed her eyes again.

"Amie, oh god, Amie, talk to me," Eric implored, and she felt him drop to the ground beside her.

Breaking the cardinal rule of not moving an injured person, he lifted her upper body and rocked her in his arms, willing her awake.

She felt his hot breath on hers, warming her skin and somehow familiar. Her mind flew to a memory that had been niggling at her for most of the morning, and she squeezed her eyes tighter while trying to place it. With a sudden flash of insight, she remembered and nearly groaned aloud.

Last night! She had been dreaming. But about what? She concentrated again. It was the dream she always had, she realized. She was a princess held captive in a high tower, the tall blonde knight coming to her rescue. She didn't want to remember the rest. All she knew was that she had kissed the man holding her now, and it had felt good. Dismayed, she opened her eyes and stared straight into his.

"Thank god." Relief was instantly evident in the clearing of his brow. "I thought I killed you,"

Amie forced a laugh and said the first thing that popped into her mind. "It might have been better if you had."

Her whole being was conscious of him as every bone in her body molded into his chest. Thoughts flew to her best friend, and she was filled with overwhelming shame. She struggled to sit up, but Eric held her firmly immobile.

"I think you better stay still for a while," his voice sounded quiet and subdued.

He was looking at her strangely, and fascinated, she saw his head lower. Scarcely able to breathe, much less move away, she watched his descent until he was inches from her face. Then he stopped—a questioning look in his eyes. With a barely perceptible nod, she gave him the permission he was seeking.

Without pause, Eric swooped forward, and as his lips touched hers, he felt her strain to meet them. He tightened his arms and pulled her closer still.

A sweetness Amie had never experienced before stole over her, and she sighed in pure contentment. Freeing one arm, she wrapped it around his neck and clung. In the soft cushion of leaves, their passion grew as their mouths and tongues played with each other, teasing and enticing. Eric's hand crept up over her waist to rest on a breast nearly exposed as their clothes somehow rearranged themselves. She groaned again.

At long last, Eric raised his head, a mixture of confusion, longing and lust in his eyes. Distractedly, he ran his fingers through his hair, wondering what the hell he was doing and how to extract himself.

Amie felt the emotional withdrawal even before he moved. Without thinking, she reached out a hand in understanding and touched his face, bringing his eyes back to hers. He stared down as if he had never seen her before, and she felt a chill sweep through her body. Dropping her hand as if burned, she sat up and wrapped her arms around her knees.

"No one has to know about this." Her voice was husky with passion and misuse. His eyes darkened, and she knew that he had mistaken what she was trying to tell him. She laughed then, the sound sharp and brittle in the afternoon sun.

"It was just a kiss, pal," she said, striving for flippancy, but it only came out sounding harsh. She watched his mouth tighten grimly in sudden anger, and for a minute, all he could seem to do was stare at her. She looked away first. When she heard his laugh, it was a sound equally devoid of humor as hers, and Amie felt another chill dance up her spine. This time, she kept her unwavering gaze on his.

"Come on then, pal." He stood abruptly, holding out a hand, and with one smooth movement, he pulled her to her feet.

Shivering despite the heat of the day, Amie clapped her arms around her waist. Then, seeing that her clothes were in disarray, she spent a few minutes adjusting them while trying to cover her confusion.

Eric watched dispassionately. "Ready?" he gave her a sardonic smile.

Not trusting herself to speak, she nodded and followed him to where her horse stood grazing complacently a few feet away. While Eric held her mount in one hand, the other placed intimately on her butt, he lifted her awkwardly into the saddle. His hand burned where it touched her, and she flushed a dull red.

"Sure you're okay?" He tried to keep the sympathy from his voice and ignored what looked suspiciously like tears in her eyes.

Amie nodded curtly and yanked the reins hard to the right. Her horse promptly trotted in the direction of home.

Despite his mixed emotions, the sight of her round bottom bouncing up and down on the saddle caused Eric to grin. He swung himself into his saddle and urged Capitan into a soft, gentle trot. If they kept up that pace, there would still be plenty of time to get home and cleaned up for the party. Maybe even a nap. God knew he hadn't gotten much sleep last night, and he needed to be alert if he wanted to have that long-awaited discussion with Jade. The only problem was that he had no idea what that discussion would entail.

The trail ride over, Amie and Eric tactically agreed that it was best to go back to Jade's and forgo a visit to The Jungle Bar. Instead, they hopped on the scooter, which blessedly started up on the first try, and sped down the highway. The roar of the bike made conversation impossible, each wrapped tightly as they were in their own thoughts and shame.

With relief, the golden-skinned pair walked into the house only to stop dead in their tracks. Mouths open, they took in the frenetic activity. More than twenty women were crowded in the kitchen, clothes, shoes and makeup strewn everywhere. Some ladies sat in whicker chairs, feet soaking in sudsy water, while others gave manicures. Kimberly and her daughters were there working their magic while others were trying on clothes or applying makeup. Nearly all were in one state of undress or another.

The state of attire, or rather the lack of it, was what finally hit Eric, and he blushed a deep red and bolted for the door just as Jade caught sight of his retreating back.

"Eric. Amie. What are you doing here?" The buzzing stopped abruptly as the women turned to stare at the intruders. Then, after a moment of silence, shrieks of laughter filled the room as they tried to scramble for clothes. Eric was halfway across the porch when Jade caught up with him.

"Eric, wait." Jade's voice was light and teasing as he stopped his hasty retreat and did as she asked.

"I'm sorry, Jade. I didn't realize that you were going to have everyone here for this." He indicated the house, where the sound of laughter and chatter could be heard over the birdsong in the garden. He winced.

Laughing at his confusion, Jade took his hand to reassure him.

"Don't apologize, Eric. No harm done. In fact, I think you gave the girls a thrill in there." She jerked her thumb over her shoulder and laughed again. "I would have warned you, but it was a last-minute decision to have a hen party before the festivities tonight. Besides," she peered closely. "You weren't supposed to be back for hours. How did the ride go?" Her face was bright, open and curious. He brazened it out.

"The ride was wonderful," he drawled as if he were a cowboy born in Texas rather than a city slicker from Canada. Jade looked delighted until he imparted the news, "Too bad that Amie had to go and fall off her horse."

"No!" Jade stared first at him, then back at the house, where Amie had opted to stay. Concerned, she made a move towards the kitchen, but a touch of Eric's hand on her arm stopped her.

"Don't worry, Jade. Amie is fine. The only thing I think bruised was her pride. Well, maybe her butt," he amended, making Jade laugh despite her concern.

Jade visibly relaxed and regarded him thoughtfully. Eric was such a wonderful man. She knew that any woman would be happy to have him in her life, just as she knew that she was not that woman. She took a deep breath, impulsively deciding that now was as good a time as ever to tell him it was over. Just as she opened her mouth to speak, a voice called out to her, effectively stymieing what she was about to say. Jade looked up at the house to see Eli's face poking around the screen door, Celia and Delilah hovering in the background.

"*Ven*, Jade." Come.

Jade laughed at the trio and held her thumb and fingers a couple of inches apart, meaning she would be there in a minute. Satisfied, they giggled and shut the door behind them.

Jade turned back to Eric and smiled an explanation. "I have to go."

"I can see that." Suddenly, he pulled her into a bear hug as his lips brushed her hair. Then, as quickly, he set her away from him. "I am going to go to the beach until this shindig is over, Jade. See you later?" With another smile, he grabbed his knapsack and left her to return to her friends.

For a long time, Jade remained where she was, watching as he made his way down the craggy path to the beach below. She heard her friends call out to her again, urging her to come back to the party, but her mind was far from what her friends were doing in the kitchen. They were on the man she considered one of her best friends. She only hoped that after what she had to say, he would still want that dubious honor.

With a shrug, she walked to where her friends gleefully welcomed her back into their midst and pushed all sad thoughts from her mind. Chatting and laughing as if she hadn't a care in the world, she didn't notice Amie regarding her with mournful, guilt ridden eyes.

But Ana did. From her corner of the room, she smiled secretly, watching all that went on around her with a sharp eye. Things were moving along nicely, in her opinion. She plucked an olive from the tray on a nearby table and popped it into her mouth. Savoring the taste, she let it roll around her mouth before biting down. Then, with a smile to the others, Ana circulated around the room, offering her expert advise on clothes and makeup as it was needed.

10

Raul looked around the restaurant with a deep sense of satisfaction. Against all odds, he and Rodolfo had accomplished what some said was impossible. The Mi Corazon Dos fairly shone with elegance and style. Every plant, chandelier and chair was just where it should be for the opening night. The decorations hung gaily from the ceiling and pillars, yet because of the color scheme did not look gaudy. Merely festive, they added just the right amount of pizzazz needed to let people know there were two things to celebrate tonight. *Maybe three,* Raul thought, immediately filled with thoughts of Jade and the news they were about to impart. Hopefully tonight. *Not that Rodolfo or Lydia are going to be surprised,* he thought with an inward grin.

All day, Rodolfo had been giving him sidelong looks, smiling for no apparent reason each time he caught his eye. It was disconcerting at first—after all, he had kept his daughter out half the night. Still, it was no secret that the Perez family had harbored thoughts that he would one day marry Jade. He wanted to be sure he was worthy of her before he could formally ask for their daughter's hand in marriage.

In a rare lull that morning, he had taken Rodolfo aside and asked if he could have a moment of his time. There was something he wanted to tell him, and he knew he had better do it while he still had the courage. Surprised by his intensity, Rodolfo had readily agreed to meet him in his office. Nervously, Raul outlined his plan to his boss, mentor and partner. Then he handed over the piece of paper that would change his fortune—for better or for worse.

Rodolfo had looked askance, surprise clearly written on his face. At first, he tried to refuse what Raul proposed, but the young man remained firm in his resolve. Finally, after much discussion and after seeing that he could not deter Raul from his course, Rodolfo had grudgingly agreed. Placing the envelope on the top of the filing cabinet, he hugged his protégé closely. Unseen, the envelope slid to the floor with a soft whoosh and disappeared from view.

Raul smiled in deep satisfaction as he waited for the guests to arrive. In his opinion, what he did today was the only thing he could do—if he ever expected to have Jade in his life. As much of a gamble as it was, instinctively he knew he had made the right decision.

Just then, Danny approached him with questions about seating arrangements, effectively putting a halt to his daydreams. As he followed Danny into the dining area, Raul felt confident that finally all his dreams were about to come true. It was a good place to be.

Lydia walked into their bedroom to find Rodolfo lying on the bed, eyes closed. He looked pale, and, immediately alarmed, she went to sit by his side. The weight of her body on the springs woke him from his semi-conscious state.

Groggily, Rodolfo opened his eyes, and seeing her face hovering above him, he held out his arms. She fell into them with a relieved sigh.

"Lydia," he whispered, stroking her hair gently.

Suddenly, Lydia remembered what she came for and pulled back.

"What are you doing Rodolfo? You're not even dressed yet. We are supposed to be at the restaurant in half an hour. Are you alright?"

Her voice was a mixture of concern and gentle nagging. She didn't see him hide a grin as she glanced at her solid gold watch. Already six thirty. By Mexican standards, there would not be a lot of people there before eight or so, but she still felt that they should greet any early arrivals. Like the two people she had invited as a surprise. She hugged the secret to herself. She could not wait to see the look on everyone's face when Amie's parents walked through the door that night, least of all Amie's.

Rodolfo watched her from half-closed eyes. He was exhausted, pure and simple. If it wasn't for the fact that it was his daughter's birthday, he would have gladly removed his clothes and crawled under the blankets for the rest of the night. Preferably with his wife in his arms.

In hindsight, taking on two young pups in tequila-drinking contests the previous day had not been one of his better judgment calls. The whole day had been spent taking care of what seemed like a million tiny details. Thank goodness for Raul.

Thinking about him now, he smiled slightly. Just like Raul to show up bright and early, eager to go with no sign that the day before had been a rough one for him. Most likely it had not, he conceded, recognizing that look from his early days of courting Lydia. The real surprise of the day was the discussion he had with Raul earlier. Looking back at it now, however, he realized he would not have expected anything less of him. It made him proud of the young man he had taken under his wing.

He thought about the other man in Jade's life. Other than a slight green tinge around the gills early this morning, Eric returned to the house from his afternoon at the beach looking fit and rested. He too wore the look of someone in love, and seeing him, Rodolfo had felt a tinge of pity for the lad. It was clear that Jade had chosen Raul simply by the glow she tried to hide at breakfast that morning. But he knew her well. Sad. On the other hand, there was much to be said about the recuperative powers of youth! He had no doubt Eric would come away from the experience a better person, if not a slightly bruised one.

Lydia stirred restlessly in her husband's arms, wondering what he was thinking. She could almost see the wheels of his mind turning, and she would have given anything to know what was going on in there, but now was not the time. With a laugh, she pulled on Rodolfo's arm and tried to raise him from his pillow.

"Give me a moment," Rodolfo requested tiredly, his voice quiet and low.

Alarmed anew by his uncharacteristic placidity, she leaned over to plant a light kiss on his cheek.

"A few minutes, okay?" Her voice was tinged with worry as Rodolfo nodded gratefully.

"When this is over, you and I are going to take a vacation," he told her, and she stared in pleased disbelief.

She had been after him for months to do just that, seeing the lines that hadn't been there before etched in his face. He must have been feeling very badly if he was suggesting a holiday. A sharp warning raced in her heart, and she sent a swift prayer to the powers above. Keeping her voice as light as she could, she tried not to let him know how worried she really was.

"Okay, mi amor. A vacation is exactly what we will do. We can plan it together. Now I am going to finish what I was doing and then check on the girls. Eric is on the front porch ready to go. Poor boy. He looks lost."

Lydia rose from the bed and glanced down at the only man she could ever love. Then without another word she left him to pull himself together.

Rodolfo watched her go with a tired smile. His wife looked absolutely beautiful in a black chiffon dress that floated around her like a storm cloud. He should have told her so, he knew, promising that he would at the first opportunity. He didn't recall ever seeing that particular outfit before and realized she had probably bought it the day they had all gone shopping. He sighed and started to lift himself off the bed. Just then, a sharp pain shot up his arm and across his chest.

With a gasp, Rodolfo quickly lay down again. Breathing shallowly, he waited until the pain ceased. Nothing. After a few minutes, he rose gingerly off the bed and made for the bathroom to take a shower. *Just a little twinge,* he assured himself as he undressed carefully and slowly in the adjoining room. *Must have been something I ate.* With a massive effort, he put it from his mind and concentrated on getting through the night.

Later, polished and looking like his old self, Rodolfo reached to turn off the bathroom light. On the way out, he stopped at the top drawer of his bureau and opened it. Reaching inside, he lovingly removed a pink velvet pouch from the neatly pressed shirts and stuck it into the inside pocket of his black tuxedo. Then, with a merry whistle, he stepped out of the room to where everyone waited anxiously for him to make an appearance.

The group standing in the kitchen greeted him with warm smiles as he strolled nonchalantly through the doorway, and they breathed a collective sigh of relief. Now the party could get started.

Two taxis were waiting outside when they stepped onto the porch. Rodolfo hadn't wanted anyone to feel they had to drive any vehicles home, especially when there was bound to be drinking involved. It was decided that Lydia and Rodolfo would take one taxi, and Amie, Eric and Jade would go in the other. Juan and his family would follow in the last taxi, just pulling into the driveway at that moment.

Young Juan was brimming over with excitement at going to such a lavish party, but he did his best to act "cool" in front of Jade's Canadian friends. Seeing his studied air, his father reached over and mused up his hair until he couldn't help but laugh. He looked around at the group assembled as if he were seeing them for the first time.

His mother looked more elegant than he had ever seen her, wearing a soft, rose-colored dress to the floor. It reminded him of the way a cloud looks when the last rays of the sun touched them at the end of the day. Proudly, he noted her jet black hair was held with the silver barrette he had bought for her last Christmas with his own money. His father looked handsome too in a new cream and black shirt that had horses running across the chest. Alligator cowboy boots were shined and matched perfectly the sharp creased black pants he wore over them.

Juan caught a glance at himself in the taxi window. Lydia had bought him a whole new outfit, saying it was his reward for rescuing Eric and Amie. He loved the feel of his royal blue shirt tucked into a pair of white jeans. Even his shoes were new, a shiny black pair that Lydia told him were real Italian leather. All Juanito cared was that they didn't hurt his feet. He wiggled his toes in pure pleasure at the feel of them. In his young mind, his family had never looked better.

Rodolfo announced it was time to go, and before Juan had a chance to check out anyone else, he was scrambling into the back seat of the cab with his parents. He turned his head just in time to see Jade and her friends drive away ahead of them, and he smiled and waved, gratified when Amie waved happily back at him through the back window. He wondered if she would dance with him if he asked her and then decided she might. It was going to be a great party.

Ana looked around the restaurant with a critical eye. Everyone had done an incredible job of decorating—under her guidance, of course. Now, satisfied with the final outcome, she smiled with real pleasure. It had been wonderful for her to be a part of this, and she wouldn't have missed it for the world. She glanced at her Christian Dior watch, and her smile dimmed slightly.

It was nearly seven fifteen, and the Perez family still hadn't arrived. She wondered what could be keeping them. Lydia had called her nearly forty-five minutes ago and asked if she would mind going to Ixtapa as soon as she was able to greet any early arrivals in their stead. They were running behind schedule and would be there as soon as they could.

Ana had dressed in record time, looking splendidly regal in a blood red and black dress, a matching Mantilla lace shawl around her shoulders. She waved her Spanish fan against her face, her only sign that she was at all concerned. To the few early arrivals, she was composed, elegant and completely on top of things. Now and again, she glanced over at Raul, who had positioned himself near the entranceway next to her. With one eyebrow raised, she asked him if he had heard from anyone yet.

Raul leaned gallantly across the podium and took her hand.

"Don't worry, Ana, they'll be…" He broke off as a new group of people were heard talking and laughing in the corridor beyond. Unconsciously, he straightened his spine. In a minute, they came into view, and suddenly, he felt his world was complete. He barely heard Ana as she let out her breath in pure relief. As for Raul, he only had eyes for Jade.

"Look, Jade, there's Raul." Amie was tugging on her friend's arm in excitement.

She needn't have worried. Jade was completely aware of Raul the minute she stepped into view and her green eyes drank in the sight of him. *He looks so handsome in a tuxedo.* Then she laughed as Amie immediately echoed her thoughts.

"Oh my God, he looks so handsome." She fairly cooed the words, and Eric, who heard, winced in disgust.

"For God's sake, Amie, can you just for once stop acting like a schoolgirl?"

"That's not what you thought today," Amie shot back at him without thinking.

Puzzled, Jade looked from one to the other, and Amie flushed. "I mean he…"

"She has no idea what she's talking about, Jade." Eric broke in smoothly and took Jade's arm. "I think the fall must have addled her brains."

Amie threw him a grateful look. "He's right, Jade. I'm sorry, and I promise for your birthday Eric and I won't fight even once tonight. Right, Eric?"

Eric gritted his teeth but smiled back.

Jade beamed and pulled them close on either side of her. "Excellent. It would be nice to see you two kiss and makeup. Now let's party."

At the word "kiss," Amie and Eric exchanged guilty glances, but by then, Jade had spotted Ana. She hurried them forward until they joined the crush of people at the podium. Immediately, Ana enlisted their aid, and soon they were caught up with assisting people in finding their name cards set on each table. Somehow, Eric and Amie managed to avoid all contact with one another.

Through all the commotion, Raul and Jade found themselves miraculously alone. Taking full advantage of the situation, he grabbed her hand and pulled her back down the corridor. At the moment, the space was empty, and they would be able to enjoy a brief bit of privacy. Not wanting to waste any time, he pulled a willing Jade into his arms and kissed her soundly.

"I have wanted to do that all day." Noticing how he looked as if he wanted to memorize her features, she laughed shakily.

"You look as if you want to eat me. Like a wolf, as my father says."

Raul's eyes gleamed dangerously, and he moved closer. She laughed merrily but decided she would be safer with a little distance between them and stepped out of his reach.

Raul took the opportunity to give an appreciative wolf whistle, which made her laugh again. She knew she looked good. Her silver dress fitted her like a glove, the shimmering material wrapped like a shroud from the low cut neckline to her silver-sandaled feet. A long slit up one side freed her so that she could move, but when she did, the lights of the crystal chandeliers would reflect on the dress. "Like a silver moon," Raul said poetically, the compliment pleasing her greatly.

Jade purposefully kept her makeup sparse, mostly only a touch of pale pink gloss and mascara. There was a healthy glow in her cheeks, the love in her eyes at this moment doing what no artifacts could do. Jewelry was at a minimum too—a simple pair of silver hoop earrings inlaid with tiny diamond chips, her fingers bare.

"We better go in," Jade suggested, reluctant to leave his side. She wanted to stay there more than anything else, but of course, she knew that was impossible.

Raul nodded in silent agreement and kissed her again. "Yes, you are the guest of honor. We better go back."

His voice was light as he tried to keep the disappointment he was feeling from showing. It was obvious to him that she had not yet spoken to Eric. No matter. However, there was something very important he had to tell her, and he didn't want to wait a moment longer. As far as he was concerned, this was as good a time as any. Just then, Ana appeared around the corner, and he sighed, knowing the opportunity was lost. Anything he had to say would have to wait until later.

"Jade. Raul. There you are. Come on, you two. There are people here who want to see you." Ana waved her fan and stood, waiting impatiently but with a smile on her face to show she understood.

It was as if the gods themselves were against him, Raul mused even as a smile formed his lips. He would be content to hold Jade in his arms all night if he could, but duty first, he reminded himself. Tonight was definitely an important night for them. With a cheeky wink at Ana, he excused himself and hurried to attend to his duties.

"That boy is going places," Ana remarked sagely and flipped her fan open to cool the air around her. Jade merely laughed in agreement and, taking Ana's arm, escorted her regally into the fray.

Rodolfo heard Lydia catch her breath as they stepped into the main dining room. He felt her squeeze the muscle of his forearm, and he turned to watch her shining, upturned face.

"*Te gusta*, Lydia?" he asked needlessly but wanting to hear it from her lips anyway.

"*Si, mi amor.*" She moved closer. "I like it very much. I can't believe how beautiful everything looks. You have done a wonderful job. You and Raul," she amended, her eyes sweeping the room and locating him next to the bartender on the other side of the dance floor.

Raul looked busy, but happier than she had ever seen him. Nearby, she spotted her daughter talking to a group of friends, Amie and Eric flanking either side of her. *They make a good pair*, she realized once again. She knew she was not thinking of Eric with her daughter but of the other young woman next to him.

Amie looked fragilely ethereal in a pure white gauzy dress shot with gold streaks that shimmered around the floor length hem. When she had first tried it on in the boutique, virtually every woman in the place had stopped and stared with envy and admiration at the angelic apparition before them. Ecstatic, Amie had gaily twirled in the full length mirror so that the full skirts floated around her.

"This," she had declared with deep conviction, "is the best salsa dress I have ever owned," as if she bought salsa dresses in Canada, as a matter of course. They had laughingly agreed it was perfect for her. Apparently, many of the young men around the room thought so too, all of whom couldn't seem to take their eyes off the petite blonde goddess in their midst.

While Rodolfo was occupied with one of the waiters, Lydia's eyes moved to scrutinize Eric. Hands down, he was the handsomest man in the room, aside from her husband of course. Standing head and shoulders above everyone, he was devastating in his black tux, but not arrogantly so, she noted with approval. She felt a twinge of sadness. She had grown to care for him very much in a short time. He was unfailingly polite, had a wonderful sense of humor and was extraordinarily kind and gentle to everyone he met.

After the complicated birth of her daughter, the doctors had told them they would be wise not to have anymore children. That they had been disappointed was an understatement. Lydia knew how much Rodolfo secretly wanted sons to carry on the Perez name. She thought now that if God had so blessed them, she would have wanted one just like Eric. But it was apparent to both she and Rodolfo that Jade had made her choice, and Eric was not it. Such was life. She thought it was too bad that he and Amie couldn't see their way to... She was interrupted by a nudge from Rodolfo as he urged her forward to greet some of their guests.

Just then, a loud gong sounded, and immediately the noise diminished. A spotlight danced over the room, finally centering on Raul, who stood smiling in the center of the dance floor. When he thought that he had everyone's full attention, Raul welcomed the guests and asked that they now take their seats so that the first course could be served. Once more, Jade was amazed by the confidence he exuded. She decided she liked the new Raul as much if not more than the old one.

Eagerly, the crowd dispersed to the various tables assigned to each family or group, the buzz of anticipation filling the room. Raul remained standing where he was, waiting until everyone was seated. Then, as prearranged, he called Father Ramirez, the local parish priest, to bless the meal.

With little fanfare, Father Ramirez did what was required, praying first in Spanish and then in English for the benefit of the non-Mexican guests in the room.

After the last amen had echoed, Raul raised his hands for the waiters to bring in the first course. Then, just as the mariachis struck up the first song, he took his place at the head table.

Jade looked surprised as he sat down on the other side of her father. Then she relaxed. After all, they had known him all his life. That he was only an employee would make no difference to either her father or mother. She smiled a shy greeting, and he winked lazily in return. Hiding her laughter, she ducked her head and dabbed at her mouth with her napkin.

"What's so funny?" Amie whispered, awed by the pomp and splendor of a real Mexican fiesta.

Jade's eyes were bright with excitement. "I guess I'm just happy," was all she would say.

Amie sighed and looked around. She would be happy too if her parents threw her a birthday bash like this. Thinking of them now made her wish they could be here for this. Her dad especially would be thrilled, she knew. For a minute, she felt alone, and she cast around the room for something to distract her.

There in the corner. Amie craned her neck and stared mightily at the doorway, hardly daring to believe her eyes. With a sharp jab, she poked Jade, who was just about to taste the delicious-looking fish soup. It spilled off her spoon and splattered the table, fortunately missing everyone.

"Amie, do you have to make a spectacle of yourself everywhere we go?" This came from Eric, who eyed her with something akin to dislike.

Amie heard him, but at that moment couldn't have cared less. With an excited yelp she leapt to her feet. "Mom! Dad!"

At her words, Jade looked up in surprise. Laughing like the pair of schoolgirls they once were, they raced across the room to greet them. Lydia and Rodolfo followed close behind but at a more sedate pace. Arms opened and kisses floated through the air to land on cheeks and lips.

Amidst the emotional scene, a lone clap could be heard followed by a smattering more, tentative at first, then stronger until, quickly, the whole room was filled with thunderous applause. It didn't matter at all to the guests present that evening what all the excitement was about. They only knew that there seemed to be a reunion of sorts, and it involved the pretty blonde.

"Seems like a good place to eat," some tourists remarked on hearing the noise outside the wooden doors. They were disappointed to note the sign tacked to it. *Closed for private party. Reopening tomorrow at six*. It was followed by the phone number. Jotting it down, they vowed to make a reservation for the very next evening.

Lina held her daughter tightly as the noise died away. She was a small woman, dark where Amie was fair, but just as fine boned. She looked like a strong wind would blow her over, but those that knew her soon realized that beneath Lina's fragile appearance, she was a woman of strength and steel. Especially Len, her affable husband.

Thrilled, Amie fired off a dozen questions all at once. How did they get there? How long were they staying? Why didn't they tell her? Laughing, Lydia held up her hand and told her all would be answered later.

"Now," she said, "there are two spots available at the head of the table, and they have your parents' names on them. Let's give them a drink at least, Amie," she coaxed.

Contrite, Amie looked at the weary faces of her parents. They had probably traveled all day just to get there, and now she was bombarding them with questions before they even had a chance to catch their breath. She slid one hand into each of her parents' arms and led them to the table, where there were indeed two seats to the left of hers. Funny she hadn't even noticed them before.

Magically, two pina coladas appeared before the Canadian couple.

Tropical and festive, they sported juicy slices of pineapple and maraschino cherries. Pretty paper umbrellas clung damply to the sides of the glass.

Lina looked at Lydia and smiled. "You remembered?"

Lydia grinned. One of the last things Lina had said to her was that she couldn't wait to be sitting on the beach with a pina colada in her hand. The beach would have to wait until at least tomorrow, but Lydia had known she would be able to fill the other request easily. And she had.

While Len and Lina answered some of Amie's questions, their first course was served. Knowing they were probably hungry, Amie graciously offered to let them eat first and talk later. For now, she was just happy to see have them here. Jade chimed in and introduced her "adoptive parents" to the others around the table, some of whom they already knew.

"Here's Ana, of course, and you remember my Uncle Roberto and Aunt Yola? And here is Andrea and her husband Hugo." They greeted the Canadian couple with wide, open smiles. "I don't think you met her children? These are Tania and Rosie. Aren't they beautiful?" At the obvious pleasure in their cousin's voice, the two little girls blushed with pleasure. Len and Lina smiled and agreed that indeed they truly were adorable.

"This is Raul," Jade shot him a special smile and then hurried on. "And, of course, I can't forget Eric, who you definitely know."

"Unfortunately," Amie muttered under her breath, then looked sheepish as her mother sent her an exasperated look.

Eric spent as much time at their place as Jade did, and they knew and liked him very much. They could never understand the intense dislike between him and their daughter but had finally explained it away as merely a personality clash. Now, as Lina exchanged pleasant greetings, she wasn't so sure. She couldn't put her finger on it, but it seemed to her something had changed. Shrewdly, she looked from one to the other, then back again. The truth nearly stopped her heart.

Disturbed by what that would mean all around, Lina's smile dimmed slightly. She turned to her husband and whispered something in his ear, then leaned back and watched his reaction. Len only smiled.

"I knew that a long time ago."

Openmouthed, Lina stared in surprise, then reluctantly grinned. Len always did have a way of figuring out what was going on before anyone else did. One of his strengths had always been his judge of character and his intuition. She smiled wider, thinking women's intuition wasn't all it was cracked up to be. It was just another example of that.

"What are you two whispering about over there?" Lydia smiled. "I know you are here for a second honeymoon, but—"

"And here I thought you came just to see me!" Amie pouted, and Jade piped up.

"And me!"

Everyone laughed, including Amie's parents, who bushed guiltily. Further explanation was halted by the timely appearance of waiters, who began to clear the tables and prepare for the arrival of the second course. While they waited, the topic turned to what they had planned for the next few days of their impromptu vacation. Amie was surprised to hear that they would be staying longer than she and Eric, who were scheduled to leave two days after the party.

"We know," Len quipped, a pleased smile on his open face. "We planned it that way." Then, to the delight of everyone, he kissed his wife on the lips.

Amie and Jade watched the interactions with interest. Both sets of parents had wonderful relationships and had been a source of inspiration to them all their lives. Each knew that they would never settle for less. Again, Jade turned to look at Raul. He caught her eye and smiled softly, almost as if he knew what she was thinking. A warm feeling stole over her heart, and she sat back, content to be exactly where she was at that moment. She was lucky, and she knew it. Her reverie was interrupted by another poke in the ribs from Amie, and with a happy grin, she refocused her attention on her guests.

11

The night was simply and utterly magic. There was no other way to describe it, Jade thought. From the wonderful decorations to the music of the mariachis, everything was perfect. Judging from the smiles of the vast number of people who had accepted the invitation, everyone was having a good time. The food at dinner was incredible too. Pleased, she had complimented her father, but he had leaned over and reminded her that it had been all Raul's doing, from start to finish. She blushed, remembering her crack about him poisoning the food, and vowed to make it up to him.

Jade was sincere in her praise of the food, which was as delectable as it was varied. There was, of course, the fish soup, followed by a delicious cucumber, tomato and avocado salad, cool and tasty with a dressing of creamy spices. The third course was Italian prosciutto, tuna and shrimp sashimi, and fish strips finely spiced with lime, herbs and onions. The main course was a selection of Mexican dishes of enchiladas, tamales, and roasted pork in sweet mango sauce, accompanied by Mexican rice, beans and sweet rolls still hot from the oven. And, of course, hand made tortillas, but it didn't stop there.

Anxious to present some of their more continental fare, the guests were given their choice of prime rib with sauce Diane, fresh vegetables in butter and small baby potatoes. It was a virtual feast! The *piece de résistance* was a selection of several delicious deserts they planned to carry nightly as part of their regular menu. These included a rich chocolate cake—a recipe of Lydia's—a decadent banana creme pie, coffee flan, and Jade's favorite, Cherries Jubilee.

Impishly, Jade convinced everyone to take something different and then vote on the best. Amie was the only one who saw through the innocent-sounding suggestion, knowing that Jade's sweet tooth had prompted the idea.

"This way she can have a taste of everyone else's," she teased, and they all laughed. Of course, since it was her birthday, they would bow to her wishes, but only this once.

The second band struck up a tune, and almost immediately, several couples got up to dance. Jade watched wistfully as her parents led the way, gliding around the floor in a sweeping waltz. *They look perfect together*, Jade thought with pride. It wasn't long before Uncle Roberto and Aunt Yola joined them, and Jade watched as her father's eldest brother jabbed him playfully in the ribs as they twirled by. Amie and one of Jade's friends from school took to the floor, and Jade laughed as Umberto tried to hold her too close. With a sweet smile but a firm hand, Amie managed to keep his body a safe distance from hers. As they passed, Amie threw Jade a saucy grin, and Jade couldn't help but laugh aloud at her antics as they whirled gaily past.

"I see you're having a good time." Raul's voice was close to her ear. "I think the guest of honor should be dancing, don't you?"

Raul held out his hand, and without hesitation, Jade took it. She was glad he would be the first dance of the evening. *As it should be*, she realized, following him to the floor.

Eric stopped in his tracks on his way to Jade's side. He had been about to ask her to dance, but Raul beat him to it. Nonplussed, he stood on the edge of the room and watched them together. Heads close, eyes locked, he realized with sudden insight what he had been avoiding all along—Raul and Jade were in love. Of course! He cursed himself for the blind fool he was. *In more ways than one*, he realized as his eyes shifted around the room.

In the center of the room, her back to him, was the unmistakable form of Amie dancing. By now, the man Jade had recognized as Umberto had been replaced with someone else, but he didn't know which one of the numerous admirers it was. A sliver of jealousy shot through him.

The couple danced by, and then Amie was facing him. Her usually smiling face looked troubled, and at once, his eyes narrowed. When Amie's cheeks were bright red, it was a sure sign she was either embarrassed or angry. He wasn't sure which, but having been the target of one or the other often enough, he recognized the look as trouble.

Suddenly, he saw Amie push her dance partner away, knocking him slightly off balance. *Angry*, Eric decided with a sardonic grin. Before he could react, Amie turned and was fleeing across the dance floor, her admirer already hot on her heels. Looking neither left nor right, she was about to pass him by when Eric caught her and pulled her close to his chest.

Instinct took over, and without thinking, Amie slammed one small foot on his instep with all the strength she had left in her.

"Be still," he cursed the pain and her roundly.

His voice stopped her cold, and looking repentant, Amie tried to apologize. "Eric, I didn't know it was you. I am sorry—"

"Shut up, Amie," Eric growled under his breath just as her would-be lover skidded to a halt in front of them.

"Gracias, senor. My turn now, I think." He smiled openly at the young, handsome Mexican panting in front of them. Then, without giving him a chance to respond, Eric smoothly whisked Amie away.

The stunned suitor shrugged philosophically, looking around carefully to see if anyone had witnessed his disgrace. No one was paying the slightest attention to him. Relieved he wouldn't have to actually fight the blonde giant for his woman, he turned to find a more willing partner.

Amie was grateful. "Thank you again, Eric," she told him, the words sticking in her throat. "Seems like all you do is rescue me these days." Her mouth twisted wryly at the pure truth of the statement.

"Seems like you're right," he told her grimly, biting out the words carefully, his voice laced with sarcastic anger. "But then again, it seems like you bring on most things yourself."

Amie's head jerked back as if he had slapped her. "I do not." Her voice was hot with anger. "If you remember, it was you who dumped me in the ocean, and it was you who caused my horse to take off and—"

"I suppose it was me who teased and led on a poor unsuspecting man to make a pass at you too?" He glared ferociously, realizing he wasn't talking about the Mexican now.

Amie turned red. "Of all the awful, untrue things to…"

She never got a chance to finish, as Eric forcefully grabbed her arm and ushered toward the back door of the restaurant. Seeing no other option, Amie reluctantly allowed him to pull her along. It was either that or cause a scene, and she wasn't about to do that. *Besides, I have a few choice things to say to him anyway,* she thought grimly.

If anyone noticed, no one seemed to think it was odd. *Amor,* they thought with a sigh as the golden couple hurried past them in the direction of the patio garden. Luckily, it was deserted.

Eric swung Amie around to face him. His hands clamped down on her shoulders, his face dark with suppressed emotion. Amie had never seen the normally calm, even-tempered man like this, and she stared at him somewhat fearfully.

"You are the most irritating, bubble-headed woman I have ever had the misfortune to know," he rasped angrily. "God only knows why I am in love with you, but…"

"What did you say?" Amie's voice was shaky in disbelief.

"I said you're the most—"

"I mean after that." Her eyes, wide and wet, regarded him, long lashes blinking rapidly to keep the tears from spilling over.

Seeing the way she looked at him, Eric softened. Of their own volition, his arms tightened, and he pulled her to him, his words muffled in the silk of her hair.

"I said I love you." There was relief in saying the words.

Against his chest, Amie's smile threatened to split her face. *He loves me?* She could hardly believe that this was happening to her.

After a few minutes, Eric moved back, and she lifted her chin to meet his gaze. With perfect naturalness, their lips met in a soft, gentle kiss. A tremble rippled through her body, and Eric heard a sigh escape her. He smiled but kept his mouth on hers.

"We have to tell Jade," he whispered, his hands moving over her generous curves. At once, he felt her body stiffen beneath him and briefly still.

As the words sunk in, Amie's eyes flew open, wide and unseeing. Neatly, she stepped out of the circle of his arms and moved as far away as she could get. With one hand, she deliberately wiped her lips. She would never betray her best friend.

"We can't," she told him, her voice a mixture of anger and sorrow. With a last look of pure regret, Amie whirled and ran to the door. Eric called after her, but if she heard, she never once looked back.

Lina was one of the few to see her daughter leave and had been on the lookout for her return. Her daughter's face told the story, and she moved to follow, but Len's steady hand stopped her flight.

"Let her go, Lina. They can work it out."

Lina was about to protest, but then she nodded. Len was right. Still, it hurt her to see their only daughter so distraught.

"I think you better dance with me then." She smiled reluctantly, and he smiled back.

"I think I better too," he agreed as he led his wife to the dance floor.

The song ended, but neither Raul nor Jade noticed. Arms wrapped loosely around each other's waists, casually as if just friends, they fooled no one. Finally, even they realized the music had stopped, and they laughed at their silliness. A couple of their friends exchanged amused grins. The band was in full swing, but they noticed that some people were heading outside to cool off in the warm summer breeze that had blown in from the south. Raul suggested to Jade that she go there while he grabbed a couple of flutes of champagne from one of the waiters. There was something he wanted to talk to her about, her told her, promising he would join her in a minute.

Jade shivered in anticipation and nodded her agreement. As he left her side, she spotted Amie nearly running across the dance floor in the direction of the bathroom. She frowned slightly. *She looks upset*, was her first thought as she moved to follow. A firm grasp on her elbow prevented her from taking a single step.

Jade turned quickly and looked into the smiling faces of three of her best friends. In minutes, Elisabeth, Delila and Eva surrounded her and wished her a happy birthday once again. Other people joined in, and soon she was caught up in a throng of people moving outside and away from where Jade last saw Amie.

The night air fanned her face, and Jade breathed in gratefully, looking around at the people who were there. She spoke to the ones she knew and smiled at those she didn't, realizing they must be business associates of the restaurant. Indiscriminately, she approached everyone and thanked them for coming, moving across the courtyard until she found herself alone in the furthest recesses of the garden. She sat on a hidden bench to rest, grateful to be off her feet for awhile. *Let's see if Raul can find me*, she thought mischievously and pulled back deeper into the shadows.

Carlos looked at his wife of nearly two years. They had known each other all their lives, yet as a married couple, it somehow made it better, especially with the arrival of their precious daughter. His job at the hotel gave them a certain financial security, and if asked, he could honestly say that life was good for him. Across the room, he spotted Raul and waved, watching happily as Raul changed direction and joined them.

"*Hola*, Maria, Carlos." Raul beamed at the couple, kissing Maria's cheek and shaking his best friend's hand in greeting. *Marriage certainly looks good on them*, he thought enviously.

"Wonderful party, Raul," Maria complimented him shyly.

She had always liked Raul. Ever since that night when he had comforted her and encouraged her to talk to Carlos about their baby, she carried a soft spot for him. When their daughter was born, she had insisted that Raul be the godfather. Looking at him now convinced her they had made the right choice.

Maria watched him closely as he and her husband chatted. In her opinion, it was a shame that he and Jade never got back together, although she had seen them dancing earlier. Maybe there was still a chance. Carlos had not told her the details of their breakup, but over time, she had put two and two together on her own. Without knowing exactly how, she realized they had something to do with it, and she felt bad. If there were two people who deserved each other and the happiness that she and Carlos shared, she felt certain it was Jade and Raul. She wished there was something she could do.

Raul and Carlos were finishing up their conversation, and she pulled herself from her daydreams to join in.

"You two should go out to the garden," Raul was saying now. "I was just getting some champagne for me and Jade. Why don't you say hello and tell her about that beautiful baby of yours? I'll be there in a minute."

Eagerly, Maria nodded her head. Maybe there was something she could do after all. Taking her husband's hand, they took his suggestion and made their way out of the restaurant. Once past bedeviled glass doors, they looked for Jade in the mob of people, but she was nowhere to be seen.

Maria sighed with disappointment, and Carlos looked down at her in concern. She was expecting their second child, a fact they planned to share with Raul and Jade tonight if they ever got the two together.

"Let's sit over there," he suggested solicitously, leading the way to the far corner of the garden.

Maria took the lone chair offered her gratefully. She hadn't wanted to say anything to Carlos, he was always so concerned, but she would be relieved to be off her feet for awhile.

Carlos looked around the courtyard in amazement. The perspective of how vast the restaurant was changed greatly out here. The garden was a treasure trove of flowers and plants and would be a great place to have a romantic dinner for two. There were several statues surrounded by bird baths, and there was even a small stream that meandered at the outside wall. The sound of the bubbling fountains made a nice contrast to the strains of music from inside. He whistled with admiration. To think that someday this would all belong to his best friend? If he had only known that Raul envied him, he would have laughed. He told Maria about the arrangement.

"What do you mean, Carlos?" Maria's huge brown eyes regarded him with amazement. "This restaurant belongs to Rodolfo and Lydia. And Jade too, of course."

Carlos nodded. "True, Maria, but Rodolfo has given Raul a fifty percent share in the *Mi Corazon Dos*. The other half goes to Jade if she wants it."

"And if she doesn't?"

"Then Raul has the first opportunity to buy it outright when Rodolfo retires, which Raul thinks will be any day now. Certainly by this time next year, he says. Either way, Raul can't lose."

"I don't understand." Maria was still puzzled.

Carlos explained. "If by some chance Raul ends up with Jade, and they get married, then he gets the restaurant. The only thing is that it won't cost him anything that way. But even if they don't get together, and she goes to Canada, he still gets the restaurant. Get it? That Raul is one smart guy."

"I see," Maria said slowly. "Does Jade know?"

"From what I can tell from talking to Raul, I don't think so." Carlos frowned. "Personally, I think he should have said something to her, but they were broken up at the time, and I think Raul wanted to get his..." He stopped when Maria shivered. "What?"

"I thought I heard something in the bushes." She looked around, suddenly nervous. "Let's go in. I feel a little cold now."

Instantly, he was remorseful. "Yes, let's go in then. I don't want you to catch a cold. Not in your condition." They stood, and he put his arms around her gently.

Marie smiled warmly, secure in her husband's arms. A tiny doubt niggled in the back of her mind, and she asked the question troubling her. "Don't you think Jade is going to be upset when she finds out Raul is after the restaurant?"

"Yes, she might be, but there's something else. You see..." he began as he moved her gently down the path.

Jade sat mesmerized in the shadows. The voices drifted out of earshot and were soon lost to her. A tinkle of laughter and the sound of a low male voice drifted back until that too was gone.

The devastation left behind by the young couple stunned her. Jade felt tears stream down her face unchecked, hardly believing what she had heard. *Raul had used her to get her family's business?* Not content to get the partner's share, he had arranged it so that one day he would have it all whether she married him or not. Of all the low down... Not even to herself could she finish the thought.

Rage replaced sorrow and flowed through her veins like hot ice. With a determined hand, Jade wiped her tears, her face frozen in a caricature of a smile. Jade stood straight and determined. Then she went to look for the one person who could help her.

Raul stood in the garden, holding two glasses of chilly champagne. Eyes searching, he raked the thinning crowd with anxious eyes. Jade was not here, and he frowned. Some details had taken his attention, and he was longer than he expected to be. He hoped Jade wouldn't be upset with him. Then he relaxed. She was the daughter of a restaurateur. She would understand. He asked the first person he saw, but she only shrugged and said that she hadn't seen her. Just as he was about to return inside to look again, someone tapped him on the shoulder. Thinking it was Jade, he whirled, a huge smile lighting his face.

"I didn't realize you would be so happy to see me again." Carlos's voice was amused as he saw the smile dim a little to be replaced with worry.

"I thought you might be Jade," he grinned sheepishly. "I can't find her."

"Obviously," Carlos remarked dryly. "Sorry to disappoint you. We came out here to talk to her, but she wasn't here. I was just about to find you to say good night. Maria is tired." He leaned closer. "We wanted to tell you and Jade together, but since you're here…"

"What?"

"We're pregnant again." Carlos laughed happily as Raul handed him one of the glasses of champagne and clapped him on the back.

"Congratulations!" he told him heartily. "Might as well drink this. I'll get another one for Jade."

By now, Maria had joined them, and Raul kissed her cheek and congratulated her too. She smiled her pleasure.

"If you're looking for Jade, she just slipped past us and is inside." She jerked her thumb over her shoulder. "I think Rodolfo and Lydia are about to make a speech, though."

Hastily, Raul handed her the other glass.

"I better get inside then," he said smoothly, as he tired not to let his surprise show.

The speeches were not supposed to be for at least another half hour, and certainly would not be given without him. Abruptly, he hurried inside, leaving his friends to stare after him.

Jade stepped inside the glass doors and gazed around the room anxiously. Above all, she wanted to avoid Raul. She saw him heading in her direction and swiftly ducked behind an enormous potted plant, relieved when he passed by without seeing her. A waiter stopped and engaged him in conversation, and Jade watched Raul listen intently, his handsome face a study of concentration. She saw him shrug and follow the waiter to the kitchen, and she let out the breath she had been holding. Quickly, she stepped out of the shadows and went in search of Eric.

136

She found him easily on the far side of the room, talking to some of her friends. Laughing uproariously, they nevertheless encouraged and applauded his attempt to speak Spanish. Jade claimed him with a hand on his arm and a smile for the group, explaining she needed to steal her boyfriend away for a moment.

Jade's friends stared at her retreating back in confusion. Somehow, they had the impression she was back with Raul. Then they shrugged. Obviously they were wrong, they agreed as Jade led Eric away. In a moment, they disappeared around the corner, and the topic turned to other things.

Eric could see right away that Jade was stressed. *Probably she is feeling guilty. Poor thing*, he thought sympathetically. If only she knew that he was happy for her. He had something to tell her too, and his heart was heavy with the burden. He hoped that she would understand and be as happy for him as he was for her. He braced himself as Jade began.

"Eric, I've given a great deal of thought to your proposal. I promised you an answer today, and I am ready to give it."

Good, he thought with a sigh of relief. *She's going to tell me that she and Raul—*

"...and so I have decided that yes, I will marry you."

From what seemed like a far off distance, Jade pulled the large diamond ring he had given her out of her tiny jeweled pouch and handed it to him. Eric blinked and shook his head slowly, unsure if he had heard correctly. Numbly, he took the ring and stared at it as if he had never seen it before.

"You have decided to...?"

"Yes, Eric. My answer is yes." Jade's eyes shone brightly and expectantly as she held out her hand.

Hardly knowing what he was doing, he slipped the ring on the third finger.

"I don't—" Eric began, staring down at her upturned face.

Just then, the sounds of a dramatic drum roll came from the dining room and interrupted them. Jade turned around.

"Come on, Eric." Her eyes were as brilliant as the ring on her finger. "My father and mother will be making some speeches now. We can announce our engagement to everyone." She sounded excited with the prospect, her face flushing a becoming color.

Even as he followed, Eric tried to protest. "Jade, there's something I..."

The words stuck in his throat as Amie stepped out of the washroom, nearly bumping into them. Eric could see that her eyes were rimmed with red, but surprisingly, Jade appeared not to notice.

With a happy cry at seeing her best friend, Jade held out her hand, the diamond flashing brightly in the light of the tiny chandelier overhead.

"Amie!" she cried. "You are just the person we wanted to see." Then, in a rush, she said, "Eric and I are getting married! Isn't that wonderful?" Without waiting for a response, she enveloped her in a crushing hug.

Amie's arms floundered for a minute before closing around Jade's slender form. Over her shoulder, she caught sight of Eric's face, but he flushed and looked away. Feeling as if he had just kicked her in the stomach, Amie said the words Jade expected to hear.

"That is wonderful, Jade. Congratulations. To both of you." Amie pulled away, somehow avoiding another look in Eric's direction.

"We are just about to announce it to the guests, but we better hurry."

Jade laughingly grabbed the pair's hands and drew them into the dining room. Rodolfo stood in the center of the room, looking ill at ease with a microphone in his hand. Even with Lydia's coaching over the years, he had never been comfortable with public speaking, preferring to leave that to her instead. Now, in a sign of support, Raul stood erectly close to his one side, and Lydia stood on the other. He spotted his daughter as she entered the room.

"Ahhh," he smiled as the trio entered and walked toward them. "The birthday girl has finally made an appearance."

The crowd laughed and applauded as Jade took her rightful place next to them, Amie and Eric firmly in tow.

At the sight of Jade, Raul's face lit up, and he tried to catch her eye, but she blatantly ignored him. He frowned, puzzled until he looked down and saw her hand in Eric's. Something sparkled in the bright lights, and against his will, he peered closer. He saw the diamond ring gleaming wickedly on her finger, and his eyes narrowed with a sudden premonition.

On cue, the lights dimmed slightly, and four waiters appeared in the doorway to the kitchen. Hoisted on their shoulders was the largest birthday cake anyone had ever seen. Three-tiered with white icing, it stood a good two meters high. With measured steps the staff proudly paraded into the center of the room. Carefully, they placed it on the table before Jade and her family, the candles glowing gaily and illuminating their faces. As the mariachis struck up the traditional Mexican birthday song, the crowd joined in singing. After, cries went up for Jade to blow out the candles.

Jade leaned forward cautiously and drew in a deep breath, exhaling mightily. As she extinguished each one on the first try, a classmate stepped into the circle and gently pushed her head downward. The crowd roared its approval as the birthday girl straightened and, with good humor, showed her cake-plastered face to the crowd. A napkin was quickly produced, and a smiling Lydia assisted her in cleaning it off. The crowd cheered again.

By now, Rodolfo had passed the microphone to Lydia, who graciously but briefly thanked the crowd for coming. Then, with a wave, she indicated to the waiting staff to come forward with their baskets. Laden with small wrapped gifts, they moved around the room to disperse them among the crowd. Lydia turned to smile at Ana and mouthed a thank you. The thoughtful gesture was Ana's idea and added a touch of class to the already elegant evening. She had no doubt that this was a grand opening few people would forget anytime soon.

"And now we would like to give Jade her birthday present." Lydia addressed their guests again while Rodolfo reached into the inside pocket of his jacket and produced a velvet pouch. He handed it to Jade, a nervous smile on his face

"Open it, *princessa*," he encouraged her with a nod.

Jade bent to untie the silken cord. With a soft smile, she pulled a finely wrought necklace from inside and held it to the light for all to see.

"It's beautiful," she breathed. She turned to look expectantly at her father.

"It is obsidian," he told her quietly, pointing to the enormous black stone that hung from the elegantly wrought silver chain. As the crowd cheered, he told her quietly. "This is a special stone, Jade. It is known as the 'truth stone.' They say that it helps people reveal the truth about who they really are. My father told me it is a healing stone, physically and spiritually. We hope that this stone will bring you happiness and good health." He hugged her warmly.

Lydia stepped closer, took the necklace from Jade's hand and placed it around her daughter's neck.

"Your father made this so that you will know what is in your heart and follow it wisely. With this stone, we hope that you may overcome any obstacle in your life and that it protects you always." She kissed her daughter's cheek and stepped away.

Overcome with emotion, Jade could barely speak. As she struggled to hold back her tears, she whispered so softly only those closest could hear.

"I will try, Poppa. Thank you, Mama." She suddenly looked unsure of herself.

The guests started to cheer again, a few wiping their eyes and laughing at their foolishness.

Lydia gave a shaky laugh and, as prearranged, turned to pass the microphone to Raul when Jade stepped between them. She held out her hand.

"May I, mother? There is something I would like to say. I…that is…we…" She turned to Eric, who remained stoically still. "We have an announcement to make." Her voice sounded nervous and shy.

Lydia frowned and looked at Raul, his face a cold stone mask. Confused, she passed the microphone to Jade, who was still holding tightly to Eric's hand.

The crowd quieted, sensing perhaps something unexpected was about to happen. As Lydia moved a few paces to stand by her husband's side, she shot him a puzzled look. It was clear by the expression on his face he was as surprised as she was. With a sense of foreboding, they waited for their daughter to speak..

"Good evening ladies and gentleman," Jade began almost formally and then giggled nervously.

Like her father, it was difficult for her to be in the public eye. She took a deep breath and tried again. Speaking in Spanish, her beautiful voice filled the corners of the room without effort. You could have heard a pin drop, Ana related later to those who were not there.

"I want to thank you for making my twenty-fifth birthday special by your presence. I hope that I see more of you before I return to Canada."

A collective gasp followed her words, but Jade ignored them. She looked up into the eyes of the man standing rigidly beside her for courage to continue. For a brief moment, she faltered, unable to read his expression. Then he smiled a slow sweet smile, and her breath released softly into the air. With a new confidence, she turned back to her guests.

"I have an announcement to make." She smiled at the guests. "Eric and I are engaged to be married."

For a moment, there was stunned silence. Then, just as quickly, the crowd's confusion turned to understanding, then joy as the room filled with applause. As one, they surged forward and offered their congratulations.

Lydia and Rodolfo remained rooted to the spot. They were disappointed their daughter had chosen this way to make the announcement. It would have been better that she had come to them first. Still, Jade was their only daughter, and it was their duty to put aside their personal feelings. By unspoken agreement, they acted as if they had known all along, and swallowing their initial distress, they embraced Eric, warmly welcoming him into the family.

Amie slowly edged her way out of the happy circle and made her way along the outskirts of the crowd. She had already given them her best wishes and now made room for the others. A smile firmly on her face, she greeted people on all sides, agreeing that it certainly was a happy occasion. Easing away, she breathed a sigh of relief and headed for the garden. Her escape was blocked by Ana, who stood like a Roman sentinel in front of the huge doors. At the look on Amie's face, she gently pulled her into her arms.

"Come on," she said kindly, and together they backed their way outside.

Raul stepped out the front doors of the restaurant and slammed them violently behind him. He was angrier than he had ever been in his life. With a hurt so bottomless it took his breath away, he searched for the first person or object he could find. He decided on the latter. Drawing back, he crashed his hand into the podium outside, sending it sailing into the bushes next to the sidewalk. Pain shot the full length of his arm, and he thought he might have broken his wrist. *Better that than the pain in my heart,* he thought as he kicked the unfortunate block of wood for good measure. *How could she do this to me?* It was the only thought he had, playing over and over like a litany in his brain, torturing him.

He cast around for something else to smash when a hand on his arm stopped him. Whirling sharply, he was face to face with Carlos and Maria. The compassion in their eyes stopped him cold, and his shoulders slumped forward in abject misery.

"I'm fine," he lied. "I am going to go home now. Don't worry," he hastened to add as he saw the alarm in his friends' eyes. His voice was harsh. "I'm not going to do anything stupid over that…" *Puta* was the word he wanted to say, but he knew it would upset Maria even more. Instead, he spat the unspoken word out on the sidewalk, his anger rising higher in his throat.

Maria looked about to protest when Carlos laced his fingers in hers, quieting the impulse.

"Good," he said easily. "I will see you tomorrow, *compadre?*"

Raul nodded, neatly avoiding their eyes as he bid them goodnight. Already, his mind was on how he was going to handle this. *She has played me for a fool,* he thought. *Now the real question is what am I going to do about it?*

Carlos and Maria watched their friend slip away into the shadows and flag down a taxi. They heard him tell the driver to take him to the pier in Zihuatanejo. It was obvious he was going to spend the night on the *Jade.* Carlos fervently hoped that the tranquil waters of the sea would somehow lull his friend to the calm demeanor he was famous for, but watching his rigid back disappear down the street, he somehow doubted it. Sighing, he hugged his wife, thankful once more for the lack of drama in his life, and headed for home.

Rodolfo and Lydia swung quietly on the wooden swing on the front porch of their home. In many ways, their thoughts were similar—how wonderful the party had been, how great it was to see the many friends who had accepted the invitation, and how much they all seemed to enjoy themselves. But their most important reflection was one neither was up to verbalizing at the moment. Then again, they didn't need to. Years of togetherness had welded their minds in such an uncanny way it was almost mystic. But as similar as they were, there were differences too.

Lydia worried about her daughter. The announcement Jade had made that evening had taken her by surprise. Lydia had always thought of herself as someone who had great insight into the actions of others, especially those of her daughter, but this had come from nowhere, and she was still reeling from the shock.

Rodolfo, on the other hand, was surprised too, but not for the same reasons. He usually understood the impetuous nature of his daughter, but this time he was baffled. What had made her decide to marry Eric when she was clearly in love with Raul, he had no idea, but something had. He cast his mind over the events that led up to the previous night, but he came up empty. In a tired gesture that Lydia was coming to know all too well, he ran a hand over his face.

"Time for bed, *mi amor*." Her words, loving but firm, brought a smile to his lips. He turned to her in the dim candle-lit night.

"If you want an argument about that, Lydia, I am not going to give it to you," he teased, loving the self-depreciating smile she gave him in return.

She knew she was being overbearing, but she didn't care. She had never seen her husband look so tired, and it worried her now more than ever. The stress of the last few days was taking its toll on him, she could see. Gratefully, she took the proffered hand and allowed him to lead her wordlessly to their bedroom. The next day was a new day and a new beginning. For that, she was grateful.

12

aul woke to the sun streaming into the boat, blinding him as he lay on the hard wooden deck. Carefully, he moved his head to one side. A lone empty bottle of tequila faced him accusingly. Blinking rapidly, he tried to recall how it got there, then decided it didn't matter. He sat up quickly, groaning as pain shot through his head. Gingerly, he hoisted his aching body to the side of the boat and vomited over the side. When he finished, he felt slightly better. Scooping up the ocean with both hands, he washed the sickness from his face and hands. The cool water coursed over his back, wetting the tuxedo shirt he still wore from the night before. *Probably ruining it.* He grimaced. No matter. It was unlikely he would wear it again anyway.

Pulling it over his head, he threw it carelessly across the boat. Quickly, he followed it with his pants, shoes and socks until he stood completely naked and alone somewhere in the middle of the ocean. He had no idea how he had gotten here, only dimly remembering hoisting the sails and setting out of the bay. With a heavy heart, he stood up on the nearest rail and looked over the vast blue seascape. Then, taking a deep breath, he dove cleanly over the side.

Amie stood at the edge of the water at Playa La Ropa and gazed out over the water. In the distance, she thought she caught a flash of something but just as quickly discounted it. *Must be my imagination playing tricks on me again*, she decided with a wry smile. Seems like an ongoing thing lately, imagining things not real. *Like imagining Eric is in love with you.* Unbidden, the pain tore across her breast, and her hand flew up as if to stem it. It was no use.

Amie sighed and turned to walk along the sandy beach. At this hour in the morning, no one else was around save for a lone jogger far down at the other end. Squinting, she tried to make out who it could be, but she gave up as the sun streamed into her sensitive blue eyes, causing them to smart and tear. She wiped her face with the back of her hand and was surprised to find her cheeks wet. *Get a grip,* she told herself angrily, setting off at a brisk pace in the opposite direction of the runner.

Keeping her head down, she kicked at the tiny pebbles scattered on shore. Occasionally, she stopped to pick up a particularly attractive seashell to examine before dropping it back in the sand where it belonged. With each step, she found herself becoming calmer and more relaxed. More able to face what had occurred last night, she held out her feelings in the brilliant sunlight. Like the seashells she picked up along the way, she knew her emotions were multi-faceted.

There was no question she was hurt by Eric's proposal, especially in light of what he had told her moments before in the garden. How he could have done such an about-face was beyond her ken. She would never have suspected him of such cruelty. The pain it brought her was almost worse than what he had actually done, that and the fact she had been so obviously wrong about him. Or rather, that she had been right all along and hadn't stayed with her first instincts.

But there was more to it than that, she knew. She was in love with him. The truth of that was real, and she knew it would be a long time before she would get over it, if ever. More than anything. in her mind was the realization that Jade was going to marry him. Amie was at a loss as to how to deal with that. If Eric could so callously use her, then what would he do to Jade in the future? And what could she do to stop him?

She sighed aloud in frustration, masking completely the sound of footsteps running closely behind her. So bent on thinking up ways to extract her best friend from Eric's clutches, she nearly jumped out of her skin as a hand clasped her shoulder from behind. Whirling, she opened her mouth to scream.

Throwing off the cover of the light Mexican blanket, Eric slipped quietly out of bed. Moving noiselessly across the room, he located his shorts and t-shirt from the day before and slipped them on over his naked body. Picking up a pair of flip-flops, he let himself out into the quiet hall. No one was about as he stole the length of the house to the front porch and beyond. Stopping briefly to slip into his sandals, he took the path to the right and headed to the beach below.

As he walked, he thought about the events of the night before. It was a mess, pure and simple, and he had no idea how he was going to set things right. He had already hurt Amie far more than anyone had a right to, and now he was trying to come up with a way to call off his engagement without hurting Jade. Impossible!

He had been so sure that Jade was going to tell him that she was in love with Raul. Anyone with half an eye could see that. So what had happened to change her mind?

The topper had been announcing their engagement. At one point, he had glanced at Raul out of the corner of his eye, the look on his face telling him that Jade's ex-boyfriend was as surprised as the rest of them—Lydia and Rodolfo included. *Poor guy,* Eric sympathized. It was almost as if she wanted…what? Revenge? Was that it?

For the first time in several hours, Eric's smile was genuine. Maybe there was a way out of this after all. Now all he had to do was find Amie and try to straighten the whole thing out. With that thought prominent in his mind, he picked up the pace and hit the beach running.

Pouring herself a cup of coffee, Jade strolled outside in search of Amie and Eric. Earlier she had knocked on their bedroom doors, poking her head around to find that the two of them were gone. Now, standing on the porch and also finding it empty, she frowned. *Where could they be?*

Just then, little Juan strolled around the side of the house and called out a happy greeting. Glad to see a familiar face, Jade invited him on the swing with her. With a quick glance over his shoulder, Juanito bounded up the stairs to sit next to one of his most favorite people in the world.

"Did you have a good time last night?"

Jade gave him a welcoming hug and passed him one of his mother's croissants.

Juanito smiled and nodded politely, his mouth full of the delectable pastry.

"Me too," she told him softly, her voice suddenly sad.

Jaunito glanced out of the corner of his eyes at her and swallowed. "How could you?" he blurted. "You're not going to marry Raul, and now Momma says you're going back to Canada." His young voice was filled with reproach, and she flinched under his wide-eyed, accusing stare.

Jade placed an arm around him and drew him closer. At first, he resisted, but as she spoke, she felt the tension ease from his small body.

"Yes I am, Juanito, but I will come back often to visit you. You will see."

"Like you did before?"

His young voice was slightly defiant, and Jade realized then that her absence had been hard on him too. She turned so that her face was in front of his, and with one hand under his chin, she looked him directly in the eyes.

"I promise I will come back often." His look told her he didn't quite believe her, and it cut through her like a knife. She hugged him again. "I promise, Juanito," she repeated.

"I hope so, Jade." The young boy's voice was so low she had to bend her head to hear him. "I miss you when you are gone."

The heartfelt confession nearly brought tears to her eyes, and for a minute, she could hardly speak. "I promise, Juanito. I promise." As she tried to think of something else to say that would reassure him, a huge shout came from the back of the house.

Startled, Jade and Juanito leapt to their feet just as the screen door flew open. It was Juanito's mother.

"Jade, you must call the doctor and get an ambulance. There is something wrong with your father."

"What?" Jade was uncomprehending as she stared at their housekeeper and family friend of many years.

"There is no time to explain, Jade," Juanita's voice was suddenly harsh with worry. "Do as I ask, *por favor*." She hurried back into the house, the door slamming behind her.

The sound galvanized Jade into action, and she sprang to the extension phone on the small table outside. With shaking fingers, she dialed the emergency numbers her mother kept tacked there for just this purpose and waited anxiously for someone to answer. While she waited, she began to pray.

"Please, God, let him be alright. Please, God, let him be alright. Please...*Hola?*"

A voice sounded down the line, and with relief bordering on panic, Jade relayed the reason for the call. Swiftly, they took her name and address and promised they would be there as soon as they could.

"Please hurry," she said softly as she heard the click in her ear. She let out her breath in a slow hiss. Help was on its way. Suddenly terrified, she turned toward the front door. Despite her fear at what she would find, she entered the house and walked swiftly but calmly to where her mother hovered over the bed. At the sight of the still, pale form of her father, she touched the amulet he had given her the night before and stroked it lovingly for strength. Then, falling to her knees beside the bed, Jade began to pray harder than she ever had in her life.

"Whaaaaat?"

"Shut up for once, Amie." Eric stopped her from screaming by clapping a hand over her mouth. *Nice touch,* he grinned, watching the furious woman lash out with one small ineffective fist.

"You scared me half to death. What the hell do you think you're doing?"

Amie's protest was loud and angry as she tried to knee him. For the sake of his manhood, he backed a safe distance away. Suddenly, as quickly as her anger began, it stopped. Looking as deflated as a balloon with the air out of it, her blue eyes filled with an unfathomable hurt so deep he was immediately ashamed.

"What do you want?" she asked dully.

"We need to talk, Amie. I need to explain. Please."

The words were filled with need even as he moved closer. Reaching out, he gently tucked an errant strand of her pale hair behind her ears. She flinched as the water swirled around her ankles, wetting the sarong she had tied loosely around her hips that morning. She paid no attention, her eyes riveted on Eric.

The hospital was a mass of confusion and disorganization, with people milling around the emergency room. Jade sat nervously next to her mother, her hands clasped tightly together as if in prayer, but her mind would not stay still long enough to concentrate, and after a while, she gave up.

Thankfully, the ambulance had arrived in record time, whisking her father away with a speed that both frightened and gratified. Immediately, they had started CPR, taking over where Lydia and a frightened Juanita had left off. Jade was grateful once more for her mother's insistence that they all learn it. The ambulance attendants had reassured them that their efforts would go a long way in ensuring that the patient would recover completely. Jade hoped with all her heart it was true.

Just then, the doors broke apart, and their family doctor, Rogelio Grayeb, stepped through. He paused in the doorway, casting his eyes around the bedlam. Seeing him, Lydia vacated her chair and flew to his side, Jade right behind her.

"How is he?" Lydia asked anxiously, clasping one of his hands, the other holding tightly onto Jade. Juanita hovered anxiously in the background, ready to help in any way she could, her husband and son next to her

Dr. Grayeb nodded his head in greeting, his voice low and soothing as he regarded the distraught woman.

"At this moment, Lydia, Rodolfo is stable. The next twenty-four hours will be crucial, but he is a strong man."

Lydia closed her eyes at his words and bent her head. He placed a comforting hand on her shoulder, this time addressing Jade, who stood pale and wan beside her.

"I think he is going to be fine. Don't worry. You can go in now for a few minutes. He is groggy but still awake. We're going to give him something to help with the pain and to let him sleep."

"Is it his…?" Jade's voice faltered on the word she couldn't bear to voice aloud, and she bit her lip to keep from crying.

She needed to be strong for her mother. She touched the stone around her neck again for courage and felt a surge of energy run up her arm "Is it his heart?"

Dr Grayeb nodded slightly. "It is his heart, yes, but he hasn't had a full blown heart attack this time. More like a warning. As I said, the next few hours will be crucial. Now, if you would like to follow me, you can see him for a few minutes."

Leaving the waiting room, Jade looked back at the family that had cared for them for as long as she could remember and smiled bravely. They nodded and sat back down in their chairs to wait the two women's return. There was no question of going home. As part of the family, they were exactly where they should be.

Rodolfo opened his eyes as his wife and daughter entered the room, followed by his doctor and long-time friend. He tried to smile.

"You look like you're going to a funeral," he joked lightly to ease the fear and tension he saw on their faces. The joke fell flat.

Lydia took a deep breath and hurried to his side. Blinking rapidly, she fought to push the tears from her eyes, but despite her efforts, a lone tear made its way down one cheek. Rodolfo reached up and brushed it tenderly away.

"Don't cry, Lydia," he begged. "You know I can't bear it when you cry."

Lydia laughed shakily and wiped her face. Not trusting her voice, she smiled bravely and kissed his hand.

He understood. Turning his head slightly, he sought his daughter perched anxiously at the foot of the bed, her face a mixture of concern and fear. At his request, Jade moved closer and was immediately enveloped in his arms. In gratitude, she laid her head gently on his shoulder for a brief moment. No one spoke; there was no need for words between the tight-knit family.

After a few minutes Dr. Grayeb stepped in and placed a hand on Lydia's shoulders.

"It's time for Rodolfo to get some sleep," he told them kindly, watching the touching scene. He had known this family for a long time, had even brought Jade into the world.

Lydia and Jade lifted their heads, anxious to do everything to help but reluctant to leave his side. With a quick kiss on her father's cheek, Jade did as the doctor asked and moved to the other side of the room to give her parents some privacy.

"I'll be fine," Rodolfo tried to assure his wife. "I just need to rest. I'll be as good as new tomorrow," he promised her rashly.

"And that's just the attitude that got you here in the first place," Lydia spoke sternly.

Rodolfo chuckled, delighted to get a rise out of her. It was better than her tears, he thought.

At his laughter, Lydia's lips twitched slightly, and she changed her tact to mirror that of her husband's. "You are going to stay in this bed if I have to tie you to it," she threatened with mock sternness.

Rodolfo's eyes lit up, and he crooked a finger for her to come closer. "I'm going to hold you to that," he whispered so only she could hear. Despite herself, Lydia blushed and grinned back.

His smile turned to a grimace as a sharp pain ran across his chest. Instantly, Dr. Grayeb moved closer and beckoned to the nurse. Knowing she was overstaying her welcome, Lydia kissed her husband's cheek. There was fear in every line of her body, and she tried valiantly to keep it from showing now.

"I won't be far," she promised him as she stepped out of the way of the medical team. She watched with pain-dulled eyes as the nurse administered a shot and began another IV bottle. Rodolfo winked at her from his bed before closing his eyes. Soon, the powerful drug began to take effect, and his breathing slowed into a deep sleep.

Outside the room, Jade murmured words of comfort, and gratefully, Lydia sagged against her for support. Delivering her mother into Juanita's loving arms, she returned to the room where her father slept. Walking slowly past the surprised doctor and nurse, she slipped the obsidian stone necklace from her neck and, with a kiss, placed it lightly over her father's heart. Then, without a word, she slipped away to rejoin her mother

"So now what do we do?" Amie's look was confused and unhappy.

They were sitting at one of the restaurants on La Ropa Beach, two cold beers on the table in front of them. Amie took a hearty swig and set it back down.

Eric took his time in answering. Right now all he wanted to do was scoop this woman up and carry her off to his room. He grinned.

Seeing it, Amie arched an eyebrow, a smile tugging the corners of her full mouth and she tried to look stern. "Not that," she told him with a laugh.

She felt silly and childish and supremely happy all at once, and she wasn't sure how to handle it. Then she sobered. Her happiness meant that someone else would be unhappy, and that was not something she wanted, no matter what the cost to her. She said as much to the man watching her intently a mere foot away.

"That's just it, Amie," Eric tried to explain again, patiently, as if to a child.

"I know what I saw, and I saw Jade and Raul together last night. They are in love. They may not realize it, but those two are in love."

Amie brightened. "Maybe the reason Jade hasn't said anything is because she didn't want to hurt you?"

But Eric was shaking his head. "If that was all it is then we wouldn't have this problem. I could just go to her and tell her that I know she loves Raul and that I am bowing out. No, I think it's something more than that. One minute they were all over each other, and the next, she was announcing our engagement. There's something we're not seeing here."

Amie sighed. "Well, until we figure out what it is, we have to stay quiet about us."

"But..."

"I mean it, Eric. I don't want Jade to be hurt, and neither do you."

Eric nodded reluctantly. Although he wished things were different, Amie was right. He stood.

"We better get back. I'm sure everyone will be up by now, and I don't want them to worry."

Eric threw a few coins on the table, and Amie stood also. At the last moment, he reached out and pulled her close against his broad chest. "We may not get to do this for awhile," he said, kissing her thoroughly. "There, that should hold you," he grinned down from his great height as she blushed.

"You really are an ass sometimes," she told him, but instead of her usual ire, this time her voice was soft.

Hands clasped, they strolled slowly across the sand to the path that would lead them to Jade's house, only breaking apart at the last moment. Then, as if nothing had gone on between them, Eric strode forcefully ahead, leaving a thoughtful Amie to follow in his wake.

13

ou're back." Jade flew off the front porch and into the arms of her fiancé standing below the steps. Her voice shook slightly, and suddenly, without warning, she burst into tears.

Automatically, Eric's arms tightened around her, concern for her washing over him like the waves of the ocean he had left below. By now, Amie had caught up, and he turned to throw her a confused look.

Instinctively, Amie knew this was more than someone worried about where they had been, and concerned, she laid her hand on Jade's shoulder.

"Jade, what's wrong? What happened?"

Jade transferred her arms to her best friend while Eric looked helplessly on. Leading her back to the porch, Amie consoled her at the same time, urging her to explain what the matter was. At first Jade could only cry helplessly, her words coming out in short, garbled and confused sentences. Finally, through patience and extreme tact, Amie was at last able to get the full story.

"It's my father, Amie. He's in the hospital. They think it is his heart."

Amie's head snapped back. Of all the things she had expected to hear, this certainly was the last thing on her list.

"Oh my God," she whispered. "Is he going to be alright?"

"I think…so…they don't know for sure." Jade hiccupped, her voice low with anxiety and stress.

Amie pulled her close again. "Can we go and see him?" she asked fearfully.

Her Uncle Rodolfo was an important part of her life, and the idea that he was sick was terrible. A thought struck her. "Do my mother and father know?"

Jade nodded. "They're at the hospital with my mother now. I came back with Juan to pack a few things he might need and to find you two." She looked over at Eric standing where she had left him.

"Where were you?" Even though her voice was devoid of accusation, Eric flushed guiltily and stammered.

"We went for a waa…walk on the beach," he told her, relieved when Jade nodded.

"I should have realized that's where you would be," was all she said.

"Is there anything we can do, Jade? Should we go with you to the hospital?" Amie turned the attention away from she and Eric and back to the matter at hand.

Jade shook her head. "Thank you, Amie, but I think that everything is under control. I hope you don't mind if I go back to the hospital now. I need to be with my family."

"Of course not," Amie's voice was firm and decisive. "We'll stay here and keep the fires burning. Will my parents be coming back here, do you think?"

Again, Jade shook her head no. "I almost forgot, Amie. They asked if you and Eric would join them for dinner this evening at the Mi Corazon here in Zihua. There are some things they want to take care of for my mother. Is that okay with you?"

Overcome with emotion, Jade bowed her head over her tissue again and dabbed at her eyes while Amie shot Eric a look. Eyes locked on his, she reassured her friend and helped her to her feet.

"You go do what you came to do, Jade. Eric and I will be fine on our own. We both still have to pack anyway. We're leaving tomorrow, remember?"

Jade's eyes filled again with tears. "Oh, God, I forgot."

Her voice was filled with apology, and she glanced over at Eric. She was supposed to go with them, but there was no question of that now. She was needed here. At her obvious distress, Eric gave her an almost brotherly hug. Briefly, Jade allowed herself the luxury of resting her head on his chest, liking the feel of his warm, strong arms around her shoulders.

"Don't worry about us," he told her earnestly. "Just go do what you need to do. Amie and I will meet with her parents, and then we will see you later." He gave her a chaste kiss on the brow and stepped back. Holding her at arm's length, Eric regarded her thoughtfully.

"Give my best to your parents for us. And don't worry," he ordered with a smile, "your father is going to be fine."

The smile she gave him in return was tremulous, but it was there. Eric

153

nodded his approval and then, with another kiss, went into the house to take a shower and start packing some of his things for their departure. He didn't need Jade to tell him she wouldn't be coming with them.

One thing he did know was that with all that was going on, anything other than the health of her father would have to be put on the back burner for now. He wasn't sure if he was relieved or not.

Amie watched Jade closely as her eyes followed Eric. The only thing she was able to discern on her friend's face was worry and a touch of regret. She wondered about it but kept her counsel. Now was not the time to bring up anything unrelated to Uncle Rodolfo's illness. *Speaking of which...*

"Does Raul know what's going on?" she asked suddenly.

Jade's head snapped back, her eyes narrowed into slits.

"Why does he need to know?" she asked coldly, her chin lifting slightly higher in a look Amie had seen on rare occasions but knew it for what it was—pure stubbornness.

"Well...I..." Amie was momentarily at a loss for words.

"Exactly," Jade said in that cold voice again. Then she shrugged in a deliberately offhand manner. "On second thought, maybe you better tell him. He should be working tonight. After all, he practically owns the place now. I think he'll be overjoyed."

Amie was shocked by the sarcasm. "You can't believe that, Jade," she chastised her. "You must know how much Raul worships your father. How can you say such a thing?"

Jade lifted her shoulders again. "Maybe," she said, feigning indifference.

"Jade Ana Perez," Amie spoke sternly, "you better tell me right now what's going on, and you better tell me fast."

"I guess you haven't heard, then." Amie shook her head. "Raul," Jade spat the name contemptuously, "has managed to get my father to give him a fifty percent share of the Mi Corazon Dos. The other half goes to me when my father retires."

"I don't understand." Amie sounded confused. "How do you know about this?"

"I overheard his best friend Carlos telling his wife about it last night. So it seems the only one who wasn't in on the arrangement was me."

Why didn't my parents tell me? she thought angrily, trying to push away the disloyal thoughts. She couldn't help it though. She felt betrayed.

Amie looked thoughtful. "What happens if you go to Canada and marry Eric?"

"When," Jade corrected, and Amie flushed slightly. Appearing not to notice, she continued. "My father has given Raul first opportunity to buy me out. That way he would own the whole thing and get what he wanted all along."

"You're forgetting something, Jade."

Jade looked up from contemplating the tassels on her sarong. "What am I forgetting?"

"Well, what happens if you want the restaurant? Is that an option?"

For a minute, Jade looked blank. "Yes, I guess so. It would mean that Raul would own fifty percent, and I would own the other," she said slowly, realizing the implications as soon as the words were out of her mouth.

"Right." Amie smiled widely. "So the business would not leave the family after all, and," she suggested triumphantly, "maybe you could buy Raul out? Instead of the other way around?"

A slow smile lit Jade's face at the thought, then just as quickly faded.

"But Amie, I am marrying Eric. How can I own a restaurant and live so far away? I know Eric loves it here, but he has a career in Canada. I could never ask him to give that up. No Amie—I am going to Canada, too." She shrugged helplessly again. "At least I will be when my father gets better, but I would do almost anything to make sure that Raul doesn't get his hands on the restaurant my parents worked so hard to build."

"I doubt that Raul would rob you blind, Jade, but that's just it." Amie sounded excited now. "You have to stay here for a while anyway, right?" Jade nodded. "Well then, maybe you can convince Raul to turn over his share of the business to you in the meantime."

"You're not listening, Amie," Jade scolded. "Then what will I do with the restaurant?" It seemed to her they were going in circles.

Amie's face fell. For a minute, she thought she had it all worked out. She knew now she was just fooling herself. It was obvious Jade was not even considering the idea of running the restaurant. She was determined to marry Eric, and that was that. In the back of her mind, Amie realized she had half hoped Jade would break off the engagement to stay and fight Raul for her inheritance. Then maybe she would realize... Her imagination was running away with her again. She sighed unhappily.

Mistaking the reason for her concern, Jade leaned over and patted her hand.

"Don't worry, Amie, things will work out. That's what my father always says." At the mention of her father, her lower lip trembled, but she composed herself quickly.

"I better get back to the hospital." She reached over to pick the small suitcase off the floor. "My mother will be wondering what has happened to me."

Amie was reluctant to let her go, convinced there was something she was overlooking. *But what?* Desultorily, she hugged Jade and walked her to the red pickup. When Jade disappeared out of sight, she turned toward the house.

All of a sudden, she had an overwhelming urge to talk to her parents. *They will know what to do*, she thought with supreme confidence. They always did. Her concerned expression changed instantly from despair to one of hope, and with a lighter step, she hurried inside to get ready for the return to Canada.

Len and Lina waited in the dining room for their daughter and Eric to show up. Raul was not yet at work, a fact Arturo said was unusual for him. Neither was Rodolfo, he informed them with a worried frown.

At his words, they quickly realized that, in the confusion, no one had thought to tell the staff what was going on. In as tactful a manner as possible, Lina relayed the news of Rodolfo's illness, praying that Lydia wouldn't mind she had taken on the task.

Arturo had risen to the occasion of standing in Raul's place until he could be found. They approved his suggestion that he call over to the other restaurant in Ixtapa. Maybe Raul was there, or, barring that, they could send someone to his apartment or even the boat if that was what it took to locate him. In the meantime, Arturo promised earnestly, everything was under control.

Lina and Len thanked him, secure in the knowledge that at least one aspect of the tragedy was handled. They had just been served their first drink and were sipping it when the two people they were waiting for walked in. With interest, they watched as the pair searched the restaurant for sight of them. They glanced at each other and smiled, knowing instinctively they were looking at two people in love. No matter that they stood two feet apart and did their best not to show they were even aware of each other.

Amie glanced around searchingly and spotted them. With a wave, they saw her lean into Eric, and together they crossed the room to where Lina and Len were sitting

After kisses and handshakes, Len invited them to sit down. A waiter hurried over to take their drink order, and when he had gone, Amie turned her attention back to her parents.

"Any word on Uncle Rodolfo?" she asked fearfully.

Lina and Len shared a glance before Lina leaned over and patted her arm.

"Lydia says that Rodolfo is doing as well as can be expected. Right now he is getting excellent care and medication, and of course, both Lydia and Jade are with him. The doctor says there is every reason to believe he will make a full recovery." She glanced at her husband, suddenly fearful, knowing that if anything ever happened to him she didn't know what she would do.

"Is Raul here, Mother?" Her daughter interrupted her thoughts, looking around for the man she was starting to believe was stealing her best friend's heritage.

Her father answered for her. "They have gone to find him."

His answer was short and to the point. He was beginning to wonder where Raul was himself. Despite what he was feeling, however, he kept his thoughts to himself.

Amie was not so reticent. "I need to talk to him." Her voice was unusually strident. "Did you know that Rodolfo has given him shares of the Mi Corazon Dos?"

To her surprise, her parents nodded, and Amie's eyes went wide. "Why didn't you tell me?"

She looked from one to the other. Jade was right, everyone knew about it. No wonder she was upset.

"There was no need to tell you," Lina said simply. "This was Rodolfo's and Lydia's decision. After all, Raul is…"

"Raul is what?" A deep accented voice spoke, and they looked up to find Raul himself standing nonchalantly by their table. He wore a slight smile, but his eyes looked bleak and expressionless.

"I was about to say that you are quite capable of running this restaurant," Lina smiled at the handsome young man who had silently broached their table.

Immediately, his eyes softened, and he bent to kiss her cheek then offer his hand to the men at the table. When he came to Amie, he felt her stiffen, and he paused in his greeting.

"Where have you been, Raul?" she asked rudely, and Eric poked her in the ribs. She glared at him but stayed quiet, not trusting herself to speak.

"She means that we have been looking for you, Raul. There has been…I mean…" Eric floundered, having no idea how to break the news.

Once more, Lina saved the day. Standing up, she reached out to Raul, who looked at her warily.

"There's something we need to tell you, Raul. Please sit down."

"What? Has something happened to..." His face went suddenly pale. *Jade.*

"There is no easy way to tell you this, Raul, but its Rodolfo. He is in the hospital. They think it may be his heart, although the doctor hasn't ruled out other things at this point. We'll know more tomorrow."

Raul looked stunned. *Not Jade, then, but Rodolfo.* He felt his legs tremble as the words sunk in. Even Amie appeared affected and stood to take his other arm.

"Sit here, Raul." Kindly, she helped him into the chair. There was no mistaking his distress, and she couldn't help but feel sorry for him.

Raul sat down on the proffered chair. "Is he going to be alright?" It was the only thing he could think of to ask.

He listened intently as they filled him in, stopping once in a while to explain anything he didn't understand. Finally, he asked the question that had been uppermost in his mind.

"Where are Jade and Lydia?"

"At the hospital," Eric told him, watching his reactions carefully.

Raul stood decisively. "I have to go. They will need me."

Lina and Len nodded. There didn't seem to be much use in trying to dissuade him, and who knew? Maybe he could be of help to them all. Lina gave him a quick hug and asked him to pass along their love to the family. With a nod and a promise to do so, he strode swiftly out of the restaurant.

Once he was gone, Lina sat back down and looked at the quiet couple on the other side of the table.

"Now," she said, an understanding smile on her face. "What are we going to do about you two?"

Eric and Amie exchanged startled glances. *Was it that obvious?*

"Well?" Lina asked again. Then she sat back in her chair to wait while the pair struggled to find words with which to answer.

"Raul," Lydia lifted her head as a shadowy figure walked quietly into the dimly lit hospital room.

Jade looked up from the other side of the bed. Her heart thudded in her chest as an avalanche of emotions washed over her.

Raul paid no attention, going first to her mother and kissing her gently on the cheek. Still ignoring Jade, he looked down at the form on the bed, shocked by how pale Rodolfo looked. A lump formed in his throat, and he swallowed hard.

"How is he?" His voice sounded subdued and husky.

Lydia turned to look at her husband. "He's sleeping, Raul, and that's the best thing for him. The rest is up to him."

Raul placed a hand on her shoulder to try to offer some comfort. His eyes spared a glance at Jade, who was sitting upright and rigid, regarding him warily. Her eyes met his, their depths registering deep hurt and pain, but then the figure on the bed moved, and anxiously she directed her attention back to her father.

Rodolfo opened his eyes and blinked. A slow smile crossed his face on seeing the trio around his bed.

"My three favorite people in the world," he whispered.

"Shush now, Rodolfo," Lydia chided him. "The doctor says you're—"

"Not to die today." Rodolfo gave a small chuckle, the dimples in his cheeks deepening briefly.

In that moment, Lydia knew he was going to be alright. She reached across the bed and took his hand in both hers, keeping her head low so he wouldn't see the tears of relief. He knew, of course, and he stroked her hair where it laid spread across the white sheet in an effort to comfort his wife.

"Poppa," Jade whispered, a small hand reaching for his shoulder.

"*Princessa* Jade." Rodolfo turned his head. "I'm sorry your birthday was ruined."

Jade half sobbed, half laughed. She shook her head and couldn't speak for a moment. Finally, she declared bravely, "It was the best birthday ever." Her hand shook slightly as she adjusted the obsidian stone resting on his chest.

Seeing the necklace, Rodolfo looked briefly startled, but then he smiled. "Thank you, Jade," was all he said before turning his attention to Raul. "If you're here, who's minding the restaurant?" he teased lightly.

Raul returned his grin with a relieved one of his own. "We're waiting for you," he joked.

Rodolfo closed his eyes, suddenly feeling tired again. "Might be a little while yet." He opened them again to regard his wife. "It's time we took a vacation, isn't it?"

Lydia smiled, although her eyes brimmed with unshed tears. "I think it's time for you to get some rest now, Rodolfo."

He nodded, his eyes skimming over them once more. "Just for a little while," he agreed.

Jade stood up and, bending over, kissed him gently on the cheek. Lydia said goodbye to her daughter but indicated she would stay a little longer. She barely noticed as Raul followed her out of the room.

Once in the hallway, Jade ignored him and walked to the entranceway for a breath of air. He caught her a few feet from the sliding doors.

"Jade. We need to talk."

She shook his hand off her elbow and continued out into the night until she reached the lone bench beneath the palm tree in the courtyard. Her legs felt shaky, and abruptly she sat down.

"Talk," she ordered harshly, her hands fumbling in her purse for a Kleenex. The last few hours were getting to her, and she needed to distract herself with anything she could right now.

Raul sat down beside her, unsure how to begin. His hands dropped in his lap as he tried to delay the inevitable.

Jade watched him from under lowered lashes. Under other circumstances, she knew she would feel sorry for him. Despite what she had told Amie, she knew how much Raul really cared for her parents. But looking at him now, all she could muster was anger—and perhaps the hurt of betrayal too. Without warning, Jade laughed, a low, mocking sound.

Startled out of his reverie, Raul lifted his head.

"Well, that was an interesting conversation," she told him, her tone of voice sarcastic and cruel. "I think I'll go in now. Why don't you run along and protect your interest in the Mi Corazon?"

Raul looked stunned by the venom in her voice, and for a brief moment, she nearly felt sorry for him.

"You know about that?"

A sharp pain slid between her breasts. It was one thing to overhear it from someone else but another thing entirely to have it confirmed like this. She hardened her heart.

"Yes, Raul, I know all about it. How you wormed your way into my family when I was away and let them think we were still a couple. My father would never have given you a percentage if it wasn't for me, and you know it as well as I do."

Raul's voice was deceivingly soft. "You think so?" His eyes glittered dangerously.

"I know so," she shot back at him. "And now that I'm marrying Eric, you think you can have it all, but you're going to have a fight on your hands if you think I will ever let you buy me out."

Unbidden, the words left her mouth with no thought for what she was saying. He flinched as if she had slapped him, and she reveled in the pain she was causing. Satisfied ,Jade stood to go, but he stopped her. His hand burned hotly on her arm, and she threw it off.

"You have it all wrong, Jade. I admit that in the beginning I used our relationship to get a job with your father." Her eyes narrowed in sudden anger, and quickly, he amended, "I mean our past relationship. But did it ever occur to you that just maybe I—"

Unrepentantly, Raul stopped. Seeing Jade standing as proudly inflexible as she had been years ago brought back memories he had tried hard to forget, and resigned, he sighed. It was history repeating itself all over again.

"What's the use?" His voice sounded beaten. "You're never going to believe me anyway, Jade. You never have." Raul stood now and looked down at her white, angry face.

"Think what you want, but let me tell you something, Jade. As long as your father is lying in that hospital bed or in need of my help, I'm going to be here, whether you like it or not. Go back to Canada and marry Eric. I don't care. But remember this—the Mi Corazon is part mine, and I intend to keep it." With that, he turned on his heel and stomped angrily off into the night.

Jade stared at his back in confused anger. Briefly, she wondered what he had been about to say, and then she shrugged. *Probably a lie.* It was obvious what he wanted all along. Didn't he just say it? *The Mi Corazon is mine.*

The pain of hearing those words burned a hole in her stomach, and reflexively, she held an arm across her middle. With slow, measured steps, she made her way back into the hospital. Maybe with luck she could convince her mother to go home and get some rest. God only knew that she wasn't going to get any.

Raul stormed back into the restaurant, his face a masked fury. Nearly everyone was gone except for Sergio, the night janitor, who looked at him as if he were the devil himself. He forced himself to smile grimly and walked into his office, closing the door firmly behind him. His anger nearly dissipated, he sunk slowly into the leather chair Lydia had bought for Rodolfo the day he opened the restaurant. Leaning back in its comforting luxury, he put his feet up on the desk and closed his eyes. It had been a long day.

It had started with waking up on the *Jade* with the worst hangover of his short life and wanting to die. The impromptu swim had done little to cure him of his feeling of worthlessness. Even now, he had been shocked by how much he had wanted to keep on swimming until he couldn't anymore, then just sink out of sight. That the idea had crossed his mind for even a split second had shaken him to the core. With long easy strokes and fighting the panic that had threatened to engulf him, he made his way back to his boat. For a long while, he had lain on the deck, trying to get his equilibrium and sanity in line. Then he had hoisted his sails and spent the day sailing on the open waters before finally turning for home.

On land, he was greeted with the news that Arturo was looking for him and needed him to come to the restaurant right away. The pint-sized messenger, a street kid that sometimes hung around the kitchen, was not able to give any more details than that. Tipping him a few pesos, Raul had showered and dressed in record time and hurried to the Mi Corazon.

The news that the man who was like a father to him lay sick in the hospital had floored him with nearly the same intensity as Jade's announcement last night. The shock was only now beginning to wear off to be replaced by a profound sadness infinitely worse. Just when he thought things couldn't get any more terrible, they had.

Jade believed he was mercenary and only out to get what he could from her family. *Never mind that while she was in Canada partying, I was here in Mexico working my tail off.* If only he had been able to tell her. A knock on the door interrupted him. *Jade?*

"Come in."

A blonde head poked around the door, and his heart started beating normally again.

"Can I come in?" Amie asked, a small woebegone look on her pretty face.

Surprised, he swung his legs to the floor and stood, indicating a chair on the other side of the desk.

"Please sit, Amie." His voice was light but wary. He had seen how she had looked at him earlier in the dining room. He guessed that she must be thinking along the same lines that Jade was. He sighed and remained standing as Amie took the chair offered her.

"What can I do for you?" He asked now in as gentle a tone as possible.

Amie's eyes immediately filled with tears as she looked up at the man hovering over her.

"We need your help, Raul," she told him. "And we need it now."

As Raul stared in disbelief, Amie launched into one of the most complicated love triangle stories he had ever heard. Finally, at the end of her tale, she took a deep breath and concluded, "So you see, Raul, you just have to win Jade back." Her eyes were hopeful and bright, and Raul couldn't help but respond to her with a small smile.

"I wish I could help you, Amie. I really do. But Jade won't listen. She thinks that the only thing I want is the restaurant, that somehow I tricked her father into giving it to me."

"Well did you?" she demanded without thinking as Raul flushed a deep red. Immediately, she was ashamed. Something in his manner instinctively made her believe in him, and she apologized. "I'm sorry, Raul. That was uncalled for, but you have to convince her of the truth." She nodded sagely. "She loves you."

"It's too late, Amie." He came around to her side of the desk and lifted her carefully by the elbow.

Amie knew it was his way of saying the conversation was over, and she stood to stand beside him. "I don't know why you two are so stubborn," she said now in frustration, and he grinned.

"Like you and Eric were?" he teased her lightly.

She tossed her head. "Not the same thing at all." Although she knew it was.

Against her will, Amie grinned ruefully. She could see now her trip had been a total waste of time. Once more, she asked him to think it over and try again. Raul smiled and nodded agreeably, but leaving, Amie knew she was no closer to what she wanted than when she had first arrived. *It's time for Plan B*, she thought decisively and hurried to find Eric. With only a few hours left, she hoped that he would have better luck with Jade than she had with Raul.

Eric spied Jade wandering the halls of the hospital, looking lost and alone. Instantly, he went to her and put his arms around her waist. Surprised, her eyes darted upward and sought his.

"What are you doing here?"

A pleased smile curved her lips, and she leaned into him gratefully. As always, Eric was there when she needed him, like the good friend he was. *Friend? Fiancé*, she amended and hugged him tighter.

"I came to see how you were doing. How is your father?"

"Sleeping peacefully," Jade said, relief evident in the tone of her voice. "My mother is with him now. They brought in another bed, and I think she is trying to get some rest."

He lifted her chin with two fingers and scrutinized her wan face carefully. "That's good. And you? Have you had some sleep yet?"

Jade shook her head tiredly. "Not yet. I was afraid to in case..." She couldn't go on.

Eric hugged her again. "I think you and I should go back to the house, Jade. You need to get some rest. You won't do your father any good if you get sick too, now will you?"

She opened her mouth as if to protest, then quickly shut it again. What he said was right. With her father likely out of commission for at least a few weeks, there was a lot she would have to do to take over. Knowing her mother, she would want to spend as much time with her husband as she could. That meant it was up to her to take over some of their duties. It was time to see if her education was worth the money they paid for it.

"You're right, Eric," she said, surprising him. "Let me just get my wrap from the room, and we can go. If mother is awake, I want to tell her where we are going. Otherwise, I will leave a note with one of the nurses." She raised herself on tiptoes and kissed his cheek lightly, then silently slipped from his arms.

Eric watched her departure with a heavy heart and sat down in one of the hard benches to wait. He could think of no way to broach the subject of their engagement now. He could tell how stressed Jade was, and he, for one, had no desire to add to it. Suddenly, he wished the problem would somehow magically disappear.

Jade let herself quietly into the room. By the dim nightlight, she could see her mother sleeping on the cot provided for her, and she was relieved. Lydia was exhausted and needed to rest. She glanced over at her father, shocked to see him regarding her thoughtfully from his bed. She hurried to his side.

"Poppa," she whispered anxiously, "what are you doing? You're supposed to be sleeping."

Rodolfo lifted a finger to quiet her, but his eyes were lively and alert. "I'm fine, *mija*," he assured her, and indeed, as she looked closer, it seemed that he was. "I think your necklace saved me." He smiled broader, and she laughed a little, muffling the sound in one hand so as not to wake her mother. "We told you it had healing powers."

Jade nodded, her eyes bright with tears.

"Don't cry, *princessa*. You know I can't stand it when you or your mother cries." Rodolfo's expression was pained, and for his sake, she tried to control her emotions. Her father was going to be all right. She knew it.

Jade's tremulous smile gratified him. It was the absolute truth when he said he hated when either of his girls cried, for whatever reason. He suspected that lately Jade had been doing more than her fair share. The thought saddened him, and he reached over and laid a hand on her head, a gesture that never failed to comfort her in the past.

"I think you should go and get some sleep now, Jade." When she looked about to protest, he held up his hand again. Then he gave her a look he rarely used but that clearly said there would be no argument, and she gave in.

"I will, Poppa, but I will be back in a few hours. I need to make sure that Amie and Eric get to the airport okay. They leave today."

"I want you to give them a good last day to remember, Jade," Rodolfo ordered. "I promise I will be fine. I only need some rest. If we are lucky, the doctor will let me go home very soon. With your mother ordering me around and making sure I eat and rest, there really is no need for me to stay. She is a crazy woman sometimes."

Jade laughed at her father's inaccurate description of her mother. Everyone knew she was a pushover when it came to anything to do with him.

"There is something else though," Rodolfo continued, gratified by her laughter. "I would ask a favor of you, Jade."

"Anything."

"I need you to stay here in Zihuatanejo for a little while."

"Of course, Poppa. I have already told Eric I won't be going—"

She stopped as her father continued as if she hadn't spoken.

"I need you to help Raul run the restaurant and the gift shop for your mother."

Her jaw dropped, but he held his hand up again, effectively stemming her words. "Please, Jade. Your mother has convinced me we need to take a holiday. And I need you here."

Pause. "Yes, Poppa." Jade's voice was softly compliant, and she bent her head to hide her emotions.

No matter what she was feeling now, her first priority was with her family. Somehow, she would have to do this for their sake, even if it meant working with the devil himself.

"How long will you need me?" It came as an almost whisper.

"For as long as it takes, Jade," his voice was rueful, and she peered at him closely, searching for an underlying meaning. All she met with was a steady gaze, and she thought she imagined it.

"Alright, Poppa," she meekly complied with his request.

"There is something else, Jade. It's about Raul. There's something I think you should know." This time it was she who interrupted him.

"I already know about it, Poppa," she told him, her voice shaking with anger and a deep disappointment she tried hard not to show.

"What is it that you know, Jade?" he asked, curious as to what her answer would be.

"I know you gave him fifty percent of the new restaurant." Her voice sounded flat, and she strove to keep her face expressionless.

Rodolfo looked surprised. "Well, yes we did."

"I know that he used me to get you to believe we were an item—even though we had already broken up."

Rodolfo nodded reluctantly. "Yes, Jade, that may be true, but there is something you need to know."

"Please, Poppa," Jade cut in, "let's not talk about this now. You need to get some rest. We can talk later. Besides, Eric is waiting to take me home. Thank heavens for Eric." She leaned over and kissed his cheek gently, then straightened. "You better keep the necklace a little longer, though," she told him solemnly. "Just in case."

Rodolfo stroked the obsidian stone lovingly. "I will Jade. Just in case. But I promise you, I will give it back. I think that we should talk though."

"Later, Poppa," Jade promised. "Mother will have my head if we talk about this now when you need to sleep."

Rodolfo smiled grimly, and he allowed his daughter to pull the blankets up around his chin as if he were the child not she. What he had been about to say would have to keep until later, he could see that now.

At his compliance, Jade smiled and kissed him once more. Then, wordlessly, she turned and walked silently out of the room. Rodolfo watched her go with a sad smile. He knew that she was hurting, and that wounded him deeply.

I think you need the stone more than I do, hija. He reached for the necklace again. *Soon, little one. Soon.*

14

"I wonder what the poor people are doing today." Lydia turned to her husband, basking on a lounge chair in the sun, and grinned.

Rodolfo returned her smile but made no reply. None was necessary. Instead, he closed his eyes and sighed with pure delight. This vacation, much needed and appreciated, had done wonders for him. He almost hated the thought of going home and said as much now to Lydia.

"Maybe we won't have to," she smiled as he took off his glasses to regard her.

"What do you mean?"

"Well, maybe Raul and Jade will come to their senses and see that they are meant for each other, and then we can retire. Finally!"

Rodolfo laughed. "You're forgetting one thing, Lydia."

"What's that?"

"Your daughter is very stubborn."

Lydia laughed and swatted him playfully. "Oh really? How is it that when Jade is less than perfect, she's my daughter and not yours?"

"She'll always be my daughter," he said firmly. "It's just that sometimes she is more like you than me. Like now." He grinned and neatly ducked another swing aimed at his chest. Grabbing a hold of one small fist, he lifted her bodily from her lounge chair to join him on his.

Lydia happily settled herself next to him. They were on a secluded part of the resort with only the Mediterranean Sea before them and a bottle of cold champagne cooling in a bucket beside them. There was no one close enough by to see the way Rodolfo played his hands over her tanned skin, teasing her nerve ends until they tingled. She sighed with contentment and kissed his cheek gently.

"Have you talked to Raul today?"

"Yes. He says that everything is fine, and we're not to worry. I don't, not with him in charge."

Lydia laughed. "Poor Jade," she said shaking her head. "I know she didn't like it when you put him in charge."

Rodolfo grinned mischievously. "There was no other choice. I'm afraid it was a bit of a blow to her ego. I am proud of the way she took it, though."

"So am I." She tilted her head to look at her husband. "Do you think they will ever get together?" Her voice was serious, and he answered in the same vein.

"I don't know, Lydia. I hope so. It sure would solve a lot of things for us. Now that Jade has postponed the wedding to Eric, there may be some hope."

"Yes, but that was really to help us out," Lydia put in. "She said that they will make plans when we get home."

"Maybe, Lydia, but on the other hand, maybe it was just an excuse."

Lydia looked startled. "Really?"

"Sure," he grinned again, showing the dimples she loved so well. "You don't really think she's in love with Eric, do you?"

She looked thoughtful for a minute then nodded her head in agreement. "I think you may be right," she said slowly. "About not marrying Eric, I mean. But I think Raul and Jade have a long way to go before they come to terms with each other."

"Ahhh, but we have a secret weapon, now."

"We do?"

"*Si, mi amor*. Remember, we have the obsidian stone."

Lydia threw her head back and laughed long and hard. "You are crazy, Rodolfo. I mean, that stone is beautiful, but…"

"Didn't it just save me?"

Lydia stared at him. "You can't for one minute think…"

"I can, and I do." His look was decisive, and she laughed again.

"I bet you didn't know that this stone is from Canada?"

She looked at him in surprise. She hadn't known, but how like him to know.

"Yes, Lydia, it is from east of the Rocky Mountains and over to the Pacific. You know where the Haida come from?"

She nodded. Some of Canada's greatest native artists in painting and pottery came from that region. They carried a few pieces in the gift shop. "Only Canada?" she asked, curious now to learn more.

"No, it is also found wherever there is volcanic action. Places like Mexico of course, but also California, Washington, and even Russia and Norway."

"Really? I didn't know that."

"Well, I do remember my father saying that the obsidian stones are the tears of their ancestors."

"What a lovely sentiment," Lydia said softly, her voice a low murmur over the sound of the waves. Rodolfo continued.

"But each color stone is used for different things. For example, mahogany puts people at ease with their sensuality," he pinched her lightly, and she giggled.

"Rainbow colored stones balance energy, and silver and gold stimulate activity and health. There are lots more, but those are some of the main ones."

"What does black do?"

"Oh that. The reason I chose black is because it helps aid in eliminating bad habits." He laughed, and Lydia joined in.

"Jade will need that all right. She has a very bad habit of jumping to the wrong conclusions."

Rodolfo agreed. "I hope she realizes Raul's worth before it's too late."

"Do you think we should have told her what he did?"

Rodolfo shook his head. "No, Lydia. I admit I tried, but she wouldn't listen. She will just have to find out on her own, and we will have to trust that things will work out."

"You always say that," she remarked while thinking once more that he was right. She decided it was time to reward him.

"No more stories now," she told him, her intent clear in eyes, which reflected the sea.

"If you have a better idea, Lydia, I'm always at your service."

Lydia bit back a laugh. "Oh I do. I most certainly do," she told him lightly, drawing his head down for a kiss. "And I'm going to show you, right now."

Rodolfo never doubted it for a minute.

Jade sighed as she lifted the heavy crate into the back of the pickup. She brushed her arm across a weary brow and looked over the top of the truck bed at the market she had just exited. As usual, it was noisy, dirty and crowded, but the sight of it made her nostalgic. Nothing felt more like home to her than this place.

The tiny kitchens that lined the sidewalks were cooking tacos and other Mexican dishes. Now the smells wafted across the humid air, assailing her senses and overwhelming her.

Suddenly, she felt sick and valiantly swallowed hard against the nausea that threatened to rise in her throat. Blindly, she made her way to the driver's side of the truck, her skin feeling cold and clammy. She slid gratefully onto the seat and rested her head against the steering wheel, hoping she wasn't coming down with something. She was far too busy to get sick these days.

Over two months ago, her parents had left for an extended holiday somewhere in the Greek Islands, and then they were going to Italy. Since then, she had been nearly run off her feet. It was one thing to learn how to run a business in college, but as she was learning quickly, it was another to actually do it in the real world. No wonder her father had been so exhausted.

Coupled with that was the fact she was required to work with Raul, who told her in no uncertain terms that he was the one in charge. When she had complained to her father, he had, to her consternation, backed Raul up, gently explaining that his experience far outweighed hers. Not wanting to cause her father any stress, she had complied, albeit unwillingly. Her revenge was to speak to Raul only when absolutely necessary and then only on matters of business. Any other time, she completely ignored him. However, even she had to grudgingly admit he did know what he was doing.

As much as she wanted to think that he was incompetent and had tricked her parents into trusting him, she found that she no longer could. His record keeping was precise and organized, his food costs consistent and restrained, yet the quality of the food was always top notch. His staff, both the old and the new at their second location, obviously admired and respected him. They certainly jumped to attention whenever he gave an order. On top of that, they liked him too. From observing him when she thought he wasn't looking, she had been amazed at his skill in handling people.

There was the time their cook threatened to chop everyone's head off with a meat cleaver. Jade had watched with horrified fascination the way Raul managed to calm down the staff and jolly the cook into seeing the humor of a not-so-funny situation. By the time Raul had left the kitchen, everyone was laughing and talking and treating the incident as a huge joke.

Then, last week, little Rosie had cut her finger on a butcher knife, nearly severing it. At the sight of so much blood, Jade had almost passed out, while Raul, on the other hand, calmly took charge of the situation. With infinite care and expertise, he had staunched the flow of blood, at the same time calming the near-hysterical young girl. Then he drove her to the hospital and stayed with her to make sure she was properly cared for.

At the last moment, Jade had jumped in the truck with the intention of coming along. Raul had shot her a long considering look over Rosie's head, and for a moment, she thought he was going to tell her to get out. Finally, he shrugged and allowed her to accompany them while she, still embarrassed by her near fainting episode, tried to redeem herself by comforting Rosie. After it was over, Raul had grudgingly rewarded her assistance with a small smile of thanks. She was amazed at how much his approval meant to her.

There were other incidents too, but each time some crisis came up, Raul would handle it in a calm, relaxed manner. Consequently, things went, for the most part, smoothly. Reluctantly, Jade began to believe her father was right in giving the reins over to the former playboy/fisherman instead of to her. As much as it galled her, she was a fair person and knew she would never have been able to deal with all of this on her own.

But soon, she promised herself. If it killed her, she was going to learn this business inside out. Judging by the way her tired bones felt today, that was exactly what was going to happen. She grinned weakly at her feeble joke.

With enormous effort, Jade turned the key in the ignition, and the ancient truck rumbled to life. Fumes rose from the street below, and once again, she felt the sickness rise in her throat. Fearing she was about to vomit, she quickly clamped an icy hand over her mouth until it passed and took quick, deep breaths. She rubbed the obsidian stone around her neck, secretly hoping it would do what it was meant to. She laughed. Despite what her father said, she really didn't believe a stone could heal her. That was just plain old-fashioned superstition as far as she was concerned. But the way she was feeling now, she was almost willing to try anything, and Poppa did feel better after she had placed it around his neck, so who knew?

She knew from stories told to her that her grandfather on Rodolfo's side had been a great Shaman of the Tarahumara tribe far to the north. Maybe some of his magic would rub off on her? She took another deep breath.

When she finally got herself under control, Jade put the truck into gear and edged out into the traffic. *I need to see a doctor*, she thought as she roared through the green traffic light. She made a mental note to call Dr. Grayeb and set an appointment as soon as possible.

Raul looked at the column of numbers and tried to concentrate. It was no use. His headache prevented him from focusing on anything, and he realized that none of what he was seeing made any sense. With a muttered oath, he slammed the book shut and stuck it back into the drawer of the desk. Then he leaned back in his chair and put his feet up.

"It's nice to see that someone is able to take it easy around here."

He heard the door slam and the icy sound of a female voice piercing the air, reverberating like a rocket through his pain-filled head. Raul winced but kept his eyes closed.

"Is there something you want, Jade?" The irony of the question was not lost on him, and for a minute, his expression was wistful.

Momentarily confused, Jade regarded him while his eyes were still closed. *He looks tired,* she thought with some surprise, although she knew she shouldn't be. He worked harder than anyone in their employ, and she had to grudgingly give credit where it was due. With his head tipped back on the chair like it was, he looked like the small boy he had been when she first met him in grade school. His hair was as unruly now as it was then, and for a moment, she had an uncontrollable urge to run her fingers through his thick, silky curls. Hastily, she folded her arms across her chest.

"I came to see what you wanted to do about the produce I bought while you were resting." Her voice was sharp with sarcasm.

Raul barked out a laugh and opened his eyes, tempted to say something rude.

"For your information, Jade," he began on the defensive and then thought better of it. "Forget it."

Raul stood abruptly and moved to stand inches from her body, his breath warm on her face. He saw her eyes grow huge and almost frightened. Her back hit the wall, and he knew that, for her, there was nowhere to escape. Defiantly, she lifted her chin, and Raul chuckled, as amused by her courage as he was filled with admiration. Then her tongue darted nervously out of her mouth, wetting her luscious, full lips and disarming him. His eyes narrowed and darkened. He wanted nothing more than to lean forward and taste that mouth. The way she was staring at him, her generous chest heaving as if she were afraid…abruptly, he straightened and turned away.

"Get the hell out of here, Jade," he ordered harshly, his back to her now as he tried to control his emotions.

He was more than a little aware of the bulge in his jeans, and he shifted uncomfortably.

Jade didn't need to be told twice. With a moan that sounded suspiciously like a sob, she turned to obey. *Why did I have to close the damn door?* Fumbling with the doorknob, it finally gave, and she fled the room. As she raced along the corridor to the kitchen, she heard a crash of glass breaking behind her, and she winced but kept going.

Raul stooped and picked up the pieces of the vase he had thrown across the room, suddenly filled with shame. It wasn't like him to lose his cool. On the other hand, it wasn't like him to be so affected by a woman either. Jade certainly held the power to do that. He knew it couldn't continue any longer.

Working with Jade day in and day out had not been easy. In fact, it was sheer torture most of the time. To have her so close, her perfume constantly tantalizing him as she stalked past him with unseeing eyes, was driving him crazy. Her body, slim and supple in the simple sheathed dresses she favored to work in, tempted him beyond reason, knowing as he did how beautifully naked she looked underneath and how she felt in his arms as she responded to him. At night, his dreams were filled with wanting her, but she was engaged to another man now, and that made her off limits as far as he was concerned. Something would have to be done.

Raul walked back to the desk and threw the shards of glass into the garbage. As he bent over, his glance fell on a manila envelope peeking out from behind the file cabinet. He was about to reach for it when there was a knock on the door.

Heike poked his head around and asked for a few minutes of his time. There was a new dish they had made, and he wanted Raul's permission before he served it. Since it was a soufflé best served hot, he insisted his boss come at that moment.

At the urgent tone in his voice, Raul forced a smile and straightened. He knew there was no sense telling Heike he was busy. Chefs were not well known for their patient nature, and Heike was certainly not that. Besides, maybe a taste of something sweet would get his mind off those luscious lips of Jade's and back onto work-related matters where they belonged. By the way his body immediately responded to that thought, he very much doubted it. With a frown, he followed his chef down the corridor Jade had taken, the envelope momentarily forgotten.

It can't be. How could this be?
The young woman sat on the edge of the examining table, her feet swinging uselessly above the floor as she tried to grasp what the doctor was telling her.

"You're not too far along, Jade. Only about three months, I would say off hand, but you are definitely pregnant."

Pregnant? She stared at the doctor in disbelief.

Dr Grayeb reached out a compassionate hand and touched Jade's shoulder. She flinched. "This is such a shock," she told him, and he nodded, knowing that Jade was not married. The good news, however, was that she was engaged to be. Thinking to offer her some comfort, he reminded her of the fact now. He was surprised when she shook her head and looked about to faint.

Seeing her as pale white as the sheet wrapped modestly around her, Dr. Grayeb gently pushed her head between her knees. When she seemed a little better, he handed her a glass of water from the bottle next to the sink. Then he waited while the color came back into her face and she recovered her equilibrium.

"Anything you want to talk to me about, Jade?" he asked, knowing full well her parents were still out of the country.

On entering the office that day, Jade, in her nervousness, had babbled how they were due home next week and how much she had missed them. He wondered briefly how her parents would take the news, then immediately relaxed. Lydia and Rodolfo doted on their only child. It would be a shock to them initially, he speculated, but she wasn't the first woman to have this happen to her and surely wouldn't be the last. He had no qualms in believing the tight-knit family he knew would make it through this just as they had every other crisis in the past.

Jade only shook her head again. She was still trying to take it all in herself. Thanking the doctor, she slipped from the examining table to the floor and slid her feet into her Mexican sandals. Dr. Grayeb asked her to come into the office when she finished dressing so he could write her a prescription for some vitamins he wanted her to take. Then, with a puckered brow, he left her alone with her thoughts.

Slowly, Jade drew the light cotton dress over her head and frowned. She had chosen this dress that morning because she had been feeling a little fat lately, and it was big and blousy. At the slight tightness around her breasts that caused the buttons to gape, she had vowed to stop tasting Heike's delicious food in the kitchen. Now she knew the real reason for her weight gain. She paused in her dressing to place a hand on her stomach. That there was an actual life in there amazed her.

With the waning of initial shock came another feeling, and unexpectedly, she was filled with a sense of pure wonder. She moved her body to face the full-length mirror on the other side of the room. Turning sideways, she stuck her belly out a little, trying to see what others would see in just a few short weeks. Then she laughed aloud, a pure delightful sound that filled the room and echoed down the hall.

That it was Raul's child, there was no doubt. Their one night together on his boat caught them both unaware, and they were unprepared for what happened next. Jade flushed at the unbridled passion that had overcome them. With no concern for safety or the use of precautions, they had given into it.

On the other hand, she and Eric had not made love for a few months prior to their visit to Mexico. And even then, without fail they always wore protection. The weeks leading up to their trip had been hectic for her with final exams and a case for him. They had barely seen each other, much less made love. Then, of course, in Mexico there had been no opportunity. At least that's what she had told herself once they arrived.

The truth of the matter was that she had not felt comfortable in making love in her parents' house. She knew it sounded horribly old-fashioned, but she couldn't help it and had told Eric her feelings. She had been relieved when he had given in to her decision without an argument. As things turned out, she was glad now that they had refrained. Despite her predicament, Jade grinned, remembering her talk with Eric and Amie.

True to her promise to her father to show them a good time on their last day in Mexico, Jade had suggested a short boat ride to Contramar beach. On the way there, she had sensed an underlying tension between the pair, and she called them on it. Finally, over *taritas* and ice cold beers, red-faced and embarrassed, Amie and Eric told her of their feelings for each other and begged her forgiveness.

Of all the things she had expected to hear, that they were in love was certainly not one of them. The revelation had hit her like a ton of bricks, and at first, Jade could only stare at them in shock.

There was no question of being angry. The uppermost thought in her mind was the time that had been wasted when Eric and Amie could have been together. As she looked from one to the other, she saw what she should have known almost from the first, and her surprise was quickly replaced with understanding and joy. If she were being truly honest with herself, they were tinged with relief too. Later, after she had dropped the happy pair off at the airport, she had time to examine her feelings more closely.

She knew her happiness for Amie and Eric was not feigned. In her heart, she knew that as wonderful as Eric was, she would never have been completely happy with him. Not as long as there was the shadow of Raul.

Raul. She almost snorted aloud at the thought of him. He barely acknowledged her these days. That it was partly her fault, she knew. Her childish behavior earlier on in their working relationship had seen to that.

She realized now that the accusations she had thrown in his face were ungrounded, and she was ashamed by them. It was easy to see why her father and mother had trusted him and wanted to reward him for his dedication and hard work by giving him a part share in the business. Quite simply, he deserved it. The problem was that there didn't seem to be a way to let him know her feelings had changed. Each time she tried approaching him, he looked at her as if she had suddenly sprouted two heads—if he even bothered to look at her at all.

The thought depressed her. What had started out as a wish for revenge had quickly turned into a grave of her own making, and she had no idea how to dig herself back out, especially in light of the news she had just received.

The other problem was that everyone, including her parents, thought she was still engaged to Eric. She didn't want them to be disappointed. Eric was a successful man and a good catch. Again, with complete honesty, she knew the real reason she hadn't told anyone the engagement was off was because she wanted to make Raul jealous. Now what was she going to do? Her mind raced over the possibilities. *Maybe I could leave.* She laughed again, imagining her growing body running anywhere, dismissing the idea as unworthy. No, she decided, she would just have to face this head on and let the chips fall where they may.

Hearing Jade's laugh, Dr. Grayeb laid down his pen and smiled approvingly. Jade was going to be alright, he had no doubt. Now, leaning back in his chair, he waited for Jade to join him for further instructions and, in the absence of Rodolfo, some good old fatherly advice.

15

The 747 Boeing touched down uneventfully in tropical Zihuatanejo. Rodolfo and Lydia exchanged satisfied grins. It was good to be home. Holding hands, together they disembarked onto the hot tarmac and made their way to the blessedly cool terminal.

Lydia looked toward the arrivals lounge and spotted Jade pressed as close to the glass as she could. She waved enthusiastically, delighting in the wide open smile of their beautiful daughter. Minutes later, with bags retrieved, they made their way to where Jade anxiously waited.

She looks different, Lydia noticed before being engulfed by Jade's welcoming arms. As her husband took his turn, she tried to see what changes time away had wrought in their daughter. *She looks more mature, more sure*, were the first thoughts to cross her mind. *But there's something else.* She peered into the Madonna-like face, and then suddenly, she knew. Her mouth hung open.

"Lydia, are you going to stand there all day catching flies?" Rodolfo quipped, the very Canadian expression sounding funny in his accented voice. She quickly closed her mouth and smiled at Jade.

"Your father has been impossible since we left," she responded while her mind whirred in excitement. "See what I put up with?"

"You love it, and you know it," her daughter predicted accurately, picking up one of the carry-on bags. "Shall we go? I have the truck waiting outside."

As Lydia allowed her daughter and husband to lead the way, she analyzed her feelings. Joy was certainly in the forefront, but following closely on its heels was worry too. She knew this meant that Jade would be returning to Canada to marry Eric. The thought saddened her. On the plane home, she and Rodolfo had agreed that they would not stand in her daughter's way if she was determined to go. Once in the truck, she broached the subject.

"How is Eric, Jade? Are you excited to be going back to Canada?"

"He's fine," Jade evaded the question and hid her eyes from the intense ones of her mother.

"We really appreciate what you have done for us, Jade." Her father spared a glance from his driving to smile at her. "Raul said you were a real asset to him."

Raul said that? Unaccountably, she glowed with pleasure but made no comment. In all her time working with him, he had never paid her a compliment, and it irked her.

"How are you feeling, Jade?" Lydia asked her daughter in what she hoped was a casual manner.

Despite the relaxed attitude, Jade shot her a searching look. Did her mother know? She shook the thought away instantly. *I must be getting paranoid.*

"I'm fine, mother, but the real question is—how do you feel, Poppa?" Adeptly, she turned the topic away from herself, concern clearly written on her face.

"Jade, I have never felt better in my life. Your mother took excellent care of me. I ate a lot, swam, took the sun and relaxed. I feel like a million dollars."

"But you are not going back to that same schedule as before," Lydia admonished in a tone that brooked no argument. Rodolfo grinned.

"Your mother can be so bossy sometimes," he complained even as his eyes smiled.

Lydia laughed then and turned to Jade to explain.

"We have agreed that Rodolfo will be spending only mornings at the restaurant. If need be, we will hire another manager to take some of the work load away from Raul. With you gone, he will need that, I think."

Jade flushed guiltily. "If you need me to stay…"

"No." Lydia's voice was firm. "You need to go to Eric. It's time you got on with your own life."

Especially now that you are bringing a new life into the world, was the thought she held back. She smiled serenely at her daughter, holding the secret close and looking forward to the time that Jade would open up. That she was not in the least disappointed in her daughter would surprise no one who knew her well. Although it was preferable, in her opinion, to have the benefit of two people raise a child, she had no doubt Eric and Jade would do the right thing. The sooner the better. After all, they loved each other, right? Suddenly, a niggling suspicion worked its way to the forefront.

"Mother, there is something I have to…"

"How did you find working with Raul, Jade?" Lydia unwittingly interrupted her daughter, who, surprised, flushed to the roots of her hair.

"Uh…fine," she stammered and then pulled herself together to add, "Raul is very good at what he does. I can see why you gave him part of the restaurant." It was her way of apologizing for her reaction, and they both knew it.

Rodolfo's smile twisted. "Yeah, well, that's something we…"

"Look out, honey," Lydia tugged on his arm, and he swung his eyes back to the road as an ongoing truck crossed the center line, narrowly missing them.

By this time, they were entering the village limits, and Rodolfo turned his full concentration over to driving. Whatever he was about to say was forgotten for the moment with just getting them safely home. Then, as they pulled up to the house, the emphasis was getting bags put away and organized. After a light lunch, Rodolfo, under Lydia's orders, retired for a siesta in the cool bedroom they always shared. Promising to join him soon, Lydia led her daughter outside to sit on the porch with her, cold iced teas made especially by Juanita in their hands.

For a while, the two women chatted aimlessly. The moment to come clean with her news had come and gone. Instead, Jade asked questions about the trip, riveted as Lydia described the beautiful Mediterranean waters of Greece and the wine-growing countryside of Italy.

"It was incredible, Jade," Lydia sighed at the memory. "Best of all, your father was able to rest and take it easy. He looks like his old self, don't you think?"

Jade nodded. "Yes, he does, and we have to make sure he stays that way. Mother, I was thinking that maybe I should stay and help out."

"Nonsense, Jade." At the bleak look on her daughter's face, she softened. *Didn't Jade want to go?* "We appreciate what you have done, *mija*. Raul said he couldn't have done it without you. It's nice to know that the money spent for your education was money well spent. Raul said you took over the books too. Both he and your father hate that part." She laughed.

Jade glowed with real pleasure for a moment and then quickly sobered. She wished he would have said something to her. Bitterly, she thought about the last few weeks. Since her change of heart toward Raul, not to mention the new life growing within her, she had tried many times to bridge the wide gap between them. Staying late and working harder than ever, she hoped he would at least acknowledge in some small way that he appreciated her efforts. He never did. Instead, he seemed to avoid being in the same room whenever she came near. Although he remained polite, it was as if they had never shared a past together. The knowledge that he had spoken well of her to her parents both surprised and gratified her. She cleared her brow and smiled back.

"I really like this business, Momma. I think I am good at it." Her response was enthusiastic. "I only wish that…" She stopped, her expression wistful.

"What do you wish, Jade?" Lydia prodded gently.

But Jade had stood up and, with a brittle smile on her face, said, "Nothing, Mother. I am glad you are home. I hope you don't mind, but I have many things to do before we open tonight, so I better get to it."

"Don't overdo it," Lydia blurted without thinking, and for a minute, Jade's smile faltered. "I just mean that you don't want to work too hard in this heat," she ended lamely as Jade regarded her with a curious look on her beautiful face.

"I won't, Momma, don't worry." Unconsciously, her hands fluttered to her stomach lightly before moving away.

Lydia caught the movement and smiled. It was obvious Jade wasn't ready to tell her anything yet, but she hoped it would be soon. She watched her walk to the edge of the porch balcony to pluck a spray of bougainvilleas from the hedge and tuck it into the comb of her hair. There was a dreamy expression on her face that Lydia knew well, recognizing it as one she wore when pregnant with her. Another thought overtook her. *I'm going to be a grandmother!*

Jade straightened from where she was leaning over the rails and saw the smile on her mother's face. It was nice to see her father wasn't the only one who had benefitted from the holiday. Fondly, Jade blew her a kiss.

"I have to go, Momma. Why don't you get some rest too?"

Lydia nodded. "I will, Jade. First, though, I am going to call Ana and let her know we're home, and then I will lie down for awhile. I don't think we will go into the restaurant tonight. Tell everyone we will see them tomorrow. Besides, with you and Raul running the show, I'm sure no one will miss our not being there for one more night."

Her mother watched Jade hop in the red truck parked in the driveway and, with a final wave, drive away. Immediately, Lydia reached for the extension and dialed a number. After a few sharp rings, she spoke into the receiver.

"Ana, is that you? We're back. Listen, Ana, you're never going to guess…"

Lydia stopped mid-sentence and laughed giddily. Then, with suppressed excitement, she lowered her voice and told Ana the wonderful news.

Jade let herself into the office and turned on the lights. Brightly-lit floor lamps flooded the room, momentarily blinding her and revealing Raul fast asleep behind the desk. Despite the animosity between them, this time her face softened, and she smiled. As always, when he was sleeping he looked vulnerable and young, the worry lines he had accumulated over the last few months smoothed from his brow. She allowed her gaze to fall to his hands clasped across his lap, and she shivered, remembering the feeling of them on her body. It seemed like eons ago now. Raul stirred, and not wanting him to catch her staring, Jade hastily turned away.

Slowly, Raul opened his eyes, blinking rapidly at the apparition before him. Funnily enough, he had been dreaming of Jade yet again, and now here she was. *Who said that dreams don't come true?* Her back to him, he could nearly see though the flimsy material of the dress she wore. He saw her shapely legs form the V at the top of her thighs, and remembering how they had felt clamped around his waist, he nearly groaned aloud. Through half-lidded eyes, he watched her fingers, the same ones that had so eagerly caressed him, flip through the files of the cabinet, pulling out one after another and setting them down on the small desk beside her. Her body—*was it fuller these days?*—strained at the bodice and hips, and he felt his own stir in response as she moved in graceful—*Por Dios*—he swore under his breath. With a crash, he swung his legs to the floor.

Startled, Jade whirled and, in the process, dropped some of the files she was holding to the floor. The others she held clasped closely to her body, her luminous eyes glowing hugely in her face.

For a moment, they stared openly across the tiny expanse of space as time stood suspended. The only sound heard was their ragged and tense breathing, the air tingling with unsuppressed excitement and attraction.

An unreadable expression on his face, Raul got up slowly and moved toward her, his steps measured and sure. As he drew closer, her arms lowered from her breasts, and she watched his eyes flick over them and widen slightly in admiration. Subconsciously, she straightened her back, thrusting her chest forward. It was all the encouragement he needed, and his hands lifted to touch her.

Hardly daring to believe he would finally approach her, Jade remained where she was. His hot breath warmed her neck, and anticipating his kiss, she closed her eyes. When it didn't come, she peered out from long, dark lashes to find him regarding her with a look of contempt. Involuntarily, she took a step back, shocked by what she saw in his eyes.

Raul's sensuous mouth curled in a cruel smile.

"So. This is what engaged women do?" His voice was heavy with sarcasm

Jade flinched as if he had just slapped her. Humiliated by the effect he had, she took a step back, unwilling to listen to anything more he had to say.

"Don't flatter yourself, Raul. I have no idea what you are talking about. Now, if you don't mind, I have work to do, unlike some people I know," she glanced pointedly at the easy chair behind the desk, gratified as he turned red and moved away. She waited to speak until he was safely on the other side of the room.

"My parents are back, and they said to tell you they will be here tomorrow." Message dutifully delivered, Jade turned back to the files. "I will be leaving this week to go back to Canada," she informed him offhandedly, not seeing or caring what his reaction would be. Suddenly, the idea that she leave had merit. Only her shaking hands showed she was more affected than she let on, and to hide them, she jammed them back into the drawers of the file cabinet.

The thought of never seeing her again hit Raul with a violent blow to his stomach. "I think we need to…"A knock sounded on the door, and he swore softly under his breath. Grabbing the doorknob, he swung it open aggressively. "What?" he growled at the small figure cowering in the doorway. It was Rosie.

Seeing her looking so terrified, Raul was immediately ashamed, and he forced himself to change his manner. "Yes, Rosie. What is it?" his voice was deceptively soft.

In a halting, breathless voice, Rosie quickly explained that Heike wanted him to come to the kitchen immediately.

Sighing, Raul held up his hand to staunch her words and told her he would be right there. Then, as she fled down the hall, he scooped his keys off the desk.

"Jade," he tried again, but she kept her back to him, and he knew it was no use.

"I am busy, Raul," she said in a voice that clearly stated the subject was closed.

Cursing himself for being every kind of fool there was, Raul grimaced angrily and stomped out of the room.

When he was gone, Jade sank dejectedly to her knees, embarrassed by the need he must have seen and rejected in her eyes. Picking up the files as quickly as she could, she scrambled to stand. As she rose awkwardly off the floor, her eyes caught the edge of a file peeking out from behind the cabinet, and she frowned, wondering how it had managed to get there. Flattening her body, she arched her back and wiggled under the tiny side table. Then, stretching her arm as far as she could, she pulled the manila folder away from where it was caught. Triumphantly, she reversed direction until her head cleared the obstacle and she could sit up. Her files scattered haphazardly around her she took a deep, satisfied breath. Thinking to organize them first before putting them away again, she opened the file she was holding and began to read.

As her eyes skimmed the letter made out to her father, a series of emotions ran rampant across her features. First was surprise, then shock so deep she could hardly breathe. *Raul had given back his rights to the restaurant.*

She glanced at the date, hardly daring to believe what she was seeing. *The day of her birthday!* That meant that Raul must have done it after they had...she couldn't think anymore. *Why?*

She knew, of course, and again shame washed over her. Cursing herself for her behavior, she realized she should have known he was too proud to come to her on any other terms but his. That must have been what he wanted to tell her the night of the party. Why hadn't she trusted him enough to listen? She flushed again, knowing how her subsequent actions must have torn at him.

For a long while, Jade stayed where she was, thinking. It was only after she heard footsteps down the corridor outside her office that she finally decided it was time to get up. She needed to talk to Raul right now and straighten this out.

Resolutely she grabbed the corner of the desk and tried to stand. As she did, a sharp pain bit into her, shocking her with its intensity. She gasped and fought for air. The room swam suddenly, and she saw spots forming before her eyes. She felt a tingling between her legs, and briefly she wondered at it. The room began to spin. Vaguely, she heard the office door open and a shout as if coming from a long way off. After that, everything turned black, and then there was nothing.

"Phone for you, Raul," Arturo passed the message on to his boss with his usual grin and continued on to the dining room.

"Thanks," Raul said. "I'll take it in the office."

He strolled nonchalantly down the corridor, hoping Jade would be still there.

Then he dismissed the idea as readily as it had come. Probably she had already gone home to spend the evening with her parents. After what happened earlier, he couldn't blame her. Outside the office door, he paused, trying to steel himself for another confrontation. Finally, when he could delay no longer, he entered the room. What he saw lying there on the floor very nearly stopped his heart completely.

"I lost the baby, didn't I?" Jade stoically turned dry eyes toward her parents standing next to her hospital bed. Her tone was more a statement than a question, and she valiantly fought back the tears that threatened to overcome her. "I'm sorry," she whispered.

"Jade, you did not lose the baby." Jade's eyes scanned her mother's face in disbelief. "I didn't? But what…"

Her fingers searched and found the pendant still hanging around her neck. *Magic*, she thought with a wondering smile.

"It was only a little dizzy spell, Jade. The doctor says it was probably caused by stress or maybe hunger. Did you eat yesterday?"

Jade thought back, then shook her head. "No, I didn't." She remembered now the strange tingling in her legs. She looked up again at the faces looming above her for reassurance and found it.

Lydia continued. "All you need, Jade, are a few days of rest and some proper nutrition, and you will be as good as new. Both you and the baby are going to be fine. If you're up to it, the doctor says we can take you home tomorrow, but he does want to keep you overnight for observation. Just to be on the safe side."

At her reassurance that the baby was fine, Jade's face lit up. Then she remembered. "You must be so ashamed of me." She could barely meet their eyes.

This time, it was Rodolfo who spoke, his voice firm with conviction. "We could never be ashamed of you, Jade. Besides, you and Eric are going to be married."

Jade took a deep breath. "Eric and I are not getting married," she told them flatly, watching as their faces registered shock. It was time she came clean with them, she knew that now. Quickly, she filled them in on all that had happened, starting with the night before her birthday and ending with the present. She omitted nothing, and when she was done, she closed her eyes with relief.

"And so that means that…"

"Raul is the father," Jade finished her mother's sentence bleakly.

"Does he know?" Rodolfo asked grimly, unsure how he was supposed to behave at a time like this. As a father, he wanted to break Raul's neck, but as his mentor, he wanted to welcome him into the family with open arms.

Jade shook her head, not trusting her voice to speak. Her mind raced back to the letter she had been reading before her incident. Now that he had severed his ties with the restaurant, maybe he would sever all ties with her too?

"He thinks I am still engaged to Eric. Please don't tell him," she begged, her voice shaking with emotion.

"Why not, Jade?" Rodolfo was clearly shocked. "He has a right to know. An obligation. He will have to marry you,"

"That's just it, Poppa. The last thing I want is for him to marry me because he feels obligated." Her eyes were wide with horror at the thought.

Seeing her distress and not wanting to add to it, Lydia held up a hand. Then she took charge. "First things first," she told them with a determined air and, turning to Rodolfo, asked him to wait outside. He grumbled a little but did as she asked. When he had gone, she turned to Jade and tucked the covers around her neck. "Things will work out," she told her, "but now you need to get rest." With a final kiss, she left Jade alone to rejoin her husband, who was pacing impatiently in the corridor.

With relief, Jade lay back on the bed and closed her eyes. It felt good to have her mother home again, she thought as she drifted off to sleep.

16

Raul expertly guided the luxury fishing boat into the harbor and threw a line to one of the attendants on the dock. His body ached with the kind of hurt you can only get from a day of hard physical labor. Today had certainly been one of them. The group of rowdy Americans he had "entertained" was drunkenly clambering to the dock, one of them nearly losing his footing on the slippery deck while the others laughed uproariously at his antics. Raul sighed and turned away to busy himself with the catch.

"Hey amigo," Jeff, one of the more sober of the bunch, called out. "Thanks, eh?"

Raul smiled automatically and looked up just in time to see a small pouch sail through the air in his direction. He caught it neatly just before it hit the water. Hiding the disgust he felt at the poor manners, he didn't bother to look inside at the tip he knew was there. God knew he earned it. Raul raised a hand briefly and turned back to his duties.

Jeff, who had expected more gratitude, grumbled belligerently, but Miguel, the boat captain, stepped in and intercepted him smoothly. With extreme tact, he thanked him profusely for hiring the *Adrianna* for their day's fishing trip, while at the same time trying to cajole them into booking another day. Still muttering something about unappreciative people, Jeff nevertheless allowed himself to be mollified by the promise of beer and maybe a second-day discount. As they strolled away, Miguel threw a look at Raul that told him he would hear about his behavior later.

Angrily, Raul tugged on the lines and began the end of the day clean up of blood and guts. The thought that he would have to spend one more day on this boat with those baboons angered him even more, and for a minute, he felt like telling Miguel where to shove it. Then he remembered it was the only job he had at the moment, and if he wanted to eat, he would have to stick it out.

There were many times when he wished he was back at the Mi Corazon Uno and Dos. Although sometimes he had to deal with unruly customers, it was the kind of trouble he seemed able to handle without a second thought. Also, given the upscale style of restaurant, they had prided themselves on the fact that their customers were usually much more restrained and polite. He missed working with Rodolfo and Lydia and the rest of the staff, even the hapless Rosie, who seemed to suffer one crisis after another, and Heike, who was always threatening murder whenever something didn't go just right in his kitchen. There was someone else he missed more than all of them. He tried to stop the direction his mind was taking, but he knew it was already too late.

Several weeks had passed since he had last seen her, looking like death lying on the office floor. No one, least of all she, knew he had spent the whole night in her hospital room. It had been relatively easy to sneak in after her parents had gone home. Alone next to her bed, he had kept a silent vigil in the dark, watching her breast rise and fall beneath the unflattering hospital gown. Sometimes he would reach over and gently stroke her face. She would stir then, but never once did she open her eyes.

At that time of the night, no one was around to tell him what was wrong with her. In the early morning, he had sneaked out the same way he had come in, no wiser than before. And for some reason, he couldn't bring himself to ask her parents, feeling rightly they had more than enough to worry about. It was then he came to the only decision he felt he could.

Waiting a few days after the incident with Jade, he had gone in to see Rodolfo and found both he and Lydia huddled over the books. Heads together, they sat closely wedged behind the desk, occasionally pausing to discuss something on the sheets before them. Then they would smile gently, and sometimes they would kiss. Watching them, Raul had felt a strange tightness in his chest, feeling as if he were interrupting something so private no one else had the right to see. He coughed slightly to get their attention, and instantly they looked up and smiled warmly.

"Come in, Raul," Lydia invited. "We were just going over the books. You have done a wonderful job while we were gone. Are you sure you won't reconsider?"

Raul smiled, pleased by the compliment but unwilling to be dissuaded from the reason of his visit.

"That's why I'm here, Lydia. To tell you that I will be leaving soon. I am giving you my notice today."

Lydia's eyes clouded over while Rodolfo frowned openly.

"Leaving? Raul, you can't leave. We have tried to understand why you gave up the partnership. But to leave? There is something you should know…"

Rodolfo broke in smoothly. They had promised Jade, and as far as he was concerned, they were bound by their word.

"I'm sure we can convince Raul to stay, Lydia. Let's hear what he has to say." He put one arm around his wife's shoulders and turned his full attention to the young man in front of them.

Raul faltered at the sadness in their eyes. Then, with grim determination, he continued softly. "I'm afraid that's not possible, Rodolfo. I have been offered another position, and I have accepted."

Rodolfo frowned. "With another restaurant?" he asked sharply, relieved when Raul shook his head.

"Of course not, Rodolfo," Raul hurriedly assured him.

"Then doing what, Raul?" Lydia asked, perplexed. Everyone knew that Raul was a natural restaurateur, and she couldn't imagine him doing anything else.

"Oh, something in the tourism business," he smiled vaguely. "Public relations. It's a very good opportunity and something I feel I am good at. A chance of a lifetime, in fact. I will tell you more once I get settled."

It was all he could do to hold his smile firmly in place until, finally, Lydia looked as if she half believed him.

"Well, if you're sure…" she let the words trail away, a trace of doubt still evident by her tone.

The last thing they would want to do was hold him back, but what kind of job could he have that would be better than the position he held with them? Feeling helpless in the face of his determination, she wished she could change his mind. Besides that fact, they would be hard-pressed to find someone they could trust as much; they cared for him deeply.

"Yes, absolutely." Willing her to believe him, Raul poured as much sincerity into his voice as he could, but his façade was cracking under their scrutiny. The announcement made, Raul took his leave swiftly.

When the two weeks were up, Lydia and Rodolfo threw him a little party, and he said goodbye to all the staff, one by one. Although he hadn't expected she would, Jade hadn't come. He pretended to accept the vague explanation that she was still recovering, even as he felt hurt by her apparent complete disinterest. He tried to tell himself it was better this way, but he fooled no one, least of all himself.

Rodolfo and Lydia had watched him go, feeling as if they had lost a son rather than a former business partner. It wasn't going to be the same without him, they knew, and there was still the matter of the baby too. They couldn't help feeling that if only they were to tell him about his unborn child, he would stay, but they knew that Jade was adamant he not know—at least not yet. When they tried to change her mind, all she would do was shake her head and change the subject. Reluctantly, they agreed to stay out of it.

Some public relations job. Raul grinned stupidly as he picked up the bucket of fish guts at his feet and tried to stuff it into the garbage bag with one hand. It fell and broke, spilling ghoulishly across the just-cleaned deck, and he cursed long and hard. By the time he finished cleaning up for the second time, he was swimming in the mess and smelling like something thrown to the garbage dump. It was disgusting. With a fastidious grimace, he grabbed an old t-shirt off the bench and tried to wipe away most of the guts from his tanned muscular arms.

He wanted nothing more than a shower, some food and to take his own boat out into the open sea. It was the one thing he knew of that could help him face the next day of work. That is, if he still had a job to go to. Raul shrugged. As weary as he was right now, he could care less. With effort, he pushed the rebellious thoughts away.

Through the grapevine, he had heard that Jade was not going back to Canada—at least not for now. He wondered how Eric was dealing with that. He stopped and reminded himself that Jade's life no longer concerned him, but he couldn't stop his thoughts.

Jade was obviously the heir apparent—that much he gleamed from occasional conversations with Danny and Arturo. Even they had to admit she was doing a good job running the restaurants. Not as good a job as he did, they hastily assured him, but well enough. His ex-coworkers told him other things too. Like the fact that Rodolfo and Lydia were pursuing other things, traveling the country for their gift store. The rumor mill had it they were investigating something called dichroic glass, which was fused glass jewelry wrapped in silver. Raul had never heard of it. Still, Raul tried to convince himself it had nothing to do with him. Jade's aversion was painfully clear. Not that he blamed her. Even now, he was drowning in guilt that he may have somehow caused her mysterious collapse.

He turned his thoughts to the present. He had other dreams to pursue now. As much as he hated it, he needed this job and the money it gave him if he was ever going to save enough to buy a restaurant of his own someday. He had already discussed the idea with Rodolfo and been gratified when his former partner had offered to help him set it up. It was a tempting proposal except for one thing. Jade. She already thought he used her to get the Mi Corazon. He could only imagine what she would say if he used her father's money to start a restaurant in direct competition with them. Not that she would ever deign to speak to him again. No, he would have to make his own way. Regretfully, he declined the generous offer, only asking for Rodolfo's best wishes.

Thinking about his future goals made Raul feel better, and he reached over and grabbed his knapsack. Then, with a nimble leap to the dock, he headed toward the pier to where his dinghy was beached. *It will be good to be alone*, he thought, especially after the annoying company of Jeff and his friends all day. He looked out across the water to where the *Jade* bobbed in the water a few hundred feet away. He could hardly wait.

"*Hola*, Aunt Lydia," Amie's young, sweet voice sang down the line, immediately bringing a smile to Lydia's lips.

"*Hola*, Amie. How are you?" Jade's mother returned happily.

They had just walked in the door from their buying trip in Jalisco, and she was feeling out of sorts at the moment. The sound of Amie's voice did much to dispel her mood. She missed having the cheerful girl around and wished she would come to visit. Jade needed a confidant now more than ever. Just as she was voicing her thought aloud, Amie piped in and interrupted her.

"Guess what, Aunt Lydia? I have some extra time on my hands, and I was wondering if you would put up with me for a little while? I know it's short notice, but…"

Lydia closed her eyes in gratitude that her silent prayer had been answered.

"Absolutely, Amie," she said without hesitation. "How soon can you get here?"

Amie's musical laugh tinkled merrily as she set about relaying her itinerary for early next week.

"Can we keep this a surprise from Jade?" she asked now, her enthusiasm contagiously infectious.

As Amie outlined her scheme to surprise Jade, Lydia's thoughts moved to her daughter. The truth of the matter was that she was worried about her. Although Jade was following the doctor's orders exactly, there had been certain listlessness in her step lately. Amie would be the perfect tonic, of that she was sure. Quickly, she made a decision.

"Amie, I think there's something you need to know before you get here." She paused and then, before she could change her mind, drew a deep breath and continued. "It's about Jade."

"You have to tell him, Jade," Amie's voice was as firm as her arms around her best friend were gentle. Jade shook her head.

"He won't listen."

"Yes, he will," Amie argued with a fierceness that belied her innocent-looking face.

She didn't often throw her weight around, but seeing Jade look so miserable made her realize that this time it was warranted. Besides, she felt guilty that while she was so happy with Eric, Jade was so miserable. She wanted nothing more than to help.

Jade smiled at the determination on Amie's face. It had been a wonderful surprise to have her show up out of the blue like this. They had been best friends for so long, it was as if one of them took over where the other left off. Peering closer, she saw something else, too. Amie looked happier than ever, and she knew it was because of Eric. She changed the subject and asked about him now.

Instantly, Amie's face transformed and infused with so much love that Jade felt a pang of envy.

Amie stopped in mid-sentence from extolling the virtues of Eric and apologized. "I'm sorry, Jade. I didn't mean to go on and on about Eric. After all, he was——"

Jade cut her off with a smile. "Don't be ridiculous, Amie. You two are meant for each other, and we both know it. I can hardly believe you tore yourself away, but I am so glad you're here. Tell me more about the wedding. I am going to be the maid of honor, aren't I?"

Pretending to not see what she was doing, Amie allowed Jade to sidetrack her again. For now. But as soon as she was able, she was going to bring the subject back to where it belonged—Raul. With a grin to let Jade she was on to her, she launched into a description of the wedding she wanted to have and had been planning since she was five years old.

17

Permission to come aboard, captain?"

Raul froze as a feminine voice cut across his thoughts, neatly slicing them in half. He steeled his resolve before turning to stare at Jade sitting primly in a small dinghy a few feet away. She was wearing a broad-brimmed hat and a pale green dress similar to the one he had last seen her in. Dispassionately, he thought the blousy feminine style suited her. In fact, he had never seen her looking so... so... With an effort, he tore his face from her lush body to her eyes. They were deep green and determined.

"Suit yourself." His voice sounded unnaturally high in his ears, and he coughed to cover it. "It doesn't matter to me." The lie stuck in his throat, and he found he had a hard time swallowing.

Jade's smile faltered slightly, but she leaned forward in the dingy and putted ahead until she was parallel to his boat. Turning off the small motor, she tied off expertly and made the small leap to stand next to him. Her gaze never wavered even as did her balance, and robotically he moved forward to catch her, but she had already righted herself with a small hand on the wheel.

Tersely, he said, "I was just about to go home."

Another lie. Home these days was the *Jade*. His apartment deemed too expensive, he had reluctantly sub-let it to a high school friend and his wife until their baby was born next month, but she didn't need to know that.

"Then I'll go with you," her tone was quietly insistent.

"No."

"Yes," came the quick reply.

An unwitting smile lifted the corners of his mouth. Unrepentant, she answered with a sweet one of her own before seating herself on one of the cushioned benches. Confused, he looked away.

As casual as she tried to appear, Jade's heart beat erratically, so loudly she was sure he must be able to hear it. Fascinated, she watched him pull his shirt off in one easy motion and sluice water from a jug over his arms and chest. His bronzed skin glistened in the dying afternoon sun, the last rays touching him lightly and turning him red gold. He straightened and looked her directly in the eyes, a sardonic smile on his face. Then, in another smooth movement, he shimmied out of his jeans, his eyes never leaving her face. He was gloriously naked from head to toe. At the sight of his muscular body, Jade paled, but not once did she consider looking away as an option.

Raul threw her another cold, scathing look and walked into the cabin. A moment later, she heard the sound of a shower running, and she closed her eyes, almost imagining him there and herself with him. For a moment, she was tempted to flee, cursing the impulsiveness that had led her to come here in the first place. That and Amie. At the thought of her, she calmed slightly and smiled.

Her mother had been right in thinking that having her best friend by her side right now was a good idea. What Jade had forgotten, however, was how persuasive Amie could be when she believed in something.

"Jade, you have to go to him and tell him you are having his child."

She had said it so many times over the last few days that Jade was starting to hear it in her sleep. Even as she had argued with her, she knew Amie was right. In a short while, it would no longer be possible to hide behind the roomy smocks she had taken to wearing lately. Now even they were becoming tight, particularly across her breasts. Still, she had hesitated.

"What are you afraid of?"

A blush stained Jade's cheeks, and at once, understanding dawned, and Amie laughed aloud.

"You're in love with him, aren't you? Eric was right!" she crowed triumphantly as Jade turned even redder. "And he has no idea?"

"You don't understand, Amie. I was wrong about Raul. I accused him of terrible things."

Amie laughed. "So what? I can promise you this, Jade—that man definitely does not hate you."

From that point on, there had been no reason in Amie's mind not to go. The only fly in the ointment, as she termed it, was where she would go to "get her man."

Together, they finally decided it was best for her to look for him on the *Jade*.

With deep misgivings, Jade dressed with care, hiding her growing pregnancy with yet another blousy dress, and rowed out across the bay, Amie's parting words ringing in her ear.

"And after you tell him he is going to be a father, Jade, it is perfectly acceptable to seduce him."

Jade had laughed along with her, but now that she was here, she trembled at the thought.

Raul stepped from the shower, furious with his inability to control his thoughts. The sight of Jade affected him more than he ever imagined it could, and he cursed under his breath. Drying his body with a worn cotton towel, he slipped into a pair of clean jeans and cotton shirt. Feet bare, he padded to the deck to find Jade swaying slightly on the bench, eyes closed and wearing a dreamy expression. *What the hell is she doing here?* He strode angrily across the deck.

At that very moment, Jade was imagining Raul lathering himself with soap and almost believing that seducing him was not only possible but a good idea. She remembered too their last time on this boat. It had been magical, special for both of them; of that she was positive. *How had it gone so wrong?* she wondered, remembering his lips, hands and body on hers. So caught up was she in her fantasy, she nearly jumped into the ocean when a low male voice whispered in her ear.

"Why are you here, Jade?"

Her eyes sprang open and raked his body, half disappointed to see he was dressed. She blushed guiltily, glad he wasn't a mind reader. To hide her confusion, she stood too quickly, losing her balance in the process and swaying dangerously on the rolling deck.

Again, Raul's hand shot out to steady her, a guarded expression on his face. The gaze held until she tore her eyes away, ready to move toward the dingy for the short jaunt ashore. *This is a mistake,* was all she could think of as his fingers caressed her face.

The feel of her incredibly soft skin did him in. Raul's eyes narrowed angrily even as he puller her toward him in one smooth motion.

Jade could feel his hardness against her thigh, and her breath caught in her throat. Spellbound, she watched as his head dipped low and his lips were fastening themselves hungrily on hers. *This isn't so bad*, she thought briefly then threw herself wholeheartedly into the kiss.

Jade's lips yielded sweetly to his, and Raul groaned deep in his throat. Of its own volition, her body molded itself to him, and he knew he wanted her like no other woman in his life. If only she and Eric weren't...

Realization hit him hard, and without warning, he thrust her angrily away him. She was engaged!

Disoriented, Jade's knees hit the back of the bench she had just vacated, and with a loud thump, she sat down.

"I repeat, Jade, what do you want?" His breath was hot and furious, and immediately she recoiled from the look of disgust in his eyes.

Confused, she tried to focus, wondering what had gotten into him. He was looking as if he couldn't stand the very sight of her. It was that look that finally penetrated her mind, and instinctively, she lifted her chin. Proudly defiant, her eyes locked on his in cold determination.

Watching the myriad of emotions cross her features, Raul felt the familiar grudging admiration he always felt when she was like this. The cold, poised woman that had first come back from Canada was gone. Now she was replaced with the Jade he had known all his life, the Jade of passion and courage. It took all he had, but he willed his legs not to move forward. Instead, he leaned back against the mast and crossed his arms.

To cover her feelings, Jade carefully composed her features into a bland mask. "I think it is time you know that I am pregnant and that you are the father of my child." Coolly, she watched the faint look of shock on his face and was immediately gratified by it. Then, before he could react, she slid over the rail and stepped unaided into the bobbing dinghy. With shaking hands, she untied the loose knot and pulled the cord of the motor. Immediately, it roared to life. She was just about to put it into gear when Raul tried to stop her.

"Wait!" he yelled and jumped into the boat, rocking it dangerously.

"Get out," she told him quietly.

"How do I know it's mine?"

Bluntly, he said the first words that popped into his head. Then, seeing her eyes narrow, intuitively he knew it was a mistake.

"I said get out."

With that final pronouncement, Jade lifted one of the oars. Before he could anticipate her intention, she tapped him forcefully on his chest, catching him off guard.

Raul teetered and grabbed for something to hold onto, but there was only thin air. Utter astonishment briefly crossed his handsome features, and he tumbled into the ocean. By the time he surfaced, Jade was already halfway across the bay. Treading water, he watched her beach the borrowed water craft and jump out, leaving the owner to pull it up on shore for her. In another minute, she had disappeared from sight.

His first thought was to chase her down. Immediately, it was followed by another, and he smiled widely. *I'm going to be a father!* A thousand questions flooded his mind as he eased his wet, sodden, clothed body back onto the deck. Stripping quickly he stepped into the shower stall he had just vacated minutes before. He found he couldn't stop grinning. *We're going to have a baby.* Already, his mind reeled from the implication of what that would mean for them and their future. Suddenly, he sobered.

What future? The thought doused his enthusiasm as surely as the cold water running out of the shower head. He groaned aloud. He had to do something, he realized. Jade would have to marry him, that was the first thing. There was no way he was going to let another man raise his child. Eric! He would probably have to fight him for her, he thought. On the other hand, Eric would realize the baby was not his. The things he had to do were seemingly endless, and he felt overwhelmed. *No time like the present,* he thought as he reached for his towel for the second time that day. In record time, he dressed and, untying his dingy, headed back to shore to find Jade.

"You did what?" Amie's voice was filled with a combination of horror and amusement.

"I pushed him into the ocean," Jade repeated with righteous indignation, still seeing the look on Raul's face. Suddenly, she giggled. It had been priceless. *Serves him right,* she thought, remembering how he had kissed her and then pushed her away. Was it any wonder she had reacted as she had?

The plan was simple, really. Once Raul told her he forgave her for jumping to the wrong conclusion, she planned to tell him that she and Eric were not getting married after all. She was sure he would understand the engagement had only been a way of getting back at him. Then she would tell him he was the father of their baby, at which point, she was sure that he would...what? *Fall into my arms? Yeah right!*

She squirmed with embarrassment at her childishness. It was all supposed to go as she and Amie planned it, but as she was beginning to learn, life didn't always work out that way. Realizing now how ridiculous her fantasy was, she groaned with disillusionment.

Amie placed an arm around her friend. "Don't worry," she comforted just as there was a knock on the bedroom door, and Juanita called out to tell Jade she had a visitor.

Jade sighed, about to ask Juanita to make up an excuse, but already her footsteps were receding down the hallway. Resigned, she pulled Amie to her feet and walked to the kitchen. At her questioning look, Juanita told her the guest waited on the porch. When Amie looked about to follow, Juanita grabbed her arm and thrust a potato peeler into her hand.

Leaning over, Juanita whispered conspiratorially in Amie's ear, making her smile. Good naturedly, Amie grabbed a potato and began to peel, keeping one eye conspiratorially on Jade, who, unaware, headed for the porch.

The afternoon sun had long set, and only the soft lights of the Japanese lanterns glowed along the paths leading to the house. The shadows on the porch deepened even as she watched them. She blinked and adjusted her eyes, breathing in the smell of the nightshade her mother had planted years ago. She said it reminded her of Canada.

At first, Jade couldn't see anyone and, looking around, decided her visitor must have changed their mind. Exasperated, she turned to go back in when a voice spoke from the shadows.

"Jade, wait," Raul stepped up on the first stair and walked to the edge of the balcony.

He took a tentative step forward. *Por Dios, this is harder than I thought it would be.* He raked his eyes over her stiff, unyielding form. If only she would say something. He got his wish.

Jade turned back, a carefully composed look of indifference etched on her smooth features. "Yes? What do you want?"

Beneath the cool tones, she could hear the slight quaver that belied her surprise at the sight of him.

"Why didn't you tell me, Jade?" In contrast, his voice sounded harsh and accusing. Seeing the stubborn look he knew so well, he immediately changed his tack. "No matter. We'll just have to get married. For the baby's sake, if nothing else. Eric will just have to get used to the fact you're marrying me and not him."

Jade stared incredulously. "What did you say?"

Raul smiled widely. Now that he had actually said the words aloud, he was cocky and sure he had the situation in control. "I said we'll get married, Jade, and Eric will just have to—"

"I have no intention of marrying Eric," Jade said so softly he could barely hear the words.

"Good then," he said with smug satisfaction, relieved he wouldn't actually have a fight on his hands. "Then it's set. We can get married and..."

"That's all wonderful, Raul," Jade interrupted coldly, "except for one small thing. I am not going to marry Eric, that is true. But I wouldn't marry you if you were the last man on earth."

Then, with one last studied look, Jade spun around and stomped furiously into the house. Face like a storm cloud, she brushed past a confused Amie and Juanita standing in the kitchen, mouths agape, and slammed the door to her room. Once safely inside, Jade threw herself on the bed and burst into tears.

Raul stayed where he was for a long time in utter shock and disbelief. What was the matter with her anyway? Why was she so angry? She should have been grateful he was going to marry her. He thought back to the conversation he had with Maria about Carlos so many years ago. *At least Jade doesn't have to go through what Maria did*, he thought self righteously. He was here, wasn't he?

He saw Amie come out to the porch, hands on her hips. Right now, he didn't feel like talking to anyone. With a muttered oath, Raul climbed into his truck and roared out of the driveway, gravel flying. Who the hell knew what that woman was thinking? He knew one thing for sure. He'd be damned if he was going to stick around to find out.

Later, after Jade had gone to sleep, exhausted from crying in her friend's arms, Amie sat alone on the front porch. She had been out there for hours trying to figure out what to do. So far, she had witnessed two shooting stars, and she wished on both—one for her and Eric, and the other for Raul and Jade. Listening to Jade's tale of woe, she saw how simple misunderstandings had ruled the lives of the two of them. She decided that it was time to interfere in a very real way. Sighing, she got up and made her way into the house. Tomorrow was a big day. If she wanted to be ready for it, she better get some sleep, she thought as she turned off the hall lights and headed for her bedroom.

The next day, Amie went in search of Raul at Municipal Beach. She knew that his boat was moored there, and probably he would be waiting for his guests somewhere near the docks. She didn't have long to wait. With a happy smile, she ran to the edge of the surf and helped him bring his dingy to shore. Then, before he had a chance to stop her, she launched into a plan of attack she assured him was foolproof.

After, Raul watched, bemused as Amie headed to Jade's house before anyone knew she was gone. Was she right? He didn't know anymore. When Jade refused him last night, he had been stunned, angry and feeling more defeated than he ever had in his entire life. He had been so sure she was going to fall into his arms. *Let's face it, pal*, he told himself sternly. *You blew it!*

Amie agreed with his assessment. "If you want Jade, Raul, you have to woo her," she told him flatly, willing him to listen. Then, she spent the next hour telling him exactly how to go about it.

Raul grimaced, not sure if he was up to doing what Amie had suggested. Initially, he was skeptical her ideas would work. Jade looked like she wanted to kill him, not marry him. Then he shrugged. What did he have to lose? With a sigh, he hurried back to the dingy that would take him to his boat for a change of clothes. Then he was going to stop off at the restaurant and have another talk with Rodolfo. If that went well, it would be time to move on to the next step. Raul's mind raced with all the details of things he had to do if Amie's idea was going to work. Then, as he puttered to the *Jade*, his face broke in an open smile. Like he said, what did he have to lose?

18

Jade leaned back, her hands on the flat of her back, and tried to ease the tension that had gathered there. All day, she had been on her feet until they felt puffy and swollen and so tired she felt like screaming. It had been a long day. Truthfully, she knew her irritation and discontent had more to do with something other than physical discomfort.

Jade almost fainted to find Raul, the day after his so-called marriage proposal, sitting smugly behind her father's desk.

"What are you doing in my father's chair?" She fought to conceal her surprise or the sudden erratic increase in her pulse.

"What do you mean, Jade?" Raul had asked innocently. "I work here now."

"What do you mean, you work here?" Jade blurted then flushed. "If this is your idea of a joke, then—"

"Don't be silly, Jade. Your parents asked me to come back. They really do need me here. Not that you aren't doing a great job," he hastened to add, "but in your condition…" He looked pointedly at her slight tummy, and she flushed deeper. "…you really should be taking it easier."

A condition you put me in, she silently threw the impotent accusation into the air. Speechless, she could only stare helplessly at him.

"Was there anything you wanted?" he had asked then, a helpful expression on his face.

With a muttered oath, Jade had mumbled some plausible excuse and then fled in search of her parents.

Their explanations, although plausible, were certainly not what she wanted to hear.

"Your father and I have decided that there is no one we can trust to help you while we are gone." Her mother's voice was quiet but firm, brooking no argument. Rodolfo was only slightly more understanding.

"Sorry, *princessa*. I hope you forgive us."

Seeing her father looking so contrite, she had softened and, in the end, knew she had no choice but to agree with them. Her father was still recovering and not able to work as much as he used to. She knew her parents were thrilled that Raul had decided to come back to work for them and pick up the extra workload. They had even booked another buying trip to the Orient and planned to combine it with another vacation. Although not thrilled with the idea of Raul's return, Jade was pleased that her father was taking more time off. In the end, she encouraged them to go.

That had been almost a month ago. Since then, Jade was forced to work with Raul on a daily basis. She had to admit, though, that things were much different between her and Raul than the last time they had worked together.

For one thing, Raul's attitude had changed completely. Unfailingly polite, he had taken to spending much more time and attention to rounding out her education from the book learning she had received to more practical application. Although the university in Canada had been excellent, no schools there could have taught her about dealing with employees with the cultural background of Mexicans. It was a law unto itself, and Jade was often exasperated by what she deemed an indifferent attitude. Raul, on the other hand, was much more patient and understanding of things like family obligations his staff deemed more important than work and was teaching her the best way to handle those situations as they arose.

"The trick is to get your way but at the same time make people think they got what they want." Sometimes Jade thought Raul could teach a psychology class, so tuned in he was to the way people thought and acted.

And then there was the way he was treating her on a personal level. At first, she had been suspicious, eyeing him closely for the ulterior motive she was sure he had. Perversely, she complained to Ana and only ended up looking foolish.

"So Raul is bringing you flowers for no reason? And getting the cook at work to prepare special dinners? And he is insisting you take a nap every afternoon? Are you telling me, Jade, that he is even driving you home and making you lie in the hammock on the porch? Let me see if I have this straight, Jade," Ana said, as straight-faced as she could manage, "You're telling us Raul is *too nice* to you at work?"

She managed to sound puzzled and faintly amused at the same time while she and Juanita exchanged furtive glances. Mumbling a lame excuse, Jade had retreated to her bedroom, the laughter of the two women following her down the hall.

Calling Amie had been even less than satisfactory, and Jade had been a little put off by the lack of concern in Amie's voice.

"Oh that," Amie had dismissed her feelings easily. "Maybe he just decided that since you were going to work together, he better be nicer. Besides, isn't that what you wanted?"

Jade had to reluctantly agree it was certainly better than before. The truth of the matter was that, try as she might, she had a hard time putting him out of her mind—the way he looked, the way his hands moved while doing the simplest of tasks, even the way he smelled all aroused her sense of awareness of him, invading her waking thoughts and her dreams at night. Sometimes she wished he would just go away again.

Jade disrobed for her long-awaited bath at the end of the day and vowed to put him out of her mind—at least for the night. Suddenly, she heard a noise, and she stopped and cocked her head to listen. *What is that?*

With her parents gone and Juanita and her family in Acapulco that weekend, she was all alone except for Ana in the guest room. She wrapped a green satin robe over her naked body and hurried to the front of the house to investigate. *It sounded like music.* As she neared the porch, she reached behind her neck and removed the obsidian stone she always wore, clutching it as if it were a talisman against danger. In the distance, she could just make out the soft, melodic sounds of a guitar. Cautiously, but no longer frightened, she approached the front door and stepped out into the night. The sight that greeted her was to imprint itself on her memory for the rest of her life.

In the moonlit yard, Raul stood surrounded by twelve mariachis. He was singing softly in the beautiful tenor she knew he possessed but was not often privy to. Eyes unwavering and unashamedly glued to hers, he sang effortlessly, and with every note, her heart rose and responded to his voice. Jade found she could not tear her gaze away. Beneath the music, she heard a soft sigh, and turning her head, she greeted Ana, who was looking approvingly at the handsome man before them. They shared a smile, then turned their attention once again to the impromptu concert in the courtyard.

Sin usted, mi vida no es nada
Sin usted no hay la esperanza,
me Dice usted me adora, y estaré con usted.
Para sin usted, yo soy
nada de nada*

(Without you, my life is nothing
Without you there is no hope,
Tell me you love me, and I will be with you.
For without you, I am nothing at all.)

As he sang, Jade remembered a story her father had told the both of them when they were still in their teens. It was about how Rodolfo's parents, Jade's grandparents, had met and fallen in love.

Jade's great-grandfather had forbidden his daughter Angelina to have anything to do with Joseph Perez, a poor Tarahumara from the mountains of Chihuahua. Undeterred, Joseph had wooed the woman he had fallen in love with at first sight. Every night without fail for one solid month, he serenaded his love until finally her father gave in.

Next to the story of her parents, Jade had always felt it was the most romantic story in the world. Raul, who was, at the time, only sixteen years old, had scoffed and declared he would never make a fool of himself over a woman like that.

Looking at him now, Jade didn't think he was a fool at all.

The last strains of the song fell away, and there was only silence. Standing before her, his arms held loosely by his sides, Raul gazed as if unsure what to do next. Inside, his heart was hammering loudly with suspense. When Amie had first come to him and told her what he needed to do to win Jade over, he had been unwilling to give it a try.

"Do you want her or not, Raul? Because if you do, you better swallow some of that macho crap and get with the program." Imagine, sweet Amie talking like that! Sweet or not, her words effectively stopped him in his tracks.

Amie was relentless. "Men are such jackasses," she had declared more to herself than him, thinking how her darling Eric had failed to see her attributes until it was almost too late. She seemed determined it wouldn't happen to these two.

"You need to romance Jade, Raul. I don't know how, but you need to show her how much you care. No woman wants to think you want to marry her because you *have* to."

It was that statement more than ever that made Raul finally see the wisdom of her remarks. He realized now his proposal was sadly lacking in the romance department, and he was ashamed of himself. She certainly deserved better than that.

With real enthusiasm, he threw himself into winning Jade over. Immediately after Amie coming to see him, he had quit his job and gone to see Rodolfo and Lydia. Briefly, he told them that he knew he was the father of Jade's child and that he intended to marry her, but first he had to make her fall in love with him again. Rodolfo and Lydia had welcomed him with open arms. Cautioning him to go slowly, they wished him luck.

He soon realized why. His initial plan was that he would work with Jade and she would see that he was the man for her just by his mere presence. After her initial shock at seeing him in the office, he thought she would come around. He felt that, as her pregnancy progressed, so would her feelings for him, and eventually she would fall into his arms in gratitude. But he had forgotten how stubborn Jade could be.

Finally, at a loss, he called Amie, who initially cursed him for being an absolute fool. After she had calmed down, though, she relented and gave him some well-meaning advice. Feeling stupid and inept, he listened intently and, to his credit, changed his attitude and approach.

He began to spend hours with Jade, teaching her about the business. His manner was that of a teacher, not as a boss. At first she regarded him suspiciously, but over time, their manner once more became easy and relaxed, the way it was before she went away to school. Sometimes they found themselves laughing over something silly until Jade would suddenly remember and turn abruptly away.

Despite the resistance, Raul persevered. Sometimes on returning from the market, he would bring her flowers. Nothing showy—just a rose or two—but it pleased him the way her face would light up at the sight of them. Most of all, he loved making her laugh, the sound of it filling him with longing for what they once had together.

Other times, he would just listen. Caught unaware, she would open up and talk to him of her experiences in another country, going to school among strangers and how hard it had been. It gave him a pang to know how lonely she had felt sometimes, and he wished that he had been there for her. When he said as much, she clammed up suddenly and turned away.

Although their relationship was certainly better than before, he had been unable to pierce that shell she had built around her. It seemed as if for every step forward, he took one step back.

The one thing she absolutely refused to discuss with him was the baby and their future. That he loved her he had no doubt, but how to make her see that was another question. It was then that he decided drastic circumstances needed drastic measures.

Now, watching her waver on the top step, he poured all the love he had for her in one look and sent it across the space between them.

"Jade," he began, softly echoing the words of the song. "Without you, I am nothing. I love you more than anything or anyone in this world." He paused, unable to read the expression in her eyes Shameless, he took a deep breath and knelt in the dirt before her.

"Jade, will you marry me?" he asked, his voice strong with love and conviction.

Jade wavered and looked deep into Raul's eyes, glowing intensely by the light of the full moon. She felt a push on her back and heard Ana's encouraging whisper in her ear. "If you don't marry him, I will."

Her face filled with hope, and she looked at her godmother, a question in her eyes.

"Go on," Ana whispered as Jade hesitated. "Remember, my girl. To thine own self be true." It was the same advice she had given Jade's mother two decades ago.

Jade turned back to Raul, and her breath caught in her throat. She could almost feel his love as a palpable thing radiate towards her. And suddenly, she knew. Slowly, one small foot slid from beneath the silky robe, and she took the first step down off the porch. She saw him stand and open his arms in encouragement.

Jade didn't hesitate any longer. She took another step and then another until soon she was running across the lawn toward him. The obsidian stone burned hotly in her hand as she flew into his arms. She heard the musicians break into song just as Raul's arms enfolded her, and she knew without any doubt that she had truly come home. In the distance, she heard the whisper of Ana's voice on the wind.

"To thine own self be true. Bravo, Jade, bravo."

Printed in the United States
41242LVS00011BB/49